PASSION FEVER

DUTIFUL WIVES #3

BEVERLEY OAKLEY

FOREWORD

Dear Reader,

Passion Fever is Book 3 in the *Dutiful Wives* series.

Charlotte, the heroine of **Passion Fever**, is the illegitimate daughter of Adelaide whose story is told in An Unsuitable Alliance.

Both stories can be read on their own but are best enjoyed together.

Happy reading!

Beverley Oakley

ABOUT THE AUTHOR

Beverley Oakley writes wicked historicals dripping with scandal, mystery and suspense.

An avid knitter and historical costume-maker, she crafts her second-chance Regency, Victorian and Georgian romances with unexpected twists and turns.

She lives north of Melbourne with the handsome Norwegian bush pilot she met in Botswana, and their two gorgeous daughters.

Visit Beverley's Shopify store:
www.beverleysbooks.com
Or her website: www.beverleyoakley.com

CHAPTER 1

A gentle wind blew through the French doors of the library. It rustled the papers on Tristan's desk, lifting one that floated through the air before settling on the Aubusson rug between the potted fern and the grate, where a small fire burned on this chilly spring morning.

Adelaide, walking in with their youngest to say good-night to papa, bent to retrieve it, saying with gentle humour, "Shall I avert my eyes in case it's State secrets?"

But when she rose and observed the unusual gravity of her husband's expression, she exclaimed, "Tristan! Tell me what's happened?"

Turning to the nursemaid, she indicated with a discreet nod that she should take three-year-old Catherine back to the nursery.

Tristan didn't immediately speak, and Adelaide's fear grew, for she knew her husband kept nothing from her.

"It's Charlotte," he said finally, nodding at the wing back armchair by the bookshelf, suggesting Adelaide might need to sit down if she were to hear any more.

But Adelaide was made of sterner stuff. While Tristan had thought he'd married an invalid, the charade that Adelaide's own mother had forced her to enter was well in the past.

Not, though, Adelaide's pain over the child she'd thought had died at birth, only to discover, fourteen years ago, that her mother had deceived her over that, too. Little Charlotte would be seventeen now.

Or so Adelaide believed. For now, Tristan's expression suggested that the direst of circumstances had befallen her lost child. Charlotte must be dead.

And Adelaide had never met the girl. She had no knowledge of her character; whether she was a lively and engaging child, like her mother had been before she'd thrown in her lot with Charlotte's father, a charismatic poet—a married man—and had all but ruined her life.

Until she'd been given a second chance when she'd married the kind, honourable politician, her beloved husband, Tristan, Lord Leeson.

"Oh." She was going to refuse the invitation to sit, but suddenly the shock felt very great, and her knees gave way. She could feel the rising sobs, and her mind began to spin.

But then Tristan was at her side, reaching down to hold her hand as he said, "No, Adelaide, Charlotte is well. I'm sorry I led you to think the worst. It's just…" He breathed deeply, then added, "She's eloped. James just told me."

He held up the brief letter. This was the only communication Adelaide knew Tristan had received from James—Tristan's best friend and Adelaide's former lover—in all the fourteen years since James had left England, condemned to being an exile after he'd murdered the man who had blackmailed Adelaide over her scandalous affair with James.

"Eloped? But… if she's in love—" It was all Adelaide could manage, for she must make what excuses she could for the child she had borne James out of wedlock when she, herself, was not much more than a child herself.

Not excuses, though, in the way her mother—Mrs Henley —had made excuses for Adelaide when she'd pretended to Tristan that Adelaide's fear of men was based on having been violated while travelling through Europe; not the truth. That she'd eloped with the scandalous poet, James Treloar.

"Even if she is in love, such recklessness is bound to end badly. James is at his wits' end!" The furrows between Tristan's brows deepened and Adelaide's alarm grew in proportion to her anger towards James.

What right had James to be at his wits' end when his daughter had only done exactly what James had done with Adelaide?

For that matter, what right had James to have secretly kept their child after Adelaide's mother, Mrs Henley—or rather, the woman she'd believed was her mother—had told Adelaide that baby Charlotte had died at birth?

Adelaide smoothed her Pomona green silk skirts as her difficult past flooded back.

Not only had Charlotte not died at birth, Mrs Henley had allowed James to have the child. Charlotte had been brought up under the pretence that she was the child of passionate poet James, and his cold, unloving, zealous wife, Hortense.

James had only revealed the truth to Adelaide, years later, when Hortense was dead, as leverage to persuade Adelaide to give up her newly discovered life of love and stability with honourable Tristan.

"Mrs Henley does not know?" Adelaide refused to call her mother. A chill ran through her just to think of the lengths to which the woman would go to achieve her spiritual aims. She'd brokered Adelaide's marriage to Tristan; and she'd organised Charlotte's kidnapping, all for the money she required to save souls and thereby guarantee Mrs Henley's soul in the afterlife.

Tristan shook his head. "He makes no mention of her, thank God."

"Thank God," Adelaide corroborated, though her fears were still not eased. "Are you sure she did not continue her association with Beatrice?" Beatrice was James's wife, which made her Charlotte's stepmother. "I can't bear the idea that that woman should have any contact with my daughter after what she did to me."

She shuddered, and Tristan gave her shoulder a comforting squeeze.

"I think our concerns right now are with the man with whom Charlotte has eloped."

It was true. And, if Tristan's expression were anything to go by, Charlotte, the beloved child whom Adelaide would never be able to claim as her daughter, was committing the same dreadful mistake that had nearly ruined Adelaide's life: She was eloping with someone very unsuitable.

"Who is the gentleman?" Adelaide asked.

Tristan breathed in. "Gentleman? Having a title does not mean one is a gentleman."

Adelaide felt the constriction in her throat tighten and waited for her husband to say his name.

"Lord Gilray."

"Dear Lord!" Adelaide gasped. "The man at the centre of the scandal with that Scottish heiress?" She hesitated, then asked, "But what if Charlotte truly loves him?"

"If he truly loves her, Gilray would go about this so that a proper marriage contract could be drawn up. Charlotte is an heiress, despite the fact her father has been stripped of his English lands and entitlements. James's writings have made him a wealthy man, and all that Charlotte has will become Gilray's the moment they are married."

Adelaide put her hands to cheeks. "And James has asked you to put a stop to this?"

Once the best of friends, Tristan and James had become estranged after James had tried to persuade Adelaide to run away with him.

"I have had no dealings with James in fourteen years," Tristan assured her, "however, he is Charlotte's father. He once saved my life, and he once was my firmest friend. His confidence that I will do what I can to bring Charlotte back is not misplaced." He kissed the top of Adelaide's head. "I know you would not want Charlotte to repeat the mistakes of the past."

"No, I would not want her to commit my mistakes," Adelaide whispered, gripping Tristan's hand, her heart racing with fear and dread. "I've always wondered what kind of child she was. Now I know. She is impulsive and reckless, just as I was at her age." She drew back and locked eyes with Tristan. "You're right! She must be stopped before she ruins her life, but what can you do? Perhaps it is too late!"

"Charlotte was noticed missing from Miss Prism's Seminary only a few hours ago, and it so happens James is in England, not France. But, of course, he cannot declare himself and risk the noose. And no one else can know." Tristan straightened, uncurling his hand, and Charlotte saw the note with a strange feeling in her belly as he added, "I am only hours away, which is why James has solicited my help."

Adelaide tried to be strong, but her mind was spinning. "We must be discreet if you are to leave here in such haste. Perhaps there is another way—"

Her words were cut short by a short, sharp rap upon the door, which opened to reveal the tallest and most elegant of the small group attending Lord and Lady Leeson's house party, a handsome young man by the name of Jasper Creighton. A young man of whom Adelaide was very fond, though she was also very glad her two daughters were under the age of twelve, for Jasper was an inveterate womaniser.

Yes, he was charming and persuasive and, at twenty-three, just the kind of young man Adelaide might have fallen for had she been a reckless, impulsive seventeen-year-old.

Like Charlotte.

But Mr Creighton was most assuredly not looking for a wife, as he'd explained the evening before when he'd taken his hostess into his confidence and poured out his heart.

Mr Creighton sent them both a genial smile. "Lord Leeson, Lady Leeson, I hope I'm not intruding, but I—" And then his smile faltered as he began again, "Something has happened! Tell me, is there anything I can do to assist?"

CHAPTER 2

I t seemed to Charlotte that for her whole life she'd been admonished for being impulsive and thoughtless. Her step mama constantly upbraided her for not being sufficiently thoughtful and nurturing of her two little brothers. In other words, not letting them win at the childhood games they'd shared when Charlotte was still at home, a boisterous ten-year-old thinking she was entertaining an aggressive four-year-old brother, and a sulky three-year-old.

By the time she was twelve, she was properly segregated from Charlie and Gervase for now she was no longer a child and the outdoors which she loved so much was more often viewed through the window of the schoolroom as she tried to attend to the lessons her governess considered mind-improving for a future wife to some worthy scion of the aristocracy.

Papa had bought Charlotte a horse, though her step-mother was afraid of horses and thought this an indulgence too far. Especially when Charlotte would use her beloved Majestic as her means of escape. Too many times she'd jump onto his back to avoid the harsh strictures of Madame

Lenore, and ride until their large, lovely home in Provence was a speck in the distance and the sun was low in the sky.

Charlotte supposed she must have done this once too often for when she returned from her last truancy, she was ushered into the drawing room where her father, looking sad but resigned, and her stepmother, clearly still full of ire, announced that Charlotte would be sent away for her schooling.

To England.

Immediately, the greatest joy had filled her.

An adventure! Charlotte was going on an adventure to the land where her father, and the mother who had died when she was only a few months old, had lived.

Finally, she would be free of the constraints of her French provincial life and the dull lessons she wearily sat through.

Charlotte knew there was some mystery surrounding the reason her parents lived in France when her father, English by birth and a celebrated poet in that country, often received visits from literary giants from all over the world, yet hardly left their small estate.

Charlotte heard he'd been a passionate man in his youth and there were occasions when that same passion erupted, and she could understand the excitement that fizzed through his veins, for she felt it too when she was performing the theatricals that her parents had encouraged her to enjoy when she was younger.

But which seemed so frowned upon when she grew a little older.

~

THE REALITY of schooling in England, she soon discovered, was not an adventure.

Attending Miss Prism's Seminary for Young Ladies in

Kensington was simply another way to put Charlotte into a straitjacket and ensure that she conform to the very narrow prescription—to Charlotte's mind—of what a lady should be.

Of course, with such a passionate father, rebellion was in Charlotte's nature; she could not help that; and she decided that if her stepmother wasn't around to tell her what she should do, then neither would Miss Prism and her sister.

With their silly ringlets—grey in the case of Miss Prism the elder; her sister's being a mousey brown—the two Miss Prisms exerted wondrous authority over their sixteen young pupils who ranged in age from thirteen to eighteen.

Both were quick to uphold order by seizing the rod—an innocuous-looking switch that exerted great efficacy when it came to sharp, intense pain, to which Charlotte could attest.

Miss Prism the elder used it to punish insubordination. Her younger sister, whose passion was mathematics, considered it an aid to the speedy resolution to finding the answer to her beloved sums. If Charlotte had learned nothing else during her three years with the redoubtable ladies, it was how to calculate with lightning speed, thus earning a grudging admiration from the junior school mistress, at least.

But Charlotte's tendency towards insubordination was always going to get her into trouble and even though she often bore the physical manifestation of a beating for days after resisting Miss Prism's attempts to squeeze the life and light out of her, as she put it, she still harboured no second thoughts when it came to the bold, even reckless course of escape that handsome Lord Gilray had unexpectedly offered her.

No, Charlotte would do anything to remove herself from her stifling existence in her Kensington prison. And if it involved a handsome, dashing young lord spouting words of high praise and passion, then all the better.

It had been Charlotte's school friend, Miss Veronica Carr, who'd introduced Charlotte to her first proper vice: novels. Novel-reading was especially frowned upon, and any books not sanctioned by the two Misses Prism were summarily confiscated. Some of the girls giggled that these ladies took them to read themselves, but Charlotte was fairly sure that Miss Prism and her older sister truly were sainted virgins laying the foundations for a heavenly afterlife which the reading of novels would preclude.

It was also Veronica who introduced Charlotte to a second, deadlier vice, nicely augmented by a foundation of wickedly heart-palpitating romance novels: Veronica's cousin, the newly minted Lord Gilray.

Now here was a gentleman who made the blood fizz in Charlotte's veins like the feeling she got when performing to an audience, though she wouldn't swear with hand on heart that his title was not part of his attraction.

Charlotte's stepmother had counselled her daughter to make her marital decision based on sound common sense. Many times, Mrs Beatrice Treloar had said that a title was not the marker of a man. Charlotte had sometimes wondered why her father was rarely addressed by his title, Lord Dewhurst, as she felt he should have been. Indeed, it seemed his title caused him some embarrassment, which was odd considering he was a man who revelled in high praise and declared, himself, that he was always aiming for the heavens.

This had been during a time when father and daughter had spent a great deal of time together; the golden phase of her early adolescence, Charlotte now considered it, when her father really had seemed interested in her mind, and proud to show her off to his literary companions, other passionate poets and painters who had showered Charlotte with compliments and begged to paint her.

And, according to her stepmother, who ruined her.

Charlotte had successfully pleaded the case that she would be far less of a trial to her parents and teachers if she were allowed to remain at home on the family estate.

Her stepmother had shown surprising compassion and agreed with papa that if Charlotte were obedient and attended to her studies, she could stay.

Indeed, Charlotte's behaviour had been beyond reproach. And as a reward for honouring her word for six months, and for diligently teaching her little brothers their sums—at which Charlotte excelled—her father had, as a reward for her fifteenth birthday, taken her to Paris where he was to deliver his first literary offerings in many years.

When Charlotte had found him sweating, shaking, and close to tears as he'd been about to step onto the podium, she had done the only thing she knew was in her power to help him: she had stepped up with a confidence she was far from feeling, and had delivered the passionate words and sentiments she only partly understood.

During those fifteen minutes, she expended so much effort in ensuring her tone and pronunciation matched the fire and passion she'd heard in her papa's voice when she'd heard him practising on the other side of the closed door of his study, that she'd been unprepared for the enthusiasm of its reception.

The praise had gone on and on, and the realisation that it was as much for her as it was for her papa's poetic offerings, had ignited a fire in her breast.

A beast, her stepmama called it after Charlotte's presence had been requested at multiple subsequent readings by ladies and gentlemen, both.

The real disaster which occurred had been far from Charlotte's fault, yet she had been punished for it.

Charlotte had grown up being praised for her long dark curls, eyes like violets, and a mouth shaped like a rosebud. It had been commonplace for her to be seated on some lady's lap during the house parties her father whipped up on the spur of the moment – to her stepmama's ire - when Charlotte had been younger.

Her stepmama had argued that such attention was damaging, even though Charlotte never felt better than when she had her hair stroked and her cheek caressed as some lady, old or young, listened to her father read to his rapt audience. These were the only times Charlotte experienced physical touch, and it made her heart open like a flower. It didn't matter if the lady were young and pretty, or old and wizened. They were conveying something beautiful in her their hearts that they felt when they beckoned her over as they settled in for an evening of papa's poems which, for a long time, Charlotte didn't really attend to. Rather, she liked the mesmeric tone of his voice, and revelled in the attention of whomever she was with.

But while her stepmama had been disapproving of Charlotte being called a little doll, saying it would turn her head, she'd not banned Charlotte from these evenings.

It was a different matter, apparently, when Charlotte was older, after her escape from school.

And it hadn't even been Charlotte's fault because Charlotte had herself been about to politely extricate herself from the situation. But when her stepmama had found Charlotte seated on old Monsieur Leville's lap in her papa's study, she'd flown into one of her rare passions – though this had been later – and that's when Charlotte had been sent to Miss Prism's Seminary for Young Ladies.

As if Charlotte didn't know that at fifteen it wasn't appropriate to be seated on an old man's lap. But he'd tricked her by putting out his foot as she'd been passing by, so that she'd tripped, and under the pretext of saving her fall, he'd pulled her onto his thighs, right in front of her papa, and right in front of her stepmama who had chosen that moment to walk in and jump to whatever conclusions she had.

Lord Gilray was an entirely different kettle of fish.

Lord Gilray had, for a brief moment, ignited the flame of passion in Charlotte's heart which she realised was what her father's poems were often about.

Now she understood why her stepmama felt some of these were scandalous.

Because if they made Charlotte want to do things she knew were wrong, yet was prepared to do them anyway, they were.

But the heart banished reason.

And Lord Gilray's inducements were very compelling.

Charlotte had first met Lord Gilray in a bookshop in Bond Street when the younger Miss Prism had taken several girls on an improving jaunt, the object being to acquire a copy of Reverend Bolton's treatise on good behaviour.

The handsome viscount had been perusing the shelves and had literally bumped right into his cousin, Vanessa, whereupon introductions had been made.

And a passion forged between that gentleman and Charlotte.

Or, at least, Charlotte had believed it was a passion of unbreakable strength.

Now, as she stared at the sleeping youth on the bed of the tavern they'd been forced to bespeak half way to Gretna Green, she wasn't so sure.

Gilray was snoring loudly, his mouth slack, his breath reeking of the copious amounts of claret he'd consumed as they'd discussed their exciting future.

Granted, their rollicking adventure had started well, and Charlotte had not had second thoughts as she'd bundled a night rail, change of under things, and her best gown into a drawstring bag before slipping the bolt of the scullery door, not even disturbing the sleeping kitchen maid snoring gently by the kitchen fire.

How could Charlotte think of regrets when Gilray had promised her his heart, a future filled with unending adventure, and all the new gowns and accoutrement she could wish for?

But now—

A loud rap on the bedchamber door startled her and Charlotte jumped to her feet, holding on to the back of the chair by the table near the window as she darted a glance at Gilray.

He did not stir.

Charlotte's stomach was growling, and she supposed if he had at least organised a late supper, she shouldn't feel too badly disposed towards him, so she said in as clear and firm a voice as she could manage: "Come!"

For the truth was, she was feeling a little tearful, and not at all sure that she was where she should be right now.

Staring out of the window at the expanse of green fields disappearing into the distance, she heard the door open.

"Set it there, please," she said, indicating the table without looking round. Embarrassment and shame were now superseding her earlier impulsiveness and she was careful not to turn for if it was the tavern keeper's wife or daughter, she did not wish to be recognised.

Until she was assailed by the very male scent of leather, sandalwood soap and, with a gasp, she spun about and found herself looking up into the face of a very handsome, dark-haired young man whose smile was distinctly assessing as he asked, "Miss Charlotte Treloar, I presume?"

CHAPTER 3

"Who are you?" Charlotte demanded, very conscious of her state of undress for she was only in her night rail. Without Gilray's help, she was unable to put on her stays or do up the tiny buttons of the travelling gown she'd worn for her escape and which happened to be her only outerwear other than the evening gown she'd selected because Vanessa had helped her refashion it into something that would be worn by a fully fledged debutante, which Charlotte would not be for another year.

And which she now would never be thanks to her hasty decision to run away with Gilray.

"Mr Jasper Creighton at your service..." The young man hesitated, cast a look at the sleeping man on the bed, then finished, "ma'am."

"Oh!" Charlotte gasped, putting her hand to her breast, as a cold draft reminded her that Gilray's enthusiastic response to finding themselves alone in a bedchamber together had caused the fabric to tear. "You must have the wrong room, sir!"

"Not if you are Miss Charlotte Treloar." He cleared her throat, then added, meaningfully, "Or rather, Lady Gilray."

She wasn't going to answer that one. "You know Lord Gilray? Pray tell, what are you doing here?" But her voice shook, for her dignity was as shredded as her night rail.

And when Mr Creighton said, "I'd hoped to waylay you before you reached Gretna Green though it appears a special licence has been obtained and that I'm too late, Lady Gilray," Charlotte put her hands to her face and wailed, "I'm not Lady Gilray. We haven't married quite yet!" before bursting into tears.

It took a moment for her to gather her wits but then she found she was sitting down and the dregs of the claret that Gilray had tossed down his throat several hours before was being pushed into her hands as Mr Creighton said, "My apologies, Miss Treloar, for brandy would be my fortifier of choice but it appears there's nothing on hand suitable for a lady in your emotionally fragile situation. Where will I find your burnt feathers?"

"I have never required burnt feathers in my life!" Charlotte responded, standing up so quickly that her chair fell backwards as she faced Mr Creighton, hands on hips, her chin thrust up to face him for he was rather a tall man and his shoulders were at her eye level. "I am a very robust young lady."

She didn't like the way he considered her in the silence that followed. In fact, her skin burned as his gaze travelled over her hair, the dark ringlets that Veronica had helped create for her romantic flight across the border now bed-tossed and knotted. Taking a deep breath, she self-consciously brushed back an errant lock that had fallen across her eye then tensed while he frowned at her left breast – discovering in horror that the act of pushing back her shoulders had caused the drawstring neckline to snap, and one breast was now on display.

"How old are you?" he asked baldly before adding, "Obviously too young to know better than to associate with this reprobate. Lord Gilray might have a title but that is all he has. There's no fortune to back it up—"

"I ran away with him because I loved him, not because of his fortune!" Charlotte defended herself hotly. "And I shall be eighteen in six months, so I am very much old enough to know my own mind."

Mr Creighton appeared to consider this. "Very well." He shrugged. "Then I shall leave you to continue your journey to Gretna Green so you might enjoy a lifetime of the delights that it has been your good fortune to experience at the hands of thoughtful, caring Lord Gilray." He took several steps towards the door, adding over his shoulder, "There are some ladies who would be most envious of you having heard them say he is most selfish in bed and that with *him* they do not get to experience the pleasure that is the whole reason for bedroom sport. I am so glad you obviously experienced a tender, considerate side to his nature. Good day, Miss Treloar. I hope you enjoy the rest of your life as Lord Gilray's most esteemed and highly regarded wife."

Charlotte watched, frozen, as he let himself out. Turning towards the bed, she summoned her most tender feelings for darling Gilray, who had fired her up with such words of passion and excitement before they'd embarked on their elopement.

"Gilray!" she whispered, needing him to wake so that he might bolster her decision to throw in her lot with him.

But his only response was a slurred, "Ready for another round, my love?" as he rolled onto his side, emitting a loud fart as his eyes fluttered open and his arms went out towards her.

With a gasp, Charlotte ran to the door, throwing it open and calling down the corridor, "Mr Creighton! Mr Creighton! Come back, if you please! I need to speak with you!"

Not that Charlotte had the faintest idea what she needed to say. But she could hardly run through the inn parading herself in public like the scarlet woman Mr Creighton no doubt thought her—and whom the whole world would think her once word got out as to what she'd done.

He'd reached the stairs, but he turned with an enquiring look and asked, "What did you wish to speak with me about?"

Charlotte looked about her, ducking back into the room as a fashionably dressed woman wearing an extravagantly trimmed bonnet passed by on the arm of a soberly dressed gentleman.

Her heart beat even more fiercely as she heard Gilray stir and suddenly she was desperate for Mr Creighton to return, and just as fearful of being recognised.

But *would* Mr Creighton return?

"I... I just need you to come back, sir. Please!"

Relief flooded her when she heard him retrace his footsteps in a leisurely fashion, for she'd closed the door all but a crack. The fashionably dressed lady had raised her nose in the air as if Charlotte were beyond the pale for simply putting her head out in her nightgown. She hoped the woman hadn't recognised her.

And she wished she'd not woken Gilray, who now drawled, "Charlotte, darling, my throat's parched. Fetch me something to drink, will you? And then I have another delightful surprise for you!" just as Mr Creighton pushed open the door and strode in.

"Gad's teeth! Who are you and what are you doing in my

bedchamber?" Gilray demanded, bolting upright then quickly covering his nakedness. To Charlotte's embarrassment, she observed for the first time in daylight evidence of what had made the fumblings under the covers so uncomfortable. Was that what he'd used to spear her before writhing around and then collapsing, leaving her both in pain, yet strangely yearning for she knew not what?

Her cheeks burned as she turned to look out of the window, hoping Gilray would miraculously be fully dressed by the time she faced him again.

If only *she* could.

When she'd set out on this adventure, she'd felt so grown up and adventurous, but now she felt like a … child. A child who'd bitten off more than she could chew.

She also realised now that she had not been apprised of what Mr Creighton was doing here?

And then she felt the most ghastly shame and horror. Had her father sent him? Her beloved father, who had himself shown no care for public opinion? Who forever frustrated her stepmother with his arrogant disdain and yet who showed such concern that Charlotte be moulded into something that the world could live with.

That he could live with.

Or, Charlotte supposed, that her stepmother could live with.

"Actually, I'm here to elicit Miss Treloar's wishes regarding her future."

Gilray's eyes bulged. "Miss Treloar's future? Why, I thought that was obvious." He settled back against the pillows and looked smug as he indicated the room and then Charlotte's state of undress. "Miss Treloar will be my wife before tomorrow night. Don't think there's a damn thing you can do about it either, since I'd say it was screamingly obvious the chit's ruined. No one'll have her except me, now."

Charlotte gasped. Why was she forever doing this yet unable to state her proper outrage? Ruined? She wanted to cry, though, for it was true.

Mr Creighton shrugged. "Yes, I was on my way out since Miss Treloar concurred with these sentiments a few minutes ago. I called on her while you were sleeping and had just been dismissed before she called me back. I'm not the kind of gentleman to pressure a lady against her wishes."

This tickled Gilray's ire. "Are you suggesting that I pressured Miss Treloar to run away with me against her wishes? By Gad, she was gagging for it. All those stolen rendezvous and kisses inflamed her passions until there was nothing for it but to head north. Make an honest woman of her so we can do all those wonderful things we've been doing all night, only this time with the church's blessing. And that of our families, of course. Anyway, you've not said who you are."

Charlotte could see Gilray's bluster stemmed from the fact he was still a little drunk. With his hair sticking up in odd places, and his lips stained purple from claret, he didn't look anything like the handsome young buck who'd so excited her. And when he let out a cry of outrage at Mr Creighton's next question, his sour breath made her take a step backwards.

"Mr Jasper Creighton is my name, and it's really no one's business as to who sent me other than that I'm here in the service of a friend who has asked me to ascertain Miss Treloar's real feelings on the idea of eloping with you. Sometimes a night of discovery is enough to make a lady realise she really doesn't want to go down that path."

"How dare you?" Gilray cried, thrusting out his arm to seize Charlotte and swing her onto his lap where he clasped her protectively—or suffocatingly— against him. "Miss Treloar will soon have everything her heart desires once she's wearing a wedding band, and this thing is legal."

"What about a roof over her head?"

Charlotte darted a look at Gilray. They hadn't talked about this, as she'd simply assumed his stately home in Hampshire would be her new abode. Where else would they go? She'd be Lady Gilray and manage a household of servants on a much grander scale than her stepmother, for all that her father's Provencal estate was sizeable.

"I have adequate lodgings in town. We'll live there until the pater slips off this mortal coil. It won't be long, I assure you, the way he rides to hounds like the devil is at his heels."

Charlotte frowned. Then asked boldly, "Why can't we live at Gilray Hall?"

"Because, my dear, my pater is not going to approve of my following my heart."

She stiffened. "Why not?"

"Well, you are not the ideal choice of a wife for his son, who has just inherited a title. Are you, my love?"

Charlotte frowned. "Why not?" she asked again, feeling indignant. "Why would he not approve?"

The two men exchanged looks and for the first time, Charlotte was aware of a palpable sense of confusion. How dare Gilray even hint she wasn't a suitable match? Charlotte was the daughter of Lord Dewhurst, not only a peer but a famous poet who, while he'd scandalised society with his poems, had grown fabulously rich on the proceeds. Charlotte had never grown tired of hearing the story from Rachel, the nursemaid who'd clearly harboured romantical ideas over her very special papa.

But now she was aware of a frisson of shared under-standing that passed between the two men before they were adversaries again, as Mr Creighton said, "That is no reason to take advantage of an innocent."

"I'm going to marry her, so what does that matter?" Gilray sounded bored as he fiddled with the empty claret glass he'd found amidst the tangled bed sheets. "Tomorrow Miss Treloar will be my blushing bride and nothing papa says or does will change the fact that she will be my eternally devoted wife and the mother of my child. My heir." He grinned. "For all I know, she may already be carrying my heir." He glanced at Charlotte's mid region, then quirked an eyebrow, adding, "And if not yet, then soon. We've certainly had a great deal of fun trying, haven't we, my love? Now get out of here, Mr Creighton, for you are too late to make Miss Treloar an offer she'd consider taking. We've risked everything for love and as soon as you leave us, I can do what a gentleman in such circumstances does and—"

"You're no gentleman."

Charlotte, still reeling from a Gilray's words was shocked by the raw disgust she saw in Mr Creighton's eye as he glared at Gilray and growled, "No gentleman would behave as you have, you blackguard. If I were the girl's brother, I'd call you out this minute. But I'm not, so I'm simply going to put the case to Miss Treloar and offer her two choices: stay with you for a lifetime of... sub optimal bedroom sport. Or come with me so I can return you, Miss Treloar, to Miss Prism's Academy before too much time has elapsed. Excuses have been made that will cover these few hours, but there's little more that can be done if we tarry."

"She is not going with you!" Gilray exploded, hurling himself to his feet, fully naked, as he glared at Mr Creighton. "Are you, Charlotte?" His voice roughened as he saw her indecision.

"Miss Treloar?" Mr Creighton cocked his head and offered her his hand. "I can convey you to another chamber where you can prepare yourself for a day on the road. Travelling with me."

Charlotte studied his handsome face a moment. It was a very appealing face. His brow was high and noble, like his very straight nose; not crooked, like Gilray's. And his jaw was firm while his mouth looked soft and extremely kissable. Not flabby, like Gilray's.

And he was not pressuring her. He'd come to rescue her.

Suddenly, he seemed her saviour.

Charlotte nodded, offering Gilray a sad smile as she took a step towards Mr Creighton. "I feel quite all right, so I'm sure I'm not carrying your heir, Gilray," she said, putting her hands to her belly. "If it's all right with you, I think I'll go with this gentleman, after all."

"Gad's teeth! What is this?" Gilray raked his fingers through his hair. "Are you mad? Why, Charlotte, what you did with me just now can't be undone. You're compromised. And even if you weren't, I don' t know who else would take you in view of your father's black cloud hanging over you."

Charlotte, who'd taken a few steps towards Mr Creighton, stopped. "What are you saying about my father? You're speaking of Lord Dewhurst, if you didn't know."

"Lord Dewhurst no longer exists, my darling girl." Gilray had never sounded so condescending. He lounged over the back of the chair, the bedsheet wound about his waist, his eyes bloodshot. "Has your papa not told you? Surely you understand that is the reason my pater will be less than delighted with my choice, and why I am sacrificing so much for love; sacrificing so much to make you my wife."

Amidst her swirling thoughts, Charlotte was conscious of Mr Creighton stepping forward as if he might physically stop the evil words spilling out of Gilray's mouth, but Gilray was not to be stopped. "Your father lost his title when he murdered Gilchrist. A fellow poet. Corruption of the blood it's called when a peer of the realm forfeits his title and lands to the crown. Haven't you wondered why he's never been back to the land of his birth? Corruption of the blood—and perhaps your blood, too, only I'm prepared to take a chance on that." His nostrils quivered. "I don't know who else would?"

CHAPTER 4

The carriage rocked gently as it conveyed Charlotte and her rescuer over the rutted roads towards London. Beech forests, oak trees and swathes of emerald fields passed by, sending Charlotte who'd had little sleep, into a reverie until Mr Creighton's amused voice roused her.

"You'll hurt your neck if you don't turn it occasionally. Come now, Miss Treloar. It's not the end of the world. Though, it would have been if you'd not seen sense and come with me, but the fact is you did and now all can be set to rights."

"I was already seeing sense and would have made my own way back...only not to Miss Prism's Academy," Charlotte muttered.

"Back where? Back to France? You could hardly have travelled alone, my sweeting."

"I'm not your sweeting and I could easily have taken a disguise!" Charlotte was tired of his condescending tone. As if she were an errant schoolgirl when she could have been a married woman by now if she'd chosen that path.

She had no regrets that Gilray was not going to be her husband, and she'd initially felt very grateful that Mr Creighton had arrived on the scene. But now he was goading her and there was nothing Charlotte liked less than being reminded that she'd behaved foolishly.

"Where would you have procured this disguise?"

Charlotte jerked up her chin. "I'd have swapped my travelling gown with the stinking rags of a beggar. Then I could have gone where I wanted without a second glance from anyone!" Charlotte flashed back.

Mr Creighton traced the top of the elegantly carved stick he carried. "Bravo. So, you really are quite resourceful. I had simply thought you easily led. But the idea is… ingenious, in fact. Next time you abscond from Miss Prism's Academy and my services are sought to stymie another elopement, I shall keep a vigilant eye out for all the beggars who might not be who they appear."

"There will not be a next time, Mr Creighton." Charlotte sent him a saccharine smile. "I know when I am bested and now I shall resume my role of a dutiful daughter until…" She was going to say *until I wed*, but Gilray's words returned to haunt her and she finished with as much dignity as she could, "until someone is prepared to take me as their wife. Clearly, I am not as fine a prospect as I had thought."

"Come now, Miss Treloar, it's not as bad as all that." Mr Creighton sounded kind for the first time. "A beauty such as you will always have your pick of the crop. You chose a rotten apple who drove in the knife when he realised he was about to lose you—"

"But you concurred, Mr Creighton. You shared an understanding when Gilray said how much his father would disapprove of me. I did not know that my father—" She bit down hard on her lower lip to stop the trembling and the plaintive tone. She'd behaved like a child enough for one night. She wasn't going to shore up his impression of her as some over indulged cry baby.

"Your father is a revered poet, and one only has to read his poems to know that a passionate man such as he will defend to the death the woman he loves."

He said it looking out of the window as if he didn't know that his words were like lightning bolts in Charlotte's brain. "*Crime* passionnel" she whispered, adopting the French term for a crime that was clearly so much more serious in England than in France. Indeed, there were many differences between the French, amongst whom she'd grown up until she'd been sent to school to learn English ways. "So, my father killed this man in a duel to protect my stepmother's honour?" She tried to imagine it, but couldn't. Her stepmother was so emotionless and self-contained, unless she was berating Charlotte. Surely she'd never had a passionate moment in her life?

Mr Creighton's look intensified. "Oh, my dear Miss Treloar, I have spoken out of turn. You mean you know *nothing* about what happened?"

Charlotte shook her head. "No one tells me anything. My stepmother has always said my curiosity would get me into trouble." She fiddled with her pale green gloves. "And she was right. I only wanted a bit of fun and adventure, so when Lord Gilray a plan to elope when I met him in the shadows of the Academy, I didn't give too much thought to what would happen after I ran away with him." She sighed. "It all seemed so much more exciting when the brandy was making my head swim. I'm not used to brandy, and he knew that, so I suppose he did take advantage. It wasn't all my doing."

"Gilray is a cad. Let's leave it at that, shall we? You were an innocent, eager for adventure and he plied you with drink and kidnapped you. That's all your parents need to know, whereas your Miss Prism will be told that your impulsive papa whisked you away for a day and is very sorry he didn't inform those good ladies. I believe that's the story that is being put about."

"Well, I can pretend that whatever happened, I've had a marvellous time but am only too glad to be back, I suppose," Charlotte said sadly. "I'm a good actress."

"I can see you have the potential." Mr Creighton reached across and patted her knee. "That's good then. In another two hours we'll be in London, and this will be one grand adventure you can put behind you, and so there's nothing more to be said."

"Except for you to tell me all the details surrounding the reason my father can't come back to England and why he no longer is Lord Dewhurst, even though everyone calls him that."

Mr Creighton thought for a moment. "I'm not sure I'm the one who should be telling you, but I do think it wrong that you've been kept in the dark because it does—"

"Change everything with regard to my marriage prospects, clearly," Charlotte said crisply. "So... papa challenged a gentleman to a duel to fight for my stepmama's honour. And he killed this man who was important, clearly. And that's why he and my stepmama had to flee to France."

"Except that it wasn't a duel, and it wasn't over your stepmama. Though, that said, your stepmother stood by your father and eloped to France with him, even though his reputation was in ruins and it was possible he might hang. She was immensely loyal, to her credit and her detriment. Surprising, I would say, given the circumstances, but credit where it is due and all that."

"My father fought a duel over... *another* woman? Who?"

Lord Creighton looked evasive. "A mystery woman. Let's leave it at that. No one knows, and if they did, they wouldn't tell you. No, that scandal was hushed up very effectively and all you need to know, my dear Miss Treloar, is that your father tried to protect this woman and unwittingly killed a man with a knife in the process, after which your stepmother accompanied him to France where they immediately married."

Charlotte quickly closed her mouth, which she realised had been hanging open in shock. However, it was hard to look serene and dignified in the face of these revelations. "And this other woman?" she managed. "What became of her?"

Mr Creighton crinkled his forehead. "I suppose she went back to her husband and everyone lived happily ever after."

The carriage had been slowing for some time before it came to a complete stop as he added, "Now, let us order refreshment while we change horses, shall we?"

CHAPTER 5

Once Jasper had made arrangements for new horses and ordered refreshment, he joined Miss Treloar in the private parlour above the taproom where, he hoped, they'd remain unobserved.

He'd promised Lord Leeson that he would expedite his request as quickly as possible.

But bad weather had slowed their initial progress, and it was not going to be possible to deliver the chit back to the Miss Prisms' Ladies' Academy before midnight.

The messenger who would deliver this regrettable fact would be travelling alone and unencumbered on horseback. Jasper, therefore, had no choice but to accompany Miss Treloar back to London by coach, which, with rain and darkness, would mean a night on the road.

It was at an unprepossessing inn that he received the news—cheerfully delivered by the innkeeper's wife—that he was indeed fortunate to be able to secure the last room for his good lady wife as a convention of butchers had taken over the rest of The Four-Leaved Clover.

"So, Miss Treloar, we have a conundrum," Jasper now

said, seating himself opposite her at the table, which was laid with the saddle of beef and claret he had ordered.

"Oh?" She glanced up from where he noticed she'd been tucking into her food with great enthusiasm. Jasper supposed Gilray had prioritised his carnal appetites, for Miss Treloar appeared ravenous. "May I have some of this?" she asked, indicating the bottle of claret before querying him on his main concern.

"Of course, Miss Treloar," he began, before remembering how susceptible she'd been to Gilray's brandy, and he didn't want to be accused of taking advantage. He was doing a favour for Lord and Lady Leeson, to whom he owed a great debt of gratitude, and the sooner he got this young lady back where she needed to go, the better. "Though, on second thoughts, if you're not used to—"

She drew back indignantly. "Before today, I was not used to a great many things, Mr Creighton. I expected to be legally wed by now, and the imbibing of claret would be a small thing. I think a glass of what you're drinking is not too scandalous considering what I've already done." Deflated, she stared out of the window and into the darkness. "I should be sorrier than I am, I suppose, and I would be if, in fact, I *was* married. Well, to Lord Gilray." She shuddered as she turned to face Jasper. "How could I ever have fancied myself in love with him when it took only a short while for me to realise he was nothing like I'd thought him? But now you have saved the day and are going to return me with no one the wiser, isn't that right, Mr Creighton? Papa will rest easy once again and I shall have my come-out next year, but..." She frowned. "No one will want me as their wife, not because of what I have done—for *you* will not tell anyone and I have not been recognised — but because of this terrible scandal involving my father which you told me about. What future do I have?"

Jasper contemplated her a moment. She was young, but

she was of marriageable age and, for a young lady in her position, making a good marriage was her highest attainment.

"I mean, would *you* marry me? This is a rhetorical question because we've only just met and you no doubt think me an impetuous child who has caused you so much bother. But would a gentleman like you—or anyone in your position — consider someone like me a marriageable prospect? Knowing that my father has… done what he has done and lost his title? Why, I don't even know if papa can provide me with a dowry, so—"

"Your father might have lost his title and estates but his fortunes have been considerably bolstered by his writings. Don't worry about a lack of dowry, Miss Treloar. There are many gentlemen who would consider you a very worthy bride, and not worry about the scandal."

"But not every gentleman? What about you, Mr Creighton?"

"Well, I'm not in the market for a wife."

"If you were, would you consider me?" She narrowed her eyes. "Thanks to you my reputation remains intact." She took another long draught of her wine which seemed to loosen her tongue further for, to Jasper's alarm, she reached across the table and briefly touched his hand. "But does knowing what I have done change the way you regard me, Mr Creighton? Be honest."

Jasper did his best to evade the question. "Many men are just like Gilray. They're interested only in a young lady's fortune and, knowing how your father dotes on you, and that he'd forgive you anything, there would be many, like Gilray, who would overlook any amount of scandal."

"But I am interested in whether *you* would, Mr Creighton," she persisted. "Am I less, in your eyes, for having sinned?"

Jasper shifted uncomfortably. "My, my, but the wine is making you fretful. We all make mistakes, Miss Treloar."

"But tell me, Mr Creighton, is it of paramount importance to you that your future wife has led a blameless past?"

Exasperated, Jasper admitted, "Since the young lady I was to have married was as virtuous as any saint, it is difficult for me to answer your question truthfully without making comparisons."

Miss Treloar drew back as if stung. "Oh, my goodness! The young lady you *were* to have married? What happened?"

"She died." Jasper opened his mouth to change the subject, but not before Miss Treloar cried out, "How terrible! What was her name? When were you to have been married?"

He really didn't want to go into it. Despite the passing of time, it really was still too painful.

"Her name was Mariah, and we were to have been married two years ago. But that is in the past, Miss Treloar, and it's *your* future that I'm concerned with. I have promised to bring you home as quickly and expeditiously as possible."

"If you'd rather not talk about it, I understand, but you say she was as virtuous as any saint? Was that such a consideration in your eyes?" She nibbled the nail of her little finger and Jasper suspected that her interest in the matter was more to do with his comparison between women like Mariah and women like Miss Treloar.

"It was," he admitted.

Miss Treloar's shoulders slumped. "So, you are saying that knowing of my sins *does* change the way you think of me. Meaning, that if any other gentleman were to find out what you know, I would be damned in their eyes."

"That's taking it too far, Miss Treloar. All that will matter to most gentlemen looking for a wife is that your father provides you with more than sufficient means for you to live comfortably. A handsome dowry, in other words. The fact your father dotes on his only daughter is well known, and as for impropriety, only I know what you have done. I can promise that your secret is safe with me."

She raised her eyebrows. "How little one is aware of these things when one is confined to a schoolroom for most of one's life. Why, the last two days feel like I've only really just discovered the world. How will I get used to daily lessons after what Gilray showed me?"

Jasper should not have felt so shocked by her candour. However, he supposed this was part of her charm—and what put her in danger.

She had her father's handsome features. She was beautiful.

And reckless, like her father.

But so unlike her mother, the late, demure and virtuous Miss Hortense—as he'd heard her described by her cousin, Lord Leeson, who'd sent Jasper on this wild chase across the country.

While James Treloar had had a reputation for wildness, he had married two restrained, demure women: this chit's mother; and then Miss Beatrice Wells, her disapproving stepmother. No wonder the young lady before him chafed under her domestic strictures.

"Consider yourself lucky that you have not suffered the consequences of your recklessness, for in a few short hours it will be as if nothing has happened," Jasper reassured her, raising his glass. Then a thought struck him. *Could* there be consequences? Gilray would not have taken the precautions Jasper did when he engaged in bedroom activities. Gilray would have seen the advantages of ensuring Miss Treloar became his wife—and the mother of his heir — at the earliest.

And the blithe manner in which Miss Treloar said she felt

'perfectly alright' indicated that, even after her initiation, she still knew nothing about the facts of life.

As the girl continued to entertain him with her chatter—for she was indeed most entertaining and the liquor only brightened her spirits—Jasper was consumed by the great worry that Miss Treloar might not realise the worst had happened until she started to increase. He glanced at her midsection, just below the tabletop. He'd admired her slender waist earlier when she'd entered the room wearing a peacock blue British carriage dress with gigot sleeves, made of silk and trimmed with a belt and metal buckle.

Caroline, Jasper's last mistress, had also been a dark-haired beauty and Jasper was not ungenerous when it came to funding her penchant for keeping up with the current fashions.

His glance moved from Miss Treloar's waist, past her shapely breast, and fixed upon her face. She was telling him a story about her little brothers to which he was only half attending, though it struck him that she was fond of them.

But all he could think of were the ramifications of what Gilray had done to her.

"Did you attend to a single word I said, Mr Creighton?" she asked, dropping her hands to her lap and frowning.

Jasper had to admit he had not, and even still was unable to concentrate when she repeated her remark as his own mind was swirling with thoughts of whether he should elicit Caroline's help—for he still visited her from time to time. She'd know what to do if the worst should afflict Miss Treloar.

But how would he convey to Miss Treloar what she needed to observe?

Jasper had sisters, but he would not in a million years speak of such things to them, for all they were close.

When the meal was at an end, Miss Treloar put her knife

and fork together, yawned, said she was very tired and ready for her bed, then clapped her hand to her mouth.

Jasper smiled. "The bedchamber is yours, Miss Treloar. Did you really think I would entertain for a moment the idea of joining you?"

"But the innkeeper says there is only one room."

"And if that is the case, it is yours. I'll find accommodation elsewhere."

"But... where?"

"It really is of no concern to you. I'm resourceful. I will find some means of getting some sleep before we're on the road at sunup tomorrow. Perhaps I'll play a hand or two of cribbage in the tap room until dawn." He grinned. "Unless you really would like me to join you."

Her eyes flared with what he thought was horror, but then realised his error when she said, "I suppose that wouldn't matter, since I've transgressed so thoroughly. But... I don't think—"

"Miss Treloar, I was not serious!" he burst out for he could not have her thinking one moment longer that he meant it. "You have been entrusted to my care and I would not abuse that."

"No, my father might be renowned for his daring poems, but he would not like his daughter to be as daring as the ladies who are in them. I should hardly endear myself to him if I behaved like the *Maid of Milan*."

"Indeed, not," Jasper said, his tone non-committal, for there were few of his, or his parents' generation, who were not familiar with the scandalous poem which alluded to the sexual exploits of its heroine in so artfully a poetic manner as to confound those who would decry it outright as morally heinous.

Miss Treloar's lips twitched. "You cannot imagine my step mama's horror when she caught me reading that poem. I thought she was going to drop dead on the spot. Sadly, I never quite finished the tale about the Siren of s—" She struggled with the word until Jasper said unthinking, "Sensuality," before he realised his error and tried to deflect the conversation in deference to the concerned adults who'd corralled him to protect her innocence.

Or whatever innocence she had left.

She sighed. "And once you have deposited me at Miss Prism's, you will continue on your journey to enjoy the freedom young men enjoy, whereas I'll be imprisoned once more."

Watching her out of the corner of his eye as he took a draught of his beer, Jasper said, "Once I have dispatched you to your Ladies' Academy I shall indeed continue on my way with not a care in the world, as you predict, but I have promised to assist Lord Leeson. He is in the midst of a campaign of re-election, as I'm sure you would be aware."

She smiled, offering a slight shrug, and when he leaned forward and remarked, "I imagine you must look up to your uncle who is fast becoming one of the great reforming voices of our time," she said, frowning, "I have never met either Lord or Lady Leeson."

"You have not?"

"No," she mused. "I once heard my step mama through the drawing room door declare that she would never step foot over their threshold." She glanced up. "And you say Lord Leeson petitioned you to come after me?" She thought a moment. "How odd."

Jasper thought the same as he reflected on what he'd heard.

"I do know papa and Lord Leeson were great friends in their youth," she went on, as Jasper recalled talk of a terrible scandal having caused a schism that had destroyed the

Treloars, and Lord and Lady Leeson's, once close-knit friendship.

"I know Lady Leeson is very beautiful, though, and she was painted by Romney." Miss Treloar's pretty mouth curved into a rapturous smile as she went on. "I saw the portrait on display and when I told papa how I wished I had her graciousness and how much I would like to meet her since my nursemaid had told me what great friends papa had been with Lord and Lady Leeson, he said—" She frowned, remembering, then added with faint puzzlement, "he doubted that would ever happen."

Jasper watched as she replayed her mind over the long-ago conversation. "I remember papa sounded almost angry and I couldn't understand why." She sighed. "Now I know it's because he must have known that he would never be allowed to return to England, and that must have made him sad. Of course, he couldn't tell me the reasons for his banishment, could he? How long ago did he leave England?"

Jasper did the calculation quickly, then said, "Fourteen years ago," while his curiosity grew. Had Lord Dewhurst's first wife been dark-haired? Had she brought a cuckoo into the nest? Despite Lord Leeson's upstanding reputation, could it really be possible that Miss Treloar had been fathered by Lord Leeson, hence his Lordship's particular interest in the young woman before him? Yes, Lord Leeson and Miss Treloar's mother had been cousins, but it was not uncommon to marry one's cousin.

Still, what did the truth matter? he thought as she went on, changing tack slightly. "I don't think I ever saw someone as beautiful as Lady Leeson. How I would love to have golden tresses. I daresay one gets one's own way quite a lot if you're beautiful."

"Then you must be the most spoiled young lady at the

Academy. And there are many who far prefer dark-haired beauties, Miss Treloar."

He liked the way she blushed and giggled, as if this really was a delightful compliment. In three years' time, should he meet her again, he wondered if she would be a world-weary matron with a child or two.

Or a jade.

No, how could he think it? Soon she would be back at Miss Prism's Academy, where not a breath of scandal would taint her and she'd enter the marriage mart like any respectable young debutante.

She'd learned her lesson.

Though he had to make sure.

"Promise me you will not cause your doting papa such palpitations in future," he said, tempering his earlier praise with the sternest tone he could muster for Jasper was not inclined to play the disciplinarian.

"Papa doesn't suffer heart palpitations over scandalous behaviour, but my poor stepmother will, I hope be spared." She dropped her gaze. "I don't dislike my stepmama *all* the time. I've lived with her since I was six years old, and she's been much kinder to me than my aunt ever was. But—" She let out a heartfelt sigh --"she isn't my real mama, so she can't truly care for me as she cares for her own boys or as my real mama would if she were still alive."

"Not true, for the very reason you are with me is due to the fact you have such vigilant custodians who obviously *do* care a great deal for you." He couldn't tell her that her papa and step mama were not the real instigators of his mission.

She bit her lip then looked up. "What are you going to tell them?"

"Don't worry, you will appear nothing more than a foolish schoolgirl who, fortunately, was rescued before too much damage was done."

Now she looked stricken. "But a great deal of damage *was* done." She put her hands to her mouth. "Now that I've thought on it some more, I realise *how* much damage, though —" she shrugged then frowned, adding quickly, "though obviously not the *greatest* damage because I feel perfectly hale and hearty."

It really was not up to Jasper to offer the girl the kind of advice with which only a mother—or stepmother—should furnish her, but it did sound as if Miss Treloar's stepmama was not the sort to be frank in this area.

And, bearing in mind his earlier fears and a very real sense of duty, Jasper cleared his throat and said, "My dear, the greatest damage you refer to is something that only can be either accepted or discounted in perhaps a month or so."

She frowned, her hands unconsciously going to her waist. "I'm not sure I know what you mean, Mr Creighton."

"I mean that… if Lord Gilray had hopes of—" He cleared his throat once more—"siring his heir on you, you would not know for some weeks."

The puzzled look remained until it was replaced by patent horror. "You mean, not until my belly had vastly swollen?"

Jasper shook his head. "You'd know before then, Miss Treloar. You'd know because of changes—" He stopped, feeling his colour rise as he stumbled over his words. "I mean, changes in your… system."

"My system? What do you mean, my system?"

"A lady's… system… is different to a man's. And when that system, which is generally a regular system, encounters changes, then it's a good idea to wonder why."

She was looking at him as if he was losing his mind. "What changes do you mean?"

He felt his skin burn. "Stopping changes."

"Stopping changes?" she repeated as she clearly tried to

puzzle it out. Then, slowly, she said, "So, stopping is a bad thing?"

Jasper nodded. "Unless one is anxious to welcome an heir."

She gasped. "I cannot have Lord Gilray's heir if I am not married to him!"

"It would not be ideal," he agreed.

"Ideal? Why, I would be—" She put her hand to her mouth. "Oh, Mr Creighton, how will I know what to do?"

Tears began to flow, and Jasper put out his hand, which she grasped convulsively. "Will you help me? You obviously know so much more than I do."

She suddenly looked very young and overwhelmed. Jasper rose, drawing her up and now putting both his hands on her shoulders in what he hoped was a paternal kind of way.

"I have three sisters and also a… special friend who would be happy to call on you just to make sure you are… as well as could be hoped," he said. "Don't lose sleep over what can't be changed. And don't worry until there's something to worry about."

"You'd do that? Send your sister?"

"Well, perhaps not my sister. But a friend. A female friend. Now." He became brisk. "You've had a long and tiring day and you need your rest. Your beauty sleep." He touched her nose, smiling. It was a very pretty nose beneath two very lovely tear-filled blue eyes and he was affected, he wouldn't deny it. She was a lively, engaging young woman and Gilray was a fiend to have preyed on her for she was far too young for him.

She rose with a sigh. "I am tired," she admitted. "And I do feel bad about taking the only bed."

CHAPTER 6

Charlotte awoke with the sun streaming through her window feeling refreshed and, indeed, invigorated. It must have been the claret, she decided, for it had made her feel quite deliciously cheerful after what had been a very dampening day, all told. But the moment her head had touched the pillow she'd fallen into an instant sleep.

When she arrived once more in the breakfast parlour to dine with Mr Creighton, she couldn't help remarking on the contrast. "You look like someone has dragged you over the threshold and sprinkled sand in your eyes. Now I feel perfectly beastly for having put you through a night of such discomfort. I don't know how I can atone," she said, spreading a napkin across her knees.

"You don't look the slightest bit remorseful," her handsome companion remarked, not ameliorating his words with a smile but, rather, tucking into his food as if he'd not eaten for two days.

In fact, he looked as if he couldn't wait to reach his destination, whereas Charlotte was only too delighted to enjoy his company for the next few hours. All the while that she'd been awake and dwelling on their journey together, she'd thought how much more dashing and appealing he was than Lord Gilray.

"I have no reason to be remorseful since you *insisted* on sleeping in the taproom, or wherever it was you made your bed," she said.

"Above the stables, in fact."

"Lord, in the hay and straw? Why, that's where I used to make my bed when I was hiding from my step mama, and it's not so uncomfortable." In fact, Charlotte harboured rather fond memories of sleeping on hay and straw. That was when she was with her beloved horse and far from the cares of an exacting custodian who disapproved of everything Charlotte loved. "And if in the company of horses, then I couldn't think of anywhere nicer."

Mr Creighton merely harrumphed at this information, and Charlotte shrugged. "I suppose you can sleep in the coach, though you say it's only three hours to London."

He grimaced as he chewed his way through his breakfast, before mumbling, "I got word it's at least double due to storm damage on the road south."

"Goodness, then you're going to have to brighten your spirits considerably if you're to be endurable company for six hours, Mr Creighton." Charlotte managed a smile. Well, it was quite easy really for now that she'd done her penance for yesterday, the future was looking considerably rosier.

He raised his head and glanced at her with narrowed eyes before, perhaps perceiving her lightened spirits, allowed a reluctant smile. Then he was pushing back his shoulders and saying, "I daresay there's nothing to be done about it. I had enquired as to whether there was a suitable chaperone to take you back to London, which would enable me to saddle up and travel on my own but—"

"And consign me to the clutches of some addle-witted

matron?" Deflated and piqued beyond measure, Charlotte rose. "How could you have thought it for even one moment, sir? Am I so intolerable? Is it that it is painful to gaze upon a creature so depraved as me? Are your morals offended that I am so beyond redemption? Is that it?" Charlotte knew she was working herself up into a state, but the idea that Mr Creighton had tired of her was beyond painful.

Disinterest was a thousand times worse than anything she could think of.

"Beyond redemption? Please, Miss Treloar, you are mistaken!" Mr Creighton also rose, his tone supplicating and more than matching the expression in his eyes. "Why, perhaps there are some gentlemen who would think—" He halted abruptly, coloured, then said, "I think of you as an innocent who was preyed upon by a rake who sought to profit from you. You were entirely blameless."

"No, I wasn't. I thought it an excellent idea to run away with Gilray though I did regret it as soon as I realised that I'd have to spend a lifetime doing the things he thought was good sport in the—" she glanced down and muttered—"the bedroom."

"Enough of this, Miss Treloar. I think we should be going." He seemed embarrassed, which made Charlotte embarrassed in turn, though she really wasn't sure why she should. Marriage was the pinnacle of attainment, so obviously bedroom activities of the sort to which Gilray had introduced her were integral. And yet her stepmother had said nothing about what was involved. Nor had the Misses Prism, despite all their talk of how important it was to make a *good* marriage.

As she took his arm and he escorted her out of the building, Charlotte slid a glance over his profile and experienced a decided frisson of delicious excitement. No. Anticipation. She was going to spend another six hours on the road with this lovely man, and she was determined to make the most of it.

DRY-MOUTHED, Jasper settled his charge into the carriage and himself upon the seat opposite her before the equipage rolled down the main street of the little village.

Six hours. How was he going to manage six hours in such close confinement with a chit who was beginning to exert some strange power over him? He did not want to respond to her questions, for they were too bold for him to do so with any degree of gentlemanliness, and yet he realised that she asked not from boldness but from ignorance and understandable curiosity. If her step-mama had told her nothing of the facts of life, and everything she now knew was entirely at the hands of Lord Gilray, little wonder she was in a morass of confusion.

And yet, the blue-eyed gaze of the damsel opposite him reflected unsettling interest rather than innocent confusion.

He was relieved when the first hour passed in silence. Good. She obviously realised there were questions she'd be forbidden to ask anyone but her closest female relative.

Until she said, "As you know, I have no mama, Mr Creighton, and my closest female relative is my step mama, who has clearly decided I should know nothing until I walk down the aisle to make the match of their choosing." Her gaze was unsettling as she added, "And despite the shame I've brought upon them, I assume that your role is to ensure that their dreams for me come to fruition, even though it's somewhat dampening to realise that I'm not the catch I thought I was—"

"I spoke out of turn. Please, Miss Treloar, it's not as dire as I perhaps portrayed it."

"You say you have sisters, Mr Creighton. How old are they and what do they know?"

"They are twins, about your age, and they know nothing, as I expect is the case for all well-brought-up young ladies of seventeen."

"Why, you say that as if you think it a good thing!" Her look was reproachful as she went on, "Do you think it kind to unleash the kind of terrible ordeal Gilray unleashed upon me, with no warning? I understand that my parents and grandparents married for convenience, but what is the point of a love match if it means a lifetime of putting up with distasteful attentions from a husband? And yet…" She looked puzzled. "I'd started to enjoy it and really had thought my ruin would at least be fun. Not that I'd expected to be ruined, of course. I had thought Gilray a gentleman and that he would wait until we were properly wed. But if my step mama will not speak of it, and none of the other ladies ever do, is this a lifetime trial I must be prepared to endure?"

"Don't be downcast, Miss Treloar, for I assure you that side of things does improve over time for the lady in question and in fact, it is a sport that—" He broke off in horror. What was he telling her all this for?

He was about to atone or at least steer the conversation into acceptable channels when the carriage lurched to one side and Miss Treloar was thrown clean across the small space between them and onto his lap before the equipage righted itself.

"Goodness!" she cried, gripping his shoulders, and making no move to extricate herself. Jasper realised he too was still holding her tightly and now was faced the decision as to whether to put her decidedly back on the seat opposite him or…

Ascertain she'd suffered no injury. For she was a slight

little thing, and the violence had been teeth-rattling to the extent that she had lost her bonnet.

"Are you all right, Miss Treloar?" he asked.

She raised her right hand and stared curiously at her gloved fingers, which she wiggled in front of her eyes. "I think so," she said, seeming to notice at the same time he did that their carriage was stationary and that she was still sitting on his lap.

The shout of the coachman drew Jasper's attention, and he hurriedly settled Miss Treloar on the seat opposite as the door was opened and the fellow's red face intruded.

"We're stuck in't ditch and ain't no way to get her out afore the rain comes," he said, nodding at the darkening sky. "Now't other way than for you to stay here while I fetch help. The village is about two miles away."

Miss Treloar rubbed her hands together and seemed quite bright at the news once the coachman had departed. "I would love to stretch my legs in a gentle turn about the woods," she said, indicating the beech trees. "Please, would you accompany me?"

"We are in dire straits, Miss Treloar. This is not a promenade," said Jasper, as he helped her out.

They really should not be alone together, he knew, but she seemed oblivious to his concerns for once on solid ground, she raised her face to the sky and, closing her eyes, breathed deeply as she put her hand to her forehead.

"Are you certain you are all right, Miss Treloar? You didn't suffer a knock to your head?"

She dropped her hand, then tucked it into the crook of his elbow as she smiled. "I was thinking how strange it is to find myself here, and how sad I will be to return to the Academy."

Jasper led her a little away from the road. "There's no

saying where bold decisions will take you," he remarked pointedly.

Predictably, Miss Treloar bridled at the insinuation. "My step mama always said my fondness for the outdoors would be the undoing of me, but the truth is that while I don't mind indoor pursuits, there is a limit. And that limit was reached when Miss Prism enacted her worst punishment upon me, which was to deny me my weekly constitutional through Hampstead Heath." She fixed her gaze upon him, her tone grim as she added, "So, really, all this is Miss Prism's fault. I was forced to remain alone and bored at Miss Prism's Academy while the other young ladies—most of whom would have preferred to have stayed in—went out. It served her right that I was gone upon her return."

They were walking along a path that led amongst the beech trees now, and the threat of rain appeared to have abated.

"So, your scandalous behaviour with Gilray was more about punishing your school mistress than being in love with Gilray?" Jasper quirked an eyebrow. "What a splendid reason to elope." He sent a worried look about him. "We won't reach Kensington before dark, and I can only wonder what further untruths Miss Prism may be told to account for your truancy."

"It's enough that papa took it into his head to snatch me away for a short sojourn in the capital without informing anyone. I'm sure it'll pass muster as an excuse. Papa can tell them that, can't he?" She spoke easily, breaking off as a shower of rain suddenly burst from a dark cloud that had scudded in from the west.

In fact, dark clouds had gathered above them, as far as the eye could see.

"We can take shelter here!" Jasper had to raise his voice over the sudden noise of the wind in the trees, pointing to a woodsman's hut in the distance. He was relieved to see it appeared to have been abandoned for some time, though the door half fell off its hinges when he pushed it open, stooping to enter.

The exertion had brought the flush to Miss Treloar's cheeks, and he was just admiring how delightfully enchanting she looked when her eyes widened and she cried, "A horse!"

Startled, Jasper saw that a pair of large, equine eyes was regarding them from the other side of the window that was exposed by the scrap of burlap blown back by the wind.

"Miss Treloar, where do you think you're going?"

Charlotte was already halfway out of the door as she turned to look over her shoulder. "How can you ask such a question? That horse should not be untethered. See, it's saddled. Something's happened. Come!"

Charlotte beckoned to the gentle-eyed bay. It didn't flee as she approached him. A quick appraisal of the situation had her glancing about her before deciding her skirts were full enough to ride astride and as she was standing beside a fallen log, a burst of devilry prompted her to leap onto his back with little difficulty.

She laughed at the horror on Mr Crieghton's face and then beckoned to him. "There's room for two. He's lost, but he's sure to know his way home. We'll not stray far from here and can be back at the carriage before the coachman, I'm sure."

"I'm hardly dressed for riding, Miss Treloar—"

"And I am? Come! No one will know and that's all that matters!"

Flying over the fields once they'd left the forest with the wind in her hair made Charlotte cry out in joy. If Miss Prism had allowed her to exercise her desire for freedom with a run on Hampstead Heath, she'd never have agreed to go with

Gilray when he arrived with his sly suggestion that seemed a great deal more tantalizing than spending another day cooped up indoors.

But then, she'd never be here on this horse, riding through the countryside, and truth to tell, she couldn't imagine anything nicer than the feel of Mr Creighton's warm body caging hers as he crouched forwards to help shield her from the elements.

For there was a slight drizzle and Charlotte knew it was folly to spoil her only decent dress. But there were others. She was not short of clothes, for her father was not short of funds. As Mr Creighton had insinuated, a dowry had more power than a tarnished reputation.

Besides which, Mr Creighton was ensuring Charlotte's was as pristine as any future husband could desire.

For regardless of what anyone might say, Charlotte intended making the best of marriages.

CHAPTER 7

S he was like quickfire. Jasper had never felt such excitement and urgency roil through him at the feel of this vital young woman in front of him, laughing with exhilaration as they tore across the fields.

He should have felt a fool for not wearing the proper attire, though his breeches and riding boots did well enough. But Miss Treloar was totally improper in the way she was conducting himself.

The concern that they'd be met by opprobrium when they reached wherever it was that the horse was stabled was quickly replaced by an answering delight. Soon he too was adding his contribution to her cries of exultation.

"There!" She pointed to a wooden structure nestled near the trees, a large dwelling some distance away. "He's found his way home."

A few minutes later they were wandering into empty stables where the creature now contentedly dropped his nose to the water trough and began to drink.

Jasper couldn't help admiring Miss Treloar's ease in this environment. While her behaviour was scandalous and hoydenish, she still carried herself like a lady. In fact, anyone entering at this moment would not have imagined she'd been astride a horse for the last fifteen minutes.

"I'm glad to see he's well looked after," she remarked, settling herself on a large hay bale and looking about. "Lovely fellow. I'm glad you like horses, too."

"How do you know I do? You gave me no choice in that last little encounter." Jasper found he really didn't know how to respond. She was artless, and yet he also suspected, dangerous. Gilray had obviously been entranced and Jasper was conscious of the growing stirrings of something other than he should be feeling as someone entrusted purely with the practical task of getting this young lady home.

"Well, you'd never have leapt up with such athleticism and exercised your lungs if you hadn't enjoyed the ride like I did. Come and sit here." She patted the space beside her. "We'll have to walk up to the house and see if anyone can take us back to the carriage. But you're panting, Mr Creighton, which I suppose is not to be wondered at since you are getting on in years."

"I beg your pardon but I am—" He broke off when he realised she was teasing him.

"How old are you, though?" she asked, more seriously, before deciding to puzzle it out. "You're not a hot young blood like Gilray who thinks of nothing but the moment. A bit like me, I suppose. But I can be forgiven my impulsiveness for I'm only seventeen."

"No one who calls themselves a young lady can be forgiven that," he said, meaning to tease her back before he realised he'd wounded her, adding quickly, "But no one will ever know. Your secret—both of them—are safe with me. And, to answer your question, I'm twenty-four."

"Vastly aged, then," she said with a giggle before suddenly throwing one arm around his neck, tugging him down to her and kissing him quickly on the mouth. "There! What's one more secret? And no one will ever know. I've been wanting to do that since last night. And now I have, and the truth is that I don't care a whit. Kissing Gilray was a terrible disappointment and since he was the only man I'd kissed, I thought I might as well steal a kiss from the keeper of my growing list of secrets. That wasn't too terrible, was it?"

Jasper struggled to answer. The kiss was brief and supposedly unromantic. It was a mere touching of lips in an unexpected union between a young girl giddy with her freedom and a jaded young blade who'd promised to bring her home with as little suggestion of impropriety as possible.

And yet, it didn't feel like nothing. It didn't feel like something isolated and unromantic. Rather, it had the effect of striking a match to something combustible. Not like wildfire, exactly, but a flame to something slow burning and altogether much more dangerous if it was to account for the odd sensation of desire that started somewhere near his toes and slowly curled its way up his extremities.

"That wasn't a kiss," he countered. "Gilray doesn't know how to kiss if you thought this was."

She put her head on one side, and her eyes danced.

Before he knew what madness was issuing from his lips he was saying, "Shall I show you what a real kiss is?"

"Oh yes, she breathed. "I would like that very much."

THE FIRST SENSATION Charlotte was aware of was excitement. Not the initial excitement. Not the *I wonder what it feels like to be kissed* that she'd felt with Gilray for there'd been little lead-up before his mouth was grinding against hers and his hand had been sliding up her thigh that first illicit evening she'd met him after Vanessa had agreed to stand sentinel while

Charlotte had slipped away from the rest of the group of young ladies who were out walking home one afternoon, and she and Gilray had crept into the shadows for her first kiss.

Looking back on it, she wondered if the excitement she'd felt had been more on account of the fact that her behaviour was so wicked, for Miss Prism was only a few yards away, addressing her schoolmates, while Charlotte had been kissing Gilray. But her excitement, then, had been quickly truncated by the sense that she was most definitely missing out on something as Gilray had clearly sated his own desire.

Leaving her wanting.

Now, Mr Creighton's restraint—the antithesis to Gilray's slobbering enthusiasm —was mind-whirlingly exciting. His lips touched hers. No. They brushed hers as fleetingly as a butterfly's wing and she was the one leaning into it.

Not like Gilray, who had pressed down on her until she felt she couldn't breathe.

Well, she wasn't going to let this beautiful man get away. Seated side by side on a hay bale, Charlotte cupped his face, holding him prisoner, and he gave a soft laugh before complying.

It was a thrill for now she felt she was the one who had control in this little encounter.

As their lips had fused, she kept her eyes open, her gaze locked on his. But he was the one who closed his first with a soft groan as if what she was doing to him was as much as he could bear.

Charlotte's excitement ratcheted up several notches. She had real power. He wasn't pretending.

She curled into his side when he fell back, uncaring of the rough stalks that pricked her; and when he looked as if he might rise and end the fun, Charlotte hurled herself into his arms, caging him with her body, slipping her hands into his above his head while she brought her mouth down to his.

For a moment, she had the sense he was about to object and bring this to a definite close.

But when she flung a leg over him and breached the seam of his lips with her tongue once more, the surge of feeling from just beneath his mid region pressing into her belly made her gasp her wonderment.

It was a mistake.

"Miss Treloar!" he exclaimed, sitting bolt upright, his arms going about her to protect her from falling off his lap. "This was not what I was charged to do."

"But you liked it, didn't you?"

"That's hardly the point."

Charlotte reared back. Having fun was exactly the point. The opportunities for having fun were limited in this life, she'd discovered. She was not going to squander the few opportunities offered to her.

Was Mr Creighton really such a puritan?

Charlotte felt she should be blushing and apologising. It's what she'd been brought up to do. But her natural instincts came to the fore.

"But no one will know," she said.

"Again. Not the point. I've been charged with your safe return tonight." Through the open door, he glanced at the sky and the lengthening shadows seemed to galvanise him into action.

In one swift movement he was on his feet, setting her on the ground a safe distance from him though he put his hands on his shoulders—perhaps to ensure she didn't lurch forward, she thought with disappointment since that was exactly what she wanted to do.

"We will never make it back to London tonight and I can only imagine the concern that will occasion. But Miss Treloar, I will not be responsible for adding to the sins Gilray perpetrated against you. I might be considered a rake, but I do have some morals."

"A rake, Mr Creighton? Surely a rake doesn't marry a lady of purity and piety like you were going to do?" Charlotte tried to puzzle him out, not moving while her heartbeat slowly returned to normal. Although, just looking at the lovely man kept it at an unusually rapid resting level, she noticed.

Charlotte immediately regretted her words, for his expression shuttered.

"Knowing someone as good as Mariah spoiled me for... reality," he muttered. "He nodded at the door. "Now, let us introduce ourselves to the good people at that farmhouse on the hill and hope that someone there will be in a position to return us to the carriage where the coachman is no doubt scratching his head in perplexity at our disappearance."

It was dusk by the time they were on the doorstep.

"Who be you fair 'uns?" asked the elderly gentleman who answered. He put his hand to his ear and his brow creased as he repeated after Mr Creighton, "Your marriage is in a rut?" Shaking his head, he tried again, "Or was that a duck. Have you found my duck? She's been gone a very long time."

He looked to be in his eighth decade, an aged farmer with white hair in need of cropping.

And very hard of hearing.

"Is the farmer's wife perhaps here?" Charlotte ventured, peering past his shoulder. The night chill had set in. She was growing cold, and the warmth inside his house was enticing. The crackling fire, swept floors and polished furniture clearly bore the marks of a woman's touch.

"Farmer's wife? My daughter, d'you mean? No, she's gone

to market and won't be back afore day after the tomorrow. What did you say you wanted?"

Charlotte and Jasper glanced at one another and Charlotte wondered if Mr Creighton would be angry at her recklessness in leaving the carriage when the coachman probably had the axle fixed and would be ready to be on his way…

Once his passengers returned.

"We've had a mishap on the road," explained Mr Creighton, "and hoped to prevail upon someone to take us back to our carriage. It's fifteen minutes by horse from here—"

"No horse 'ere."

Mr Creighton frowned. "But there's a horse in your stables. We brought it back. There's fresh hay—"

"Ain't mine. Me daughter took old Silas to market."

A flurry of wind almost blew them across the threshold, and the old farmer opened the door and shooed them in. "You'll catch your death out there. What was this about your marriage…?"

And so it was that the old farmer offered them hospitality for the night, muttering, "Don't know how I can help if your marriage is in a rut, but you can't stay outside all night, so come in, come in. It's late and I have a spare bed."

Except that Charlotte's frisson of excitement at sharing a bedchamber was truncated by her disappointment to discover that the chamber to which they were led had twin beds.

Mr Creighton, to her increased dismay, looked relieved.

"The fact we're even sharing a bedchamber is scandalous," he muttered, sitting on the neatly turned bed which had obviously belonged to a pair of sisters, judging by the furnishing and feminine fittings.

"No one will ever know. And he thinks we're married and if it weren't for you, I certainly would be," Charlotte said, realising this was hardly a logical counterpoint to his argument.

He sent her a look that showed he thought the same before sighing loudly.

"So now what are we to do?" Charlotte asked, not knowing if she felt cross or relieved that he was clearly not going to take advantage of the situation.

"We're to go to bed," he all but snapped before saying very forcefully, "in our own beds. I shall leave the room while you change."

For the farmer's maidservant, a woman even older than the farmer, had rummaged in the trunk at the bottom of one of the beds, in their very presence, and with satisfaction, straightened brandishing a worn and yellowing nightrail for each of them.

At least it smelled clean, and of lemon verbena rather than the acrid smell of the herbs Charlotte's step mama used to deter the moths.

Feeling increasingly despondent, Charlotte took off her carriage dress and laid it over a chair. A few pieces of hay had adhered to the hem, and she removed these almost with a sense of nostalgia. What a magnificent, fantastical encounter that had been. She touched her lips, which suddenly burned at the memory of Mr Creighton's kiss.

Then, hurrying a little in case Mr Creighton returned too soon, she undressed, pulled her nightrail over her head and slipped into bed.

She'd expected him to enter within a few minutes and couldn't decide whether to pretend to be asleep.

But of course she could not.

Not in a thousand years for Mr Creighton was far more fascinating than Gilray, and she was dying to learn more about him. It would be even more fun than lying in bed next to her old school friend Vanessa in the days when Charlotte like to listen to her friend talk about her cousin.

Back when Gilray seemed exciting and romantic.

It was a dampening reflection, for where had that scandalous episode with Gilray led her?

To a bedroom with handsome Mr Creighton.

Charlotte's spirits took an upward trajectory, and she sat bolt upright at the realisation that she really did have the world at her feet.

Mr Creighton was quite a specimen. He was handsome, charming and—

"Miss Treloar, I thought you would be sleeping by now."

"I was waiting for you."

"For me?" When he held up the candle he was carrying, he looked horrified. At least, he clearly tried to look horrified. Charlotte, peering into the gloom, was sure there was a slightly enthusiastic glint in his eye.

"I like your nightrail," Charlotte said with a giggle.

He chuckled, looking down at his ankles displayed beneath the hem of the ancient garment, for the farmer was a good deal shorter than Mr Creighton and this most certainly belonged to him.

"I doubt you're in a position to poke fun," he said, his natural dignity asserting itself.

"See for yourself!" Charlotte hopped out of bed and threw her arms wide. "What a pair and how scandalous that we should be meeting like this, Mr Creighton. Did you enjoy this afternoon?"

"It was an exhilarating ride," he said, his eyes studiously avoiding her before he turned…

As if he were about to slide into bed. Charlotte was outraged.

"I mean after the ride," she said, dancing before him so

that his passage was blocked and he had to attend to her, in fact to the degree that his hands went to her shoulders to stop her from stumbling as she'd got between him and the bed.

"Miss Treloar…"

"Perhaps you could call me Charlotte in view of what happened this afternoon."

He looked troubled as he began, then sighed. "Nothing happened this afternoon."

Charlotte opened her mouth to object, then realised he really was intending to erase that most enjoyable part of this whole journey.

And that, in fact, he intended to slip into bed, blow out the candle and fall fast asleep.

She put her hands on her hips, which she wiggled provocatively as she said, "I've completely forgotten everything about this afternoon. Perhaps you'd like to show me what didn't happen—all over again." Placing her hands on his chest, Charlotte closed her eyes as she tilted up her face.

He'd be unable to resist. Of course he'd not resist for what man could when a young lady was offering such an invitation?

Mr Creighton, it turned out.

When she opened her eyes, he was shaking his head, his expression a touch sorrowful. "Miss Treloar, I was very wrong to do what I did. You are an innocent and I have a duty of care—"

"Yes, so you said. A duty of care to look after me. A duty of care to make sure I never make another mistake as terrible as the one I nearly made by eloping with Gilray. I hadn't, in fact, realised what a lucky escape it was until you kissed me this afternoon."

He winced and began, "I did not…"

But realising he could not possibly continue with the utter falsehood, he shrugged. "You are in even greater danger tonight and so I would suggest that you get into bed like a proper young lady and simply go to sleep, Miss Treloar."

It was a red rag to a bull. Miss Prism could instruct her to go to sleep like a proper young lady, but not Mr Creighton.

Caution, she warned herself, just as she did every time Miss Prism goaded her. Since her hot-headed childhood, she had learned a *little* restraint.

Not much, though, she realised as she reverted to her natural nature, which was to blink very rapidly, open her mouth a little as if in great hurt, and then make a sound like a whimper.

Yes, that had him regretting his harsh tone, though the brief contrition on his face was quickly swept away by clear scepticism when her tears were revealed to be reptilian. Crocodile tears, both Miss Prisms called them.

For an instant, she nearly obeyed. Like Miss Prism, he was dominant. Like Miss Prism, he held all the power. Miss Prism wasn't averse to using the rod to remind her girls of her authority.

Mr Creighton, older, more experienced, was her superior. He held all the power. Charlotte was a minion, an irritation, as he liked to infer. What power did she wield?

And yet, all it took was a flicker in his eye. The faintest clue or suggestion that he wasn't as impervious to her as he'd have her believe.

Impervious to what, though?

Unconsciously she put her hand to her chest, bare above where the night rail tied in a bow as she opened her mouth to respond with something arch and defensive—no doubt like the saucy miss he thought her. There was no intention to provoke in the movement but when she saw the rise and fall of his Adam's apple and the dilation of his eyes, she suddenly realised *how* far he was from being from impervious. His words were lip service.

In fact, it was *she* who held all the power.

Charlotte toyed with the ribbon that secured her nightrail, then carefully ran her hand down her side, feeling the swell of her breast, the curve of her waist, as she watched him carefully.

He was mesmerised.

So was she.

Mesmerised by the look in his eye. Mesmerised by the fact that such a delicious man should look at her as if *she* was the most delicious morsel on offer. She hadn't experienced this feeling with Gilray.

No, the utter want curdling in her belly was entirely new.

Slowly, she took a step forward. It was hard to breathe through the need. She wanted this man like she'd never wanted new dancing slippers or a new bonnet.

Or Gilray.

"Oh," she murmured, putting out her hand, resting it against his breast.

It was supposed to be the moment to presage their joining as one.

Instead, the touch seemed to bring him to his senses, for the mesmerised look in his eye was replaced by shock, as if he were only realising what reality was.

"Go back to bed, Miss Treloar!" His beautiful mouth transformed from invitingly kissable to censorious, and Charlotte could see the rise and fall of his chest as if he were battling some emotion that didn't seem like anger and which she was too inexperienced to identify, though she hoped it might be desire.

Desire?

Charlotte realised her mistake. Gilray had had everything handed to him on a platter. Her enthusiasm, her acquiescence.

Her shoulders slumped. She knew she was impulsive by

nature, which got her into more trouble than her contemporaries.

Despite this, obedience was deeply ingrained.

But she was also intuitive.

And, right now, highly aroused.

And she could sense this man was not quite as determined to repulse her as he would make out.

She didn't know why she knew. She just knew that was something deep within her that encouraged her to persist, even though no one liked to be embarrassed by mistaking the intent of another person.

Especially in a bedroom when the other person was a man who was immensely desirable but who had the power to make her feel like a slattern if she miscalculated.

"Please, Mr Creighton…"

"Please, what? You don't know what you're asking."

But she did. Charlotte wrapped her arms about him. He'd turned his back on her, but she wasn't going to let him freeze her out and simply get into his bed as if going to sleep was the only course open to them.

He tensed, and she pressed her face against his back, nuzzling the rough linen and murmuring. "You rescued me from Gilray. I was his wife in all but name, so I know exactly what I'm asking."

"And why would you if the experience was so unpleasant?" His voice was a low murmur. He didn't turn, but nor did he shrug her off.

Charlotte sensed she was gaining ground.

"Exactly because the experience *was* so unpleasant and yet you maintain that it need not have been. Clearly you know something I don't. And I would very much like to." She smiled as she softly breathed against his skin, her hands slowly exploring his contours. "I know nothing. Except the worst of it, it seems. And you know everything. Please show me, Mr Creighton." She sighed softly. "A girl can't be ruined twice, after all."

He turned abruptly and when she tried to throw herself into his arms, he arrested her movement by putting his hands firmly on her shoulders to hold her away from him.

"You are on the road to redemption. I am rescuing you, Miss Treloar. My reputation is not the shiniest where women are concerned, but I only take my pleasure with older, willing females. I'm sorry for speaking so plainly, but as you are determined to throw yourself into the flames, I need you to know that I will not succumb to your lures."

"Is that what they are?" Charlotte raised her shoulders and sighed. Mr Creighton was very vexing. "Lures? I thought this was a request for education, since Gilray ruined me. And you've stated yourself that you are saving me. Indeed, you saved me from Gilray, but I need you to save me from making a mistake that is potentially worse."

Mr Creighton gave a short laugh. "I hope you'd not be tempted to ever make another mistake like your mistake with Gilray. I may not be around to rescue you a second time."

"Not a mistake like eloping! But marrying! How will I know if the man I marry is just as... selfish as Gilray?"

Mr Creighton regarded her for a moment as if he had no words. Then he said slowly, "Miss Treloar, proper young ladies do not get the opportunity to know such things. A man must make an honourable offer of marriage, and the lady must—"

"Accept and take her chances," Charlotte cut in. "But now that I know the... pitfalls... I will be too wary ever to accept marriage. Please, Mr Creighton, you are the only man who knows that I am ruined. And you are the only man in a position to show me what Gilray clearly could not... and that you claim is a fact. That there's something... pleasurable in what I found only distasteful with Gilray and yet which, right now…" She put her hand to her breast. She was breathing deeply for what had begun as a desire to entice him for broader reasons had become a genuine need to engage with this man in particular. He was delightful when he was in charity with her, but she could not bear that he dismiss her.

It was more than that, though. And she hung on his answer.

Only realising how great was the blow to her pride when he simply smiled kindly at her and turned back to his bed.

This would not do. Charlotte was not used to being rejected. She'd asked as nicely as she could, and she knew he was tempted.

"Then… just kiss me!" she cried, insinuating herself between him and the bed and twining her arms about his neck, drawing him down to her.

She was prepared for another rebuff but not prepared to give up.

So when she was rewarded by the grazing of her mouth with the faint stubble of his cheeks before his lips found hers, her body was primed for more.

Tightening her hold about his neck, she cleaved closer, aware of the contours of his hard body, the jutting of his hip, the hardness of his chest, the swell of his manhood.

It was thrilling in a way she'd not experienced before.

This was her awakening. Not the tawdry, one-sided exchange with Gilray.

Or rather, this promised to be her awakening. Only Mr Creighton could arouse her and only Mr Creighton would do. One taste and then she could return to the girl she was before.

That's what she told herself as his knees buckled and she tumbled on top of him onto the bed. For the kiss was more than the kiss she'd expected.

And, it seemed, he felt the same.

His arms wrapped about her, and as she moved to balance herself, lying on top of him, she had to tug at her nightgown to allow her trapped knees to find the right position to keep her steady for she was enjoying this strange sensation of power, with Mr Creighton beneath her while she stroked his face and kissed his eyes, his cheeks, his lips.

A crescendo of pleasure accompanied the deepening of the kiss, which she thought could not be increased until it was joined by another, extraordinary feeling as his hands crept up her thigh. At first it was a gentle, rhythmic stroking of the outside, which was pleasurable enough until Charlotte's senses went on high alert when he began stroking the sensitive flesh of her inner thigh.

And then the exploration became more intimate. With a gasp, Charlotte closed her eyes and surrendered herself to the powerful sensations that seemed to have invaded her brain.

So this was what Gilray had failed to show her.

And this was what marriage to the right man offered her.

For a lifetime.

CHAPTER 8

Jasper knew he should feel guilty. It was not right that as he gazed across the small space that separated him from Miss Treloar in the carriage the next morning that he should not feel filled with remorse and self-disgust.

He might have if she'd acted like the usual innocent chit and simply gazed back at him with wonder as they rocked over the road's bumps and ruts, now only an hour away from their destination.

She'd slept for the first part of the journey and little wonder, for they'd not had much rest in the uncomfortable beds the farmer had generously offered them.

Not that it was the fault of the beds, even though they were uncomfortable.

But now she was sitting upright, her carriage gown looking as crisp and fresh as she did. Her skin looked dewy with health, her eyes bright with awareness—and interest—as they studied him.

Tensely, Jasper awaited her first words, for she'd only just woken and he'd not seen her since she'd fallen asleep in his arms. When the cockerel had jerked him to his senses before dawn, he'd carried her across to her own bed and laid her down gently before dressing quickly and taking himself outside.

He needed to order not just the day's plans for getting Miss Treloar home, but his own conscience.

What had possessed him?

Not for one moment had he ever intended to lay a lascivious finger on a young lady entrusted to his care.

Lord Leeson was a man he admired greatly. Jasper's own father was a contemporary, they were all members of the same club, Whites, but it was Jasper, with his like-minded political views, who was now often the recipients of invitations to Lord and Lady Leeson's house parties where the conversation was exhilarating, and the hospitality excellent.

Jasper knew that, since Mariah's death, his reputation was not as shiny as it had once been. But he also knew he was deeply honourable when it mattered.

And this had mattered.

Yet now as Miss Treloar smiled guilelessly at him, something hitched in his heart though he did his best to remain impervious, and was about to break the silence with something gruff and off topic when she said, "I enjoyed last night very much."

Her hands were clasped demurely in her lap and in her neat bonnet, festooned with a spray of Lily of the Valley, she looked the personification of innocence rather than the fiery vixen he'd discovered her to be last night.

How could he have been so weak? he asked himself, not for the first time.

Then another thought intruded. Was this a ruse? A means to drag him to the altar? The idea occasioned such horror as his first response that he was quite astonished to realise the idea wasn't so repugnant after all.

He forced himself to recall Mariah's image. It had always been so easy, but how strange that her features seemed to have blurred since the last time he'd conjured up the personification of purity.

That's what she was. An angel of goodness and purity, and Jasper had determined that he would only wed when he encountered her equal.

Miss Treloar might be engaging, but she was not what he was looking for in a wife.

"I'm glad, Miss Treloar." He wasn't sure how to respond, except to reassure her, so, looking out of the window rather than at her, he muttered, "This will go nor further and, of course, I took precautions."

"You mean, to ensure I'm not more ruined than I already was before?"

Jasper sighed, returning his gaze to her fresh, expectant face. "That's not to say the damage hasn't already been done, Miss Treloar. I mean, you might still *have* to marry Gilray."

"Nothing would induce me to marry him," she said decisively. "I thought it when you rescued me, but after what you showed me last night, I am determined upon it. I will *never* marry Gilray. Not if he came begging."

"But if you.... found yourself with child, then you'd have no choice."

"I'm sure that won't come to pass, Mr Creighton," she said comfortably, patting her stomach. "I don't feel any different. I feel perfectly wonderful, in fact, and that's thanks to you, not to Gilray."

After a pause she added, sounding a little more concerned, "I hope you don't think my intention is to persuade you to marry me. I'm not about to broadcast to the world what happened between us last night. No one will ever know about that. It'll be as if it never was. Well, I'm sure it can be like that for you because you're a man and there are many women to whom you've shown similar attentions. I knew that, and that's why I asked you to show me. So at least I'd know."

For some reason, her blithe disregard that it might mean something to him and that she had no intention of pressing marriage; that, in fact, she seemed not to wish it, needled him. He wasn't expecting that.

But of course he was glad.

"Then there's nothing more to be said on the matter, Miss Treloar. All that matters is that we get you back to Miss Prism's Academy at the earliest. Perhaps your papa will be waiting for you there. After all, the excuse is that he took you away on impulse."

She looked regretful. "Papa can be very impulsive and it was a very good excuse, but I do not think he will be waiting. You know he cannot return to England." She bit her lip, her brow creased in thought. "I thought that when my stepmama said there are things I should not know, that she was referring to men, in general, and that is partly what prompted me to go with Gilray. But perhaps she didn't mean that. Perhaps she was referring to papa. Well, maybe he'll tell me one day, though I doubt it. I think you are the only person kind enough to provide me with answers to any of the multitude of questions I have, Mr Creighton."

Jasper didn't think he was very kind. He made sure he didn't catch her gaze again, for he was needled with guilt. But when she turned her head to look out over the passing countryside, he found he could not stop feasting his eyes on the lovely outline of her jaw and throat.

And wondering what the future held for her.

For when they reached Miss Prism's Academy for young Ladies, it was not Charlotte's father who was waiting for her.

Nor was it Miss Prism, though Jasper spied her in the background, looking almost cowed.

And when he saw the fierce righteousness on the face of the woman who'd clearly assumed the mantle of authority when it came to Charlotte's future, he understood why.

"Charlotte, how good of you to return." The tone was like a lash. A sneer of sarcasm. Dressed soberly in a gown of dark grey with none of the bows and furbelows that were so fashionable, her headwear an unflattering black bonnet, the woman ignored Jasper as she launched into her tirade.

Jasper stared. Lord Leeson had said nothing about anyone other than Miss Prism taking charge of Charlotte.

They were now in the vestibule of the school building. It seemed the pupils had gone to bed, for only one lamp lit the room, leaving the rest of the house in darkness.

The school mistress—presumably one of the Miss Prisms — stood in the shadows while this strange woman spoke as if she were well acquainted with Miss Treloar for her tone was familiar and chastising. "Since you have shown how poorly you regard the kindness of Miss Prism and her sister, it has been decided you will board elsewhere."

Jasper watched the confusion flit across the young girl's face before she sent him an appealing look. But what could he say? He didn't have authority over Miss Treloar. This other woman seemed to want to ignore the fact he had brought the girl home, for she had not even the courtesy to introduce herself.

"Elsewhere?" It was the only question he supposed Charlotte could ask.

"Yes, with me. I am Mrs Henley and, as a dear friend of both your late mama and your step mama, I have agreed to take you in hand and school you to obey. To show the gratitude that has been so sorely lacking to date."

Fear flashed across Charlotte's face, for even Jasper could see there was little kindness in the Puritan-attired gorgon who faced Charlotte upon the top step. And there was no succour from Miss Prism, whose stony-faced expression showed no concern.

"May I ask where you are taking her?" Jasper asked, after introducing himself.

But the woman shook her head, barely glancing at him as she took Charlotte by the elbow and began leading her away.

"My carriage is over there," she said, half over her shoulder. "Miss Prism has already organised the packing of your trunk, Charlotte. All is in order. You have everything you need. Now, say your farewells to your kind benefactors of the past seven years. Miss Prism and her sister might have missed you had you been a good, biddable girl, but they were only too pleased to hand over such a trial to me. And whose fault is that, my girl? I have reassured your dear stepmama and papa that they need have no concerns over what will become of you following your disgraceful conduct." Her smile was grim as she stood by the carriage door, opened by the coachman who waited to help Charlotte in. "And, indeed, they won't, for I will see to it that no one else will suffer what you have done or experience the pain you have caused. No one, except yourself."

CHAPTER 9

THREE YEARS LATER

It had started with a bitter wind and now the relentless drizzle had driven most guests back to The Lodge, as Lord Collingwood's stately pile was termed.

Only Jasper and Collingwood continued to brave the fens, shotguns at the ready as they tramped through the gorse, flushing out the pheasant to add to their tally.

Jasper was not a particularly keen hunter. Not like Collingwood who seemed singularly determined to outbrace everyone else invited to his week-long hunting party in the highlands.

A little scandal and embarrassment in town had meant Lord Collingwood's invitation had been timely. In fact, escaping to The Lodge, the bleak, beautiful estate of the young viscount, couldn't have come at a better time.

Two shots fired ahead of him made Jasper jerk his head up in the midst of ruminating upon his stupidity; and how long before it was safe to put his head above the ramparts and return to London.

He was not usually indiscreet, but he had miscalculated when an amour had gone to his head and the passionate trysts between himself and Countess Orlov had been uncovered by Count Orlov himself who'd inadvertently walked in on them.

Jasper had miscalculated regarding the extent of Count Orlov's power and influence in the capital.

Just as he'd miscalculated regarding the count's fury at being cuckolded.

He'd not thought too much about either when Katerina had assured Jasper that her husband was at the theatre and posed no threat.

But Jasper should have exercised the caution he usually did—and would have—had he not been a slave to the Russian beauty he'd met at a Christmas Ball some months previously.

The dark-haired siren had taken an instant liking to Jasper who'd heard the rumours of her voracious appetite, taking lovers at least ten years younger than herself; and he'd been delighted to discover that her repertoire was as extensive as reported.

Count Orlov had discovered them *en flagrante* in the Orangery where Jasper had been eating grapes which the countess had artfully positioned on various parts of her flawless anatomy.

So, taking himself out of London, at least until the gossip sheets had something else with which to occupy themselves, seemed wise, and now Jasper was cooling his heels, literally, as he trudged through the mud.

Another two shots rang out, and the beaters scurried ahead to collect the dead birds. Jasper was content with his one brace of pheasant but his companion was a keen sportsman. He'd netted at least a dozen brace, his enthusiasm for blood sports apparently undimmed as he engaged Jasper in a monologue about the stag he'd shot the previous August whose head now adorned the walls of his Hampshire estate.

Now the young viscount was talking about his hunting expedition to the Cape Colony five years previously and the King of the Jungle he'd shot and skinned which now carpeted the front vestibule.

"Shot it two days after I disembarked in Cape Town," he now said as he and Jasper began the walk back to the Lodge.

"You must enjoy the hunt to travel so far from home," Jasper remarked.

The young viscount stopped to level him with a slightly contemptuous look. "For bagging tusks of a hundred and fifty pounds each? And the lion skin in the drawing room? You saw that, didn't you? Three hundred and thirty pounds of aggression and I shot it at 20 yards as it bore down on me." His nostrils flared as he ran a slightly shaking hand through his dark, oiled locks. "I am not a coward, Mr Creighton—"

"I did not infer it," Jasper defended himself in as ameliorating a tone as he could manage. He'd honed the art since the first time Count Orlov had borne down on *him*.

Fortunately Collingwood's tone modified and he continued to walk. "The game was worth every minute of the 90 days sea passage. Herds of beasts filling the horizon."

Jasper was silent as he tried for a response that would indicate how impressed he was, without sounding false or condescending. He'd not quite managed it with Count Orlov who'd threatened to blow his brains out if he ever saw him with his wife again.

Or, ever again, in fact.

But unlike the count whose power and influence could never be called into question, Collingwood appeared more like a young man desperate to impress the world with the magnificence of his trophy collection.

So, Jasper now asked in as conversational a tone as he could manage when his damp boots were causing blisters, and he really had no interest in hunting at all, if the truth be told, "Do you have a name for your magnificent lion?"

Collingwood chuckled. "It's a massive thing, isn't it? And it's right there as one walks through the front door. Lady Ogilvie shrieked when she saw it. Mahmoud, I call him. Mouth was wide open. Thought it was going to devour her."

Jasper feigned his own chuckle. "Clearly your wife is not so lily-livered," he said, though his thoughts had returned to the mole on Katerina's lily-white left breast rather than the fellow's obsession with blood sports. Lord Collingwood and he might be of similar age, but that was where all similarity ended.

"My future wife, you mean. Her temperament is of no account as long as she's obedient, and I've been assured that is the case."

Jasper glanced up at the smug look on the young man's face. "You're to be married?" He supposed the young man would make some young lady happy. The fellow was titled. More importantly, he was wealthy. Lord Collingood was the only son and heir to a vast swathe of land in the Norfolk fens. A lonely place indeed, which might account for the fellow's distant but superior manner.

"Negotiations are underway. I'm told I can anticipate February nuptials. A little later than I would have liked, but apparently the chit is in mourning and won't bring the date forward until she's out of her twelvemonth." He shrugged. "Nearly home," he added, indicating with a jerk of his chin the forbidding grey Scottish fort ahead of them.

Jasper turned up his collar and surveyed his temporary home. "A warm fire and a brandy won't come amiss," he said.

He didn't fancy spending more time with Lord Collingwood than he had to.

~

AN HOUR LATER, the roaring fire in the drawing room welcomed Jasper, who found that a change of clothes and two brandies couldn't dispel the chill he'd felt since he'd arrived. Lord Collingwood's hunting lodge might be ideally situated for hunting, but the company, and the draughts, might make him reconsider accepting his next invitation.

Though that might depend on Count Orlov.

Lord, if Mariah could see him now, he thought with a pang as he recalled the goodness in her eyes when she'd held his hand for the last time. He'd sat at her deathbed for two days, watching the life ebb from her.

So much faster than it should have, he thought bitterly, for her brother's murder had hastened the progress of the consumption that had begun to consume her not long after he'd fallen instantly in love with Mariah at a public Assembly.

"Mr Creighton?" The lilting feminine tones were familiar, and he turned, delighted to see Lady Leeson issuing into the drawing room on her husband's arm.

Lord Leeson had moved on to speak to their host and now the politician's lovely wife was conversing with Jasper as if they were long-lost friends. The warmth of her greeting was surprising.

Surprisingly appealing, in fact, as Jasper had left London feeling distinctly conscious of the chill of many of his receptions.

Katerina's husband wielded more influence than Jasper had anticipated, which had impinged upon Jasper's ability to enjoy the entertainments he usually did.

Lady Leeson, it seemed, knew nothing of all this. Fortunately.

Otherwise she would not have clasped his hand, led him into a quiet corner, and asked him in a murmur, "I haven't seen you since you were charged with that urgent mission my dear husband needed expediting three years ago. But I always did wonder if you found the young lady engaging."

Jasper blinked. The question had taken him by surprise, and he was not sure how truthful he should be. Often he thought about those two days — and nights—in Miss Treloar's company. Why, even as he kissed Katerina's mole upon her breast, he sometimes compared it to the tiny mole Miss Treloar sported in a similar place.

He could hardly tell Lady Leeson that.

So, he said, "Extremely engaging." He smiled. "Lively, irrepressible. Definitely engaging."

Lady Leeson nodded slowly, and Jasper regarded her with quiet admiration. She'd be Katerina's age, he supposed, but unlike Katerina, there was no flaunting of her almost breathtaking beauty. Her titian tresses were dressed in the fashionable plaits and coils of the day, and her gold belted and buckled evening gown showed off her neat, girlish waist. Lord Leeson had scored himself a trophy, indeed, he reflected as Lady Leeson went on, "Three years have passed since you did young Charlotte such a service, whisking her away from Gilray, who was out to snare her fortune and nothing more. At least, that was the belief of her father and stepmama who prevailed upon my husband to do what he could."

Jasper noticed how carefully Lady Leeson phrased her words and again tried to recall the details of the long-ago scandal, involving Lord and Lady Leeson, and Charlotte's impulsive, poetic father.

Poor Charlotte. She had known nothing of this. He hoped

he'd not upset her too much by mentioning that the murder of a peer in a crime of passion had been the cause of her father's exile.

This was grim history, but he smiled as he recalled the girl herself. She'd been utterly charming.

However, he said, taking his own care in responding, "I believe Charlotte was relieved to have been spared the consequences of her impulsive behaviour. I intervened just in time."

Lady Leeson clasped her hands together. "That is such a relief, Mr Creighton. How did she appear?"

How did she appear? Memory surged as he recalled exactly how she'd appeared: lovely, lithe and inviting, physically. Her neatly turned limbs and pert, well-formed bosom had been truly arousing.

As for her varying responses? There'd been indignation. Injured pride.

And then that enthusiasm, altogether more pleasing to both parties.

He cut the thought off at the root, asking instead, "I daresay she wrote to thank you and Lord Leeson for her lucky escape, as it must certainly have allowed her to make a much more suitable alliance?"

A shadow crossed Lady Leeson's lovely face. "After you returned her to the Academy, I believe her stepmama had requested that her care be entrusted to...another woman." She cleared her throat. "How... did Charlotte seem when you parted ways?"

Jasper cast his mind back. "I cannot really say. The woman, whose name I fail to recall—"

"Mrs Henley."

"Mrs Henley. Ah, yes, that's right." He recalled the gimlet eye and unfriendly greeting of the statuesque woman who'd greeted them both so coldly as he looked up into Lady Leeson's unsettlingly intensive gaze.

In as relaxed a tone as he could manage, he went on, "The details escape me, Lady Leeson. However, I've no doubt Miss Treloar enjoyed a stunning debut or perhaps has already been whisked off to become some scion's wife. She was an extraordinary creature." He coloured instantly, wishing he hadn't said that for extraordinary was not the sort of adjective a young man would use if he'd merely expedited an unremarkable duty.

"You thought that?" Lady Leeson seemed uncommonly gratified. "But no, she did not enjoy a stunning debut, for she was very ill last year and nearly died. I believe this is the year she is to shine and I daresay you will come across her at some ball or rout. If you would convey my good wishes to her, I would be very grateful. I do not spend much time in the city but, on my husband's account, I worry for the girl."

Surprised, Jasper agreed before he was claimed in conversation by another of the guests, Sir John, for a companionable fifteen minutes of conversation before the dinner gong sounded and the gentlemen led the respective ladies in to the dining room.

Not that there were many ladies, for some wives had cried off, not being hunting enthusiasts. Lord and Lady Leeson, he noticed, seemed uncommonly fond of one another and, now that Jasper was nearing the age at which he ought to settle down since the chilliness of his reception the past few months drove home the fact his behaviour was considered a stretch too far, experienced a frisson of … was it envy?

He glanced about the table, but it was a sober gathering. Only young Collingwood droning on about his sporting prowess. A dozen brace in an evening. And what had Jasper bagged?

"I don't keep a tally on my successes," Jasper responded with a smile. He was tempted, but forbore to say more. Collingwood seemed like the sniping, competitive kind, and he had no wish for any kind of provocation. Truth was that he just wanted to go to bed.

Only Lady Leeson with her dewy, unlined skin, and her sparkling eyes, held any interest but she spoke little. Collingwood, obsessed with documenting the size and magnificence of his various collections, dominated the conversation.

"A timely flight into the country."

Jasper jerked his head up. Was he imagining the veiled scorn behind Collingwood's remark?

Yet there was Collingwood, stolidly sipping his soup. Jasper had all but reassured himself he was mistaken until he caught the sly gleam in the other man's eye. He felt his hackles rise but strove to remain unaffected.

"I thought to spend a few weeks in the country, yes, before I go adventuring." He wanted to shift the focus of the conversation before anyone pondered too deeply on what Collingwood appeared to be inferring; and hoped no one would quiz him on exactly where he intended to go adventuring, but it had seemed a neat way to deflect the conversation. He sighed as he took a sip of claret. "I'm tired of London revels."

"Your departure won't break any feminine hearts?" Lady Leeson asked with a smile. "The season will soon be underway and Lord Leeson and I will be in the capital. We will miss you."

"The Cape Colony, perhaps, eh?" Sir John took finished his drink. "To find a larger, handsomer lion than Collingwood's. He'd go with you if he hadn't found himself England's fairest bride. What progress on your nuptials, then, Collingwood?" Sir John asked. "There was some delay last time we spoke."

"February, I believe, though I'd bring it forward if I could." Collingwood didn't look up from his food. "Ideally, I'd like to see my wife installed at Emsley Manor for a couple of months before I travel west."

"Ah yes, the copper mine," Sir John said. "Might she not wish to enjoy sunnier climes in Cornwall after a couple of months in so remote a location as Emsley? It will be a shock to her."

Collingwood shrugged. "She'll remain at Emsley."

Jasper, taken aback by his tone, said, "It would appear you've chosen a wife with a sober temperament. A veritable asset."

"An asset," Collingwood repeated, frowning and silent as if he truly was considering the remark before he looked up. "Marriage is a business, of course, but I would not have used the term asset."

The way he pontificated on this little matter gave Jasper the faint hope that he'd misjudged Collingwood, until the young man responded, "My future wife is the most beautiful woman I have seen in my thirty-one years. When I knew I would never find one more beautiful, I decided I would install her at Emsley as my wife—"

Sir John broke in with a laugh. "Collingwood is a collector." He emphasised the word in a way that made Jasper take stock and interrupt when the conversation was nearly diverted into other channels.

"What do you collect?" he asked.

"You've not seen my lion. There is not one larger in the British Isles. My elephant tusks? Two hundred pounds. There are none heavier in this country." He drew in a laboured breath. "I collect the finest specimen of every category on this earth." Collingwood's tone was serious. "If you are invited to Emsley you will see the finest stag mounted upon the wall, the largest, fiercest lion skin upon the floor, the finest plumage of the most exotic birds encased in glass—"

He might have gone on had not Sir John, who'd imbibed a considerable amount, Jasper surmised, said with another bluff laugh, "Collingwood is a man of discernment. A true collector, as I've said. I look forward to laying eyes on this future wife of yours, Collingwood. The most beautiful woman in all England, you say? Well, I'd have thought there were qualities other than beauty that you would consider when taking a wife."

"Like virtue." Collingwood nodded. "Beauty reflects virtue." There was no levity in his tone. He spoke as if it were an incontrovertible truth.

"And I look forward to hearing how she caught your eye." Lord Leeson's tone didn't match that of either Sir John's bluff heartiness or Collingwood's intense seriousness. He seemed a trifle concerned.

As was Jasper.

"Yes, where did you meet this vision of loveliness?" asked their hostess, Lady Bertram. "In London? For surely she can't be a provincial?"

Collingwood put down his wine glass, stared around the table at the sea of intent faces and said, "I met her at the Marshalsea."

He seemed genuinely surprised when this elicited gasps, Lady Bertram crying out, "In prison?"

"She was delivering alms," Collingwood said, frowning again, as if unsure why his remark had occasioned such a response. "Soberly dressed, she was with an older woman whom I engaged in conversation after she dropped her basket of victuals for the prisoners. Yet there was a singular quality about the young woman. She barely spoke and when I introduced myself, I was struck by the fact she showed no emotion." He shrugged. "Most young ladies respond in quite a ridiculous manner when I am introduced, in view of the fine catch I represent. I believe that is how it is termed? My curiosity was aroused." He dabbed at his smooth upper lip with his napkin, his mouth an almost prim line as he added, "My curiosity is not often aroused."

"And now you are to marry her?" cried Lady Bertram, the plumes in her elaborate coiffure waving. "Why, what a romantic tale."

"There was no romance involved." Again, Collingwood's serious look elicited a shiver down Jasper's spine, and he asked, "So this wife of yours is for your collection, Colling- wood?" Immediately he regretted his insult but was even more surprised when he realised Collingwood did not consider it as such, saying, "That is correct. I engaged her guardian, Mrs Henley, in further conversation and learned—"

He was cut off by Lady Leeson's gasp. All heads turned towards her, and Jasper was surprised to see Lord Leeson patting her arm, looking as if he were equally horrified by whatever had set off her cry.

Lady Leeson waved her hand and said, "My apologies, Mr Collingwood. I interrupted you when you were telling us what you'd learned about… this paragon."

"A paragon, indeed, Lady Leeson. What I learned about the young lady convinced me she is the epitome of every- thing I desire in a wife. She is a paragon of virtue and beauty, yet with a dedication to duty and hard work that strength- ened my resolve to make her mine."

Jasper, after a quick, anxious look at Lord and Lady Leeson, asked, "And how did you woo this paragon of beauty and—" he hesitated—"virtue?"

"Mrs Henley brokered the match—"

"Your intended has no male relative?" Lord Leeson asked,

and Jasper recognised a suppressed anger, which went unnoticed by the rest of the party.

The next course had been placed upon the table. Collingwood, who had a hearty appetite, tucked into his syllabub, taking a mouthful before replying. "Her father does not reside in England, so negotiations were conducted between us through Mrs Henley."

"And the young lady in question?" Lady Leeson asked. "She was amenable to your offer?"

"The young lady in question was only too pleased to accept."

JASPER BIT HIS LIP. Henley was not an uncommon name and he could no more imagine Charlotte quietly doing good works at the Marshalsea than—

Marrying Gilray.

Besides which, the vital young woman he had met would have thumbed her nose at Collingwood's marriage offer.

Sir John merely laughed. "Oh, Collingwood, you're too rich. I don't think your approach would have gone down too well with my wife, and perhaps the other ladies at the table, but well done, I say. I shall look forward to meeting this paragon of beauty and virtue when you bring her to the capital in February."

"She will not accompany me. I will be in the capital for business, not pleasure."

"She may not consider your proposal so favourably if you intend keeping her in a gilded cage, Lord Collingwood," Lord Leeson said.

"The match is in our mutual interests. She will be amenable to whatever I tell her," said Lord Collingwood.

Jasper felt sorry for the young woman, but his attention was diverted by Sir John's talk on the possibility of a visit to the Cape Colony, which bolstered his enthusiasm for swapping the dreary climes of England for somewhere more interesting.

After some minutes of such talk, Lady Bertram rose and took the feminine contingent off to the drawing room while Jasper and the gentlemen remained for port and talk on gold mining and hunting.

Collingwood, who'd gone quiet, was drawn out by Sir John's exhortation that he regale the company with more talk about his hunting exploits to which he readily agreed in his cool, pedantic manner.

Jasper noticed Lord Leeson said little, but that he seemed to be watching Collingwood with some intensity. No doubt he was as troubled as Jasper was by what Collingwood had revealed about his attitude towards the wife he would soon take.

As the men rose and arrived in the drawing room to join the ladies, Jasper noticed out of the corner of his eye that Lady Leeson rose and, gripping her husband's arm, spoke in a low, urgent tone. When he drew closer, he heard him say, "It cannot come from you, my love. You know why—"

But the pair drew apart as he approached, Lady Leeson rejoining the ladies, while Lord Leeson appeared surprisingly awkward for a moment before he took a step towards Jasper to intercept him before their host who was making his way in their direction.

"If I may have a word," he said, clearing his throat. He appeared uncomfortable, even diffident, which was not like the practised politician Jasper knew.

"The talk at table regarding—" He cleared his throat again as if unsure how to continue and Jasper said in a low voice, "Disturbing, I found it, if truth be told." Collingwood was out of earshot on the other side of the room, and he could tell that this was the source of Leeson's concern.

"Collingwood has not mentioned the name of this young woman he intends to wed, has he?"

Jasper shook his head.

"I believe she can be none other than my friend James' Treloar's daughter."

"Charlotte?" Jasper shook his head. "The Charlotte I know would never wed a man like Collingwood."

"You think not?" Leeson looked relieved, and it occurred to Jasper that Leeson had not met the girl.

"The Charlotte I knew was vivacious and strong-willed."

Still, Leeson appeared concerned. "The coincidence is too great. This Mrs Henley—"

"It's a common name," Jasper reassured him.

"Mrs Henley," Lord Leeson went on, firmly, "is a staunch proponent of prison reform and spends many of her days at the Marshalsea. No, Jasper, it is too great a coincidence."

Jasper didn't want to believe it but he was silent as Leeson went on, "Mrs Henley has been Charlotte's guardian since the unfortunate incident from which you rescued her. She did not return Charlotte to her father and stepmother after you delivered her into her hands when we thought the Misses Prism were accepting her back into the Ladies Academy. Collingwood can be speaking of none other."

"But Charlotte is a girl of fire and spark!" Jasper knew he spoke too peremptorily as his mind whirled with memories of the two nights he'd spent with the young woman.

Lord Leeson raised his eyebrows. "I'm glad you thought so. I have not seen her for many years, alas. Her father and I were once great friends, as I think I once told you, but since he has been exiled in France—" He shrugged. "Suffice to say that my wife and I have taken an interest in Charlotte since her birth but circumstances have not favoured a continued intimacy." He sighed and clearly made a conscious effort to relax. "Ah, well, Jasper, I'm glad you think it would be out of character for Charlotte to accept Lord Collingwood. Perhaps I am jumping to conclusions." He hesitated. "Jasper, might I prevail upon you to expedite another enormous favour on our behalf? Would you consent to visiting Charlotte at your earliest convenience?"

Jasper cleared his throat. "It would be no inconvenience, I assure you. Though I must add that I intend leaving for the continent in a few weeks."

"I'm not asking you to marry the girl."

Jasper felt foolish, adding quickly, "I did not mean to infer the two were connected," as he remembered what happened during his last intervention and the knowledge that Leeson would demand marriage if he knew the truth.

Yet who had taken advantage of whom? Charlotte had been insistent that Jasper perform when it went against his gentlemanly principles.

Pah! This was convenient talk. Jasper had wanted what Charlotte had wanted from the moment she'd pursed her kissable lips and raised an eyebrow. And that was long before she'd gone to the inventive lengths to which she'd ultimately resorted.

He tried to imagine the reception such uninhibited sexual delight would have on Collingwood. Surely she would not have behaved towards *him* with such unseemliness? Collingwood had no sense of humour. He had no spark of sexuality.

Good lord, but surely Charlotte could not have agreed to become his wife?

No, Jasper was going travelling to extricate himself from his current difficulties until Count Orlov calmed down; and to exorcise his preoccupation with Mariah who continued to needle him after all these years.

But if Leeson wanted him to play the knight in shining armour one more time, then he would be happy to do it.

Perhaps it might exonerate him for what had happened the last time Leeson had placed his trust in Jasper.

So he looked his lordship square in the eye, nodded briefly, and said, "If you wish it, I will see her next week."

CHAPTER 10

"**C**harlotte! Come away from that window! And look at you! Do you imagine I'm going to take you dressed like that?"

Charlotte turned away from where she'd been observing the passing foot traffic and sent Mrs Henley a baleful stare. She'd slept better than she usually did, and it was on these days she felt something like her old spark had returned.

"I'm quite happy for you to go alone, Mrs Henley," she said, sweetly. "I've accompanied you to the prison every day this week, and you have said in the past you enjoyed your own company." Right now, Charlotte was enjoying the feeling of the sun on her cheeks and deciding which of the fashionable ensembles of the ladies passing by on the street below the window she would wear—if she only was allowed to go about in something less drab than the Quakerism monstrosities upon which Mrs Henley insisted.

Not that she and Mrs Henley lived in a fashionable part of town but they were close enough to the centre of the metropolis that Charlotte could watch the ladies emerging from carriages to visit the dressmaker who lived in the street opposite.

When the weather favoured her, a bit of a craning of her neck would sometimes enable Charlotte to see the bolts of beautiful fabric lined up near the window and, occasionally, an exquisite gown as it was being prepared.

She glanced down at her own dreary homespun and remembered the wardrobe she'd once owned. Not the most fashionable for she'd been seventeen and had not yet made her debut before she'd come to live with Mrs Henley. But she'd had style.

And today she'd experimented with a touch of style in view of her vastly improved mood no doubt due to her good night's sleep. Clearly the addition of a pink sash and the floral decoration she'd found to adorn her simple dress had not found favour with Mrs Henley.

"And as a soon-to-be-married woman, I do have much to plan," she added, when Mrs Henley looked about to object. She tried for a demure smile though the thought of her future husband did something to her insides that made her mouth twitch as if she'd sucked a lemon.

Except that he wasn't going to be her future husband.

He was her escape plan but never, ever, would he be her husband.

No, Charlotte had it all planned.

Well, the concept of escape was all planned. After all, she'd extricated herself from one near-disastrous elopement, she surely must be able to utilise her knowledge, experience and skills to escape another. Or a marriage, at any rate, which had a much greater lead-in.

And she had friends, surely?

She might not have had contact with her school friend Vanessa for three years. Not, in fact, since the night she left Miss Prism's Academy to elope with Vanessa's cousin, Gilray.

But surely, when Vanessa knew the prison to which Charlotte was about to be consigned if she married Lord Collingwood, she'd help her?

Charlotte glanced up from her reverie to see Mrs Henley still looking at her, lips pursed. "Since I am the one doing most of the work with regard to this illustrious marriage, you're about to contract, that excuse doesn't wash with me, my girl."

"I'd have thought that was more within the realm of papa and my step-mama," Charlotte remarked. "Aren't they the ones making plans?"

Mrs Henley's look narrowed. "What's got into you, girl? You've got a very glib tongue this morning."

Charlotte stayed the response she'd been formulating. It was true that she was generally more subdued than this, but the sun was out and for the first time in literally years, she felt a tiny kernel of hope.

Yes, hope that she would achieve some autonomy in her life.

Which meant not marrying Mr Collingwood. Though when all was said and done, that surely would be preferable to remaining with Mrs Henley.

"Has papa answered my last letter?" Charlotte asked, returning Mrs Henley's look with one equally pointed. She'd long harboured suspicions that her guardian was not entirely truthful regarding communications. It didn't make sense that her darling papa would be so unfeeling as to ignore her entreaties to leave Mrs Henley and live with him. And, of course, her step-mama.

"Your papa is a very busy man. If he hasn't written to you, it's because he has more important things on his mind. Now, get changed for I'm not taking you looking like that."

Charlotte knew there was no point arguing. Her good mood had resulted in her donning the best gown she owned and adding a little adornment but she wasn't going to spoil it traipsing around a prison dispensing alms. And she knew she'd not avoid accompanying Mrs Henley.

Five minutes later, more subdued, Charlotte set out with her guardian, matching her steps to the older woman's impossibly long gait. Charlotte always did wonder where Mrs Henley got her energy, but she supposed that, fuelled by dreams of her reward in the afterlife, the woman could manage most things to which she set her mind.

Low clouds hung in the sky and the air was close and damp. If Charlotte were lucky, there'd be a downpour before they arrived meaning there was the slight possibility Mrs Henley would decide to return home. She had recently suffered a chill and Charlotte could see she was not fully recovered.

Which prompted the thought that perhaps it would be a good thing if Mrs Henley *didn't* return home and instead worsened her chill as a result of doggedly pursuing her virtuous passion.

Really, Charlotte didn't know what to think except that she could not remain under Mrs Henley's roof much longer. The woman was going to send her to an early grave.

"Chin up, Charlotte! Mind your basket! You don't want street urchins thieving from you!" her guardian hissed as she elbowed a scrawny, large-eyed boy in rags out of the way and sailed on through the throng.

Their journey from Oxford St to Southwark where the dank, overcrowded prison had been incarcerating prisoners for the past four hundred years was half an hour on this chilly Autumn day and Charlotte noticed many shivering children huddled in doorways along the way.

She wondered why Mrs Henley's charity didn't encompass street urchins whom she thought just as deserving as prisoners. She had no doubt some of the prisoners they fed and to whom they proselytised had done some very bad things.

Mrs Henley, though, was a mass of contradictions, she'd decided.

Pushing back her shoulders, Charlotte did, however, keep a more vigilante eye upon the still steaming loaves of bread in her basket for the aroma was making her stomach growl. As she'd been a lie-abed, according to Mrs Henley, Charlotte had missed breakfast. Now she was wondering if she could surreptitiously tear off a hunk of bread, for she knew Mrs Henley would keep her on her feet for hours. And missing breakfast was a punishment Mrs Henley might just stretch out to luncheon since her guardian did like to make a point.

Pushing through the dense crowd, they were nearly at the prison wall when a gentleman stepped out of the goldsmith's she was passing, hesitated as his gaze followed her, then thrust out his hand.

He was going to snatch her bread, Charlotte was sure of it, and she had no little satisfaction in swatting his hand out of the way and using her elbow in the same manner Mrs Henley had a few minutes before.

When dressed in plain homespun, Charlotte often found herself on the receiving end of a disrespectful look or a sly pinch, and she derived great satisfaction from causing the opportunist whatever discomfort she could.

When dressed in plain homespun, it was as if Charlotte were a different person. And while it was easier to go unnoticed, she missed the beauty of lovely clothes, and the attention they brought her.

She missed being treated with respect, if not admiration.

Yet, in a strange paradox, Mrs Henley was now accompanying Charlotte to a number of dress fittings for the most astonishing wedding trousseau. Lord Collingwood's concern that his future wife should be outfitted with such extravagance so thoroughly in line with fashion had been a factor in her agreeing to the match. Now, in between visits to the Marshalsea in homespun, Charlotte was attending regular fittings for the many evening gowns, walking gowns, opera cloaks, bonnets and other accoutrements that were part of the marriage contract.

So, while Charlotte had appeared compliant, she'd spent the last four weeks planning how she could escape with her fashionable new wardrobe without having to marry Mr Collingwood.

As to where she could go, she wasn't sure. Not with her papa and step-mama seemingly insensible to her pleas.

But she would make a plan. She had four weeks, some of this time surely gracing a few society balls and routs. Why else would she be so beautifully clothed?

And, oh, what a wonderful thing it would be not to have to accompany Mrs Henley on visits to the Marshalsea dressed as soberly as a Quaker, having to protect herself and her loaves of bread from opportunists like the one whom she'd just elbowed sharply.

But who, instead of crying out in pain, cried out her name.

"Charlotte! Good Lord, is it really you?" The gentleman, whom she couldn't immediately identify as he was blocked by a passing mule bearing a heavy load of pots and pans, redoubled his enthusiastic greeting as he went on, "Charlotte! It *is* you! After all this time!"

Oh, Good Lord, was it Gilray? she wondered, as she darted forward to close the distance between herself and Mrs Henley.

"Charlotte! Stop!"

But it wasn't Gilray.

And as she took in the fine physique of the gentleman who loomed up before her, Charlotte was assailed by the most extraordinary excitement and longing as she cried out, "Mr Creighton!"

But her cry drew the attention of Mrs Henley, forcing Charlotte to do what she could to block the lovely man from sight for she knew recognition would be the death knell to any opportunity of speaking to him.

And speak to him she would. Mrs Henley would not prevent her – though Charlotte knew she would if she could.

"I can't talk to you here, Mr Creighton," she whispered, pretending to check on her loaves, "for my guardian would not permit it—"

"Where are you going?"

"To the Marshalsea. We're to spend the day dispensing alms and...and bringing the prisoners to God." Charlotte shifted uncomfortably at his perplexed look.

"Yes, you're looking surprisingly nunnish, Charlotte," he remarked in that wonderfully familiar, half jocular tone of his. "Are you suggesting you'll spend *all* day at the prison?"

Charlotte nodded. Wearily. But when she refocussed her attention on the combination of strong square jaw and kind eyes that alternated between laughter and concern, she felt hope fizz through her veins.

"And you say the prisoners's welfare are the chief concern of you and your guardian?" he went on.

"Of my guardian though I must pretend to be equally sincere."

"You're very good at pretending, so I'm sure she's satisfied by your piety."

"Mrs Henley will never be satisfied with me—" Charlotte glanced about her, fear pulsing through her when she caught Mrs Henley in the distance staring back at her. Her small eyes were scrunched up in her lined face and Charlotte could only hope she did not see that Charlotte was speaking to a handsome gentleman in the street. The crowd that had surrounded them seconds earlier had dispersed.

"Oh, Mr Creighton, it is so good to see you again, but I cannot be seen to speak to you. Mrs Henley will not permit it. She has plans—" She stopped abruptly. What could she say? How could she find the words to ask him to seek her out.

If only he would help her once more, for her father had not responded to any of her letters—

"Please, Mr Creighton, will you meet me at the Marshalsea? But not like you are. Mrs Henley would never permit me to see you. And I do so long to talk to you again."

Melting back into the crowd, his parting words were reassuring. "I'll make a plan, Charlotte. You will know me when you see me."

"Charlotte!"

Mrs Henley's high-pitched, nasal tones penetrated the rabble and Charlotte raised her hand, calling, "Coming, Mrs Henley!"

Holding her basket against her chest, Charlotte hurried to close the distance. Mr Creighton had thought on his feet and now she had to formulate a response for the inevitable questioning.

So when Mrs Henley said suspiciously, "You spent too long detained by a fashionable gentleman, Charlotte. Who was he?" Charlotte simply looked ingenuous and said, "He asked to buy a loaf of bread as it smelled so delicious."

"Well, you should have ignored him. Men have only one thing on their minds. You were foolish to humour him. What would Mr Collingwood have said?"

"Mr Collingwood would never know." She knew it was a foolish response the moment the words were out of her mouth for her guardian rounded on her saying, "That is never an excuse, but it is just one more thing we must ensure

Mr Collingwood *does* never know. What would he say if he learned about your deplorable behaviour three years ago? You are an untarnished angel in his eyes and that's the fiction that must be maintained. At all costs."

Mrs Henley gripped Charlotte's arm, her fingers digging into the soft flesh as she made Charlotte walk with her.

But all the while an idea was forming.

Charlotte was never going to marry Mr Collingwood. She reflected on the cold calculation in his eye whenever he'd assessed her. Yes, first when his attention had been caught by her at the prison, and he'd engaged Mrs Henley in conversation, and then later when Charlotte had been at a small gathering at which Mr Collingwood was a guest, and he'd focused that cold, assessing gaze upon her, she'd felt like a fish skewered by a polar bear.

There'd been a detailed painting of that very scene in Mr Collingwood's London townhouse where he'd hosted a small gathering of intellectuals. In fact, above a polar bear skin, had hung a watercolour of a polar bear amidst the bleak snow-covered steppes of the Arctic, a helpless fish caught in its fiendishly long claws.

Charlotte had been the youngest there by many years and the gathering had been an eclectic mix of mostly gentlemen with the occasional female, all of whose principal conversation had been the rare specimen of bird Mr Collingwood had been sent from South America or the collection of coins which they'd managed to secure through dubious means from the African kingdom of Benin.

Charlotte hadn't questioned why she'd been invited to the soiree of a gentleman to whom Mrs Henley had only briefly introduced her. She'd only been interested in the fact that Mrs Henley was going to great pains to adorn her like a princess for the occasion.

And Charlotte had been desperate to wear something new, or at least with embellishments.

The evening had been cathartic. After more than two years of wearing the plainest garb, and then months of being ill, Charlotte had felt like a butterfly emerging from a chrysalis. Mr Collingwood's soiree was, she presumed, simply a quiet, rather odd, means of testing Charlotte before she was released properly into society.

So when Mrs Henley had told her that Charlotte's future in society depended upon how modestly she behaved, but yet how engaging she must be towards Mr Collingwood and his friends, Charlotte had been determined to prove herself the actress she knew herself to be.

Well, Mr Collingwood had made a marriage offer. She'd never been more astonished in her life.

It was, to date, the only avenue of escaping Mrs Henley, though of course Charlotte had no intention of following through with the offer to which she'd verbally agreed.

For that is exactly what she'd done when Mr Collingwood declared that he wanted his future wife to have an exquisite gown for every possible contingency.

And while Charlotte didn't want to marry Mr Collingwood, that was something she didn't need to think about for six months following his proposal.

The problem was, she reflected as she trudged obediently towards the Marshalsea, time was ticking away. Certainly, the magnificent wardrobe was growing except that Charlotte was not actually able to wear any of her new gowns, and she wasn't quite sure when she would.

Surely, she wasn't expected to wait until *after* their proposed marriage?

"Yes, Mrs Henley." Charlotte hung her head. Humility was the best way to respond, she'd learned. She'd tried defiance and that had served her as ill as it had when she'd been a pupil with Miss Prism.

Her shoulders slumped. She could feel hope sliding off them as she contemplated her prospects. At least at Miss Prism's she'd had friends.

She recalled Vanessa with longing. Vanessa, whom she'd tried to contact, only to discover that her letters to her were getting no further than Mrs Henley and the staff.

Miss Prism had called Vanessa and Charlotte 'birds of a feather'. It hadn't been a compliment. Apparently vivacity and determination were not desirable attributes in young ladies. Even when their sights were set on that for which they'd apparently been bred: the penultimate marriage.

No, vivacity was a mark of loose morals while determination suggested obstinacy. And what gentleman of distinction wanted an obstinate wife?

Therefore these traits were among the many that the Miss Prisms were instructed to eliminate in their raw charges.

"And pull your shoulders back, my girl! No one likes a slouch!"

Obediently Charlotte stood straight. The prison loomed ahead but for once she felt excitement.

Immediately followed by despair.

How would Mr Creighton manage to speak to her without Mrs Henley deciding that he was the devil incarnate for showing an interest when Charlotte was earmarked for another man? Mrs Henley had become especially vigilant of Charlotte since Charlotte had voiced reservations about her impending marriage.

"You won't get another offer half so fine," she'd say. Or, "The sooner this is done, the better, my girl, else your dirty little secret is laid bare to the world."

On one occasion, Charlotte had retorted that a providential rescue by an honourable gentleman friend of her father's had meant that her 'secret' was forever safe.

Now, as Charlotte recalled the beetling look Mrs Henley had focussed upon her and Mr Creighton—even though he had been far in the distance—she had the sudden fear that if Mrs Henley recognised Mr Creighton as the honourable gentleman who'd 'saved' her, and then delivered her to the Academy, she'd be even more determined that Charlotte not speak to him.

For some reason, Mrs Henley seemed set on Charlotte making a match with only Mr Collingwood.

As the wedding date drew nearer, Charlotte's desperation had grown more intense, as—it seemed—did Mrs Henley's desire that Charlotte wed this particular gentleman.

"Your bonnet has slipped. Cover your hair, my girl!"

Mrs Henley barked the admonishment as they arrived at the prison. A quick pat down from her guardian to ensure that Charlotte looked as unprepossessing as possible, was the usual precursor.

Strangely, Mrs Henley had never done this prior to their chance meeting with Mr Collingwood at the prison.

But ever since Charlotte had become betrothed, Mrs Henley seemed determined to ensure Charlotte look as plain as possible.

It puzzled her as she traipsed through one of the many dark, dank corridors, her hands sliding over the mildew that covered the walls as she sought to save herself from a misstep upon the uneven cobblestones.

Moans and, worse, sobbing and screeching, were familiar sounds. Charlotte always left this place with heavy heart, despairing for those who occupied the overcrowded stinking cells. She'd heard enough stories to know that justice was not meted out fairly. It was all the more surprising to her, then, that Mrs Henley continued to believe so strongly in divine intervention. There was none of that for the wretches here.

"A creature of habit, I'm pleased to note."

Charlotte swung round at the sound of Mr Creighton's voice and beheld him in a cell in company with a filthy, bearded creature who, when he raised his head, regarded her with rheumy eyes and a semblance of a smile. "The Angel has returned," muttered the prisoner. He was one of the few who had been separated, his ankle chained to the floor. His one-red hair had faded to grizzled grey and his rheumy light blue eyes raked her with a smile. "Your friend is bearing me company to evade your guardian for the necessary minutes he has to say what he must." He touched his nose. "We both know she'd not allow it otherwise."

To Charlotte's surprise, the man spoke in educated tones for in the two years she had been coming to the Marshalsea he'd not murmured more than a thank you when she'd dished out food.

"Mrs Henley allows me to speak to the prisoners," said Charlotte, her smile growing warmer as she added, "but I know she would not allow me to speak to you, Mr Creighton. You're too handsome and well dressed. She'd know you were not one of…" She indicated Mr Creighton's hirsute companion, adding, "Though you're very wily to have made it to the wrong side of the bars." She wished she could spend all morning speaking to him but that would never be allowed. However, when he said with theatrical gravitas, "Miss Treloar, what I would not do to snatch a few words with the Angel of the Marshalsea," Charlotte felt something hitch in her heart combined with a great outpouring of warmth.

He turned to his companion. "What a charming Moniker for the young lady," he said, making Charlotte smile even more until he added, "Though you hardly look angelic in that ghastly garb and with your hair all covered up. And you're not blooming like the last time I saw you. So, tell me what's happened. I can't believe you're to marry Mr Collingwood. What possessed you when you could have had—"

"Gilray?" Charlotte supplied, shocked that he should confront her so directly.

Yet, it was so good to talk to Mr Creighton again. And she didn't feel the slightest bit embarrassed that he brought up her shameful past for wasn't it a relief it could be spoken about openly? "Yes, he was a terrible mistake, I admit it. A rake and a scoundrel—"

"And marrying Collingwood isn't? You would marry a monk instead? Or rather a monk in wolf's clothing, for I fear that his piety is a disguise your dear papa has not seen through if he has agreed to this." He was suddenly serious as he went to the bars, his eyes dark and melting, making Charlotte's heart hitch again. "You cannot marry Collingwood. There, Charlotte. I have no right to say it but when your concerned uncle exhorted me to do what I could to dissuade you, I was happy to do it for I was as horrified as he was."

"My uncle?"

"Lord Leeson." Mr Creighton shook his head. "I was attending a hunting party with Lord and Lady Leeson when our host, Lord Collingwood, made known the identify of his future wife."

Charlotte frowned. "It is very good of my uncle to be concerned when I have never met Lord Leeson. It was he, also, who asked you to intervene when I eloped with Gilray."

"Charlotte!"

Guiltily, Charlotte stepped back at the sound of Mrs Henley's strident voice. To her dismay, she saw that her guardian was making her way towards her. "I cannot be seen to address you, Mr Creighton," she whispered hastily, "though I wish so much that I could."

"Do you not attend any London revels?"

"I have been to none, no."

"Does Collingwood escort you nowhere?"

"He has been in the country but comes to London next week and we are to attend a ball. My first in his company." Charlotte felt sick at the thought but her heart was beating rapidly as she added, "If you could contrive an invitation to Lady Milburne's ball next Thursday you would see me." Turning on her heel, she hurried forward to meet her guardian, saying over her shoulder, "Do try for I would so like to see an old friend."

Old friend, she thought as her body pulsed with the excited memory of what 'old friend' really constituted.

CHAPTER 11

"**I** know you."

Jasper was about to let himself into the dank corridor with the key the prison warden had supplied him for this part of the cell in return for a handsome inducement.

The man's words shocked him out of the fierce churning he was feeling at his encounter with Charlotte, though he had been taken by surprise earlier when the prisoner had addressed him like a cultured man as Jasper had entered the cell.

Now Jasper turned to face him. He supposed the man was a charlatan and that he was in here for something pertaining to false pretences. An actor, perhaps, or a thief trained to ape his betters.

So he armed himself with scepticism as he responded with equal calm, "Indeed?"

The man nodded. "I should have introduced myself earlier but you were obviously under some pressure." His thick beard made some slight movement that indicated a twist of his lips.

Jasper peered more closely at him but it was impossible to make out his features, much less his age.

The prisoner scratched his grizzled head and went on. "So you want to make contact with the young lady without the knowledge of her guardian? I've seen she is kept under close supervision. The pair of them are here often." He was silent a moment, then said, "But, yes, we have met." There was the smile again.

Jasper tried to reconcile the man's words with the pitiable specimen before him.

A rat scurried across the stone floor, and he stepped back. He'd not taken into full account the lice, fleas and other vermin of the place.

"Even the most respectable can fall so low. You'd like to know my name?" the man asked. "I'm not in the habit of playing games, but indulge me a few moments longer. It is rare I enjoy the smallest modicum of power in this place. I was cast in here three long years ago and I have been forgotten. Forgotten by those who used me as their scapegoat for a crime I did not commit. I am bitter, but while there is life, there is hope. Unlike Archie Banning, at least I still have that."

This name caused Jasper such a shock he had to grip the bars to keep his balance.

"What do you know of Archie Banning?"

"I worked with him at the exchequer. I am the man wrongly accused of a crime for which Banning was blamed in the first instance." The prisoner's nostrils flared.

"You?" rasped Jasper. "You are not only a thief, you are a murderer, for you struck Archie the blow that—"

"I was imprisoned on the false testimony of Banning's sister, and I defended myself when Banning threw the first punch."

"You are calling Miss Mariah Banning a liar?" All the

pent-up rage and pain Jasper had felt at the crime which had cost his beloved Mariah her life and thus shortened her life swamped him like a red fog.

"Well, someone is responsible for my rotting away in this prison."

"And you cannot take responsibility!" Jasper breathed deeply as he clenched his fists to stop himself from causing violence.

His hand trembled as he used the key the prison warden had given him to unlock this section of the cell, after being offered a significant bribe.

He could barely look at the man as he said, "Archie Banning was the brother of the woman to whom I was betrothed. Why did you not introduce yourself earlier? Because you feared I might kill you?" He let himself out, turning the key to keep this man—what was his name? Everingham! Rupert Everingham—where he should remain forever locked up.

This man was as much vermin as the lice that infested his clothes.

"Was it not enough to steal from your employer and accuse Banning of the crime—?" He drew in a laboured breath. "But you had to kill him, too?"

"Banning's death was an accident! I'd have hanged three years ago if I'd been convicted of his murder, too."

"It was your fist that rendered him unconscious from a sleep from which he would never wake."

"Banning was my friend and he set upon me first. There were witnesses who testified that I was not responsible for his death! You have taken the part of his sister without knowing the facts—" Everingham rattled the bars.

Jasper was unmoved. He took a difficult breath as he handed the key to the prison warden hovering nearby. "I take great pleasure in ensuring you remain where you need to stay and where you deserve to stay for the rest of your days. For the pain and suffering you inflicted on the woman I loved and who might have enjoyed a life long enough to be cured had you not sent her to a premature grave through pain and grief."

Jasper was still shaking as he went in search of Charlotte. Dutifully, he asked several prison guards if they'd seen the Angel of the Marshalsea. But the chill, dank air and the general desolation of his surroundings had further lowered his mood.

Whereas he'd felt a surge of delight at finding the girl whose liberty he'd been charged to ensure, he now felt only the deepest despondency.

CHAPTER 12

"No doubt you'll meet approval with those whose regard you seek to garner." Mrs Henley raked Charlotte with a critical gaze. As her gaze was rarely anything other than critical, however, Charlotte continued to preen in front of Madame Leville's looking glass.

The dressmaker was one of the most sought-after in London, and Lord Collingwood had given her the undertaking of providing his future bride with a trousseau that would make her the season's most admired woman.

"The guests at Lady Brigalow's ball will have eyes only for Miss Treloar." Madame Leville looked as proud of her achievement as Charlotte certainly was. She adjusted a bow on one of the pink, puffed sleeves of Charlotte's ballgown, her voice breaking with emotion as she went on, "Ah, but your mama would be so proud this evening, Miss Treloar. You look *tres* magnificent!"

"Well, her poor mama is dead, and it is my duty to ensure such compliments don't go to the girl's head if she is to have a future worth speaking of," Mrs Henley said on a sniff.

Charlotte ignored her as she did a slow turn, gazing at the cream bows around the hem of her pale pink ballgown which fell to the ankle. Ballgowns had never been so short, which had scandalised Mrs Henley.

However, Madame Leville's keen sense of fashion had prevailed, and Mrs Henley had finally been won over when she and Charlotte had arrived as Lady Byrne's own daughter had been finalising a fitting for a gown equally short. There was nothing like competition to change Mrs Henley's mind.

"With a wardrobe as extensive, Miss Treloar will not be easily forgotten." Madame Leville spoke with a sincerity that went beyond a reference to the revenue she might personally enjoy. "Not only is she London's most beautiful debutante, she is its best dressed, which is as it should be." Brandishing needle and thread, she bent to straighten a bow at the hem. "Miss Treloar's papa is making a wise investment."

"It is thanks to the man she is to marry that the girl is to be outfitted with such wanton waste." Mrs Henley sniffed again, and Madame Leville glanced up in surprise.

"I did not know the young lady had received an offer already?" She paused, shrugged slightly as she digested this, then said, "In that case, Miss Treloar will not present such a threat to the other young ladies with whom she is in competition. Perhaps she will even enjoy herself and … smile a little more."

"Oh!" Charlotte jerked around and was surprised to see that Madame Leville was serious. But then, Charlotte rarely smiled in Mrs Henley's company, she reflected. The last time she'd really felt joyful was seeing Mr Creighton again.

At the thought, her heart nearly burst out of her chest and with a reverence to hide her excitement, she touched one of the cream bows that adorned her sleeve. This beautiful gown was the one she'd wear to Lady Brigalow's ball on the first night of the house party, and Mr Creighton would be there.

Surely he would? She'd given him all the details during their too-brief conversation at the Marshalsea. Yes, he'd seemed distracted, but surely he would recognise her need for him to be there? To effect some kind of rescue, as he had before?

"And who is Miss Treloar's intended?" asked Madame Leville.

"Lord Collingwood."

Madame Leville's brow creased before she ventured, "A serious, reclusive young man, as I recall."

"You know him?" Charlotte asked, surprised.

"I attended to the wardrobe of the... young lady to whom he was affianced several years ago. Sadly, of course, that match never went ahead."

A long silence hung over the pronouncement until finally Charlotte asked—for Mrs Henley seemed uninterested— "Why did it not?"

"The young lady died."

"Oh." Charlotte did not know what else to say except that perhaps the young lady had had a lucky escape. There was no way she intended marrying Lord Collingwood, either.

She was about to ask the circumstances surrounding the demise of Lord Collingwood's previous intended, but Madame Leville rose at a knock upon the door which opened to the maid servant saying, "Miss Creighton is here for her fitting, Madame."

Miss Creighton? Charlotte felt as if her heart was about to burst out of her chest. Nervously, she glanced at Mrs Henley for a glimmer of recognition, but the woman's face was averted.

Miss Creighton? Was this one of Jasper's beloved sisters?

Through a dry throat, Charlotte whispered, "I hope Miss Creighton will be as satisfied with her beautiful gown as I am with mine." She smiled at Madame Leville in the hope of eliciting more, but then Mrs Henley was shooing Charlotte off to change and Charlotte had no choice but to go with the assistant.

Behind the screen, and feeling more confident as she heard the other two women talking, she asked, "Is Miss Creighton the sister of Mr Jasper Creighton?"

"His cousin, miss. I've heard she and Mr Jasper Creighton are to make a match."

Charlotte was glad she was not in the company of her guardian and that the assistant was behind Charlotte, helping her out of her gown. For as she caught a glance of herself in the looking glass, the devastation of her expression would have put Mrs Henley and everyone else in no doubt as to her feelings.

She gave herself a mental shake. She had *not* lost her heart to Mr Creighton. He had merely acceded to her wishes and shown her what pleasure was. It had been an education they'd both enjoyed.

And now he was to marry his cousin while she was to marry Lord Collingwood.

Except that she would find someone else.

She would not be a prisoner any longer.

At Lady Brigalow's ball, in her exquisite gown, she would meet Mr Creighton and on the strength of their past association, she would petition him to help her. Knowing that he was to marry his cousin, she would reign in her emotions and simply regard him as the friend she hoped he would continue to be in view of how much she needed the help of a friend.

For the truth was that these past three years she had never felt so friendless.

CHAPTER 13

I t was difficult to believe that this was the world she had forgone due to the foolishness of her past actions. Charlotte had to concede that, and not only because it was what Mrs Henley intimated as the older woman stood at her side while they contemplated the splendour before them.

They'd arrived at Brigalow House later than expected due to the bad roads. And while Charlotte had wished for nothing more than to dash outside onto the emerald green lawns to join in the game of ground billiards she spied beyond the pond with its splashing water fountain, she was admonished for her exuberance and told to rest quietly until the ball which was the highlight of their two-night visit.

A light supper had been brought up on a tray—even though Charlotte and Mrs Henley had been invited to join the rest of the party downstairs.

It had been pure agony for Charlotte to remain silent as Mrs Henley dismissed this invitation.

No, Charlotte must remain calm and unstimulated so that she appear the paragon of virtue Lord Collingwood would anticipate when he greeted her downstairs this evening.

Charlotte's stomach roiled with distaste and fear at the thought. She'd not seen Lord Collingwood in six weeks and in the interim, he'd grown even more unsavoury in her imagination.

Of course, she was grateful for the opportunity to leave Mrs Henley, but at what cost?

No, Jasper would help her.

Wouldn't he?

Once again, she reflected on their rushed conversation at the Marshalsea. It had been strange that the initial delight he'd exhibited at seeing her had dissipated by the time she saw him in the cell where he'd obviously gone to great lengths to appear as one of the prisoners.

In fact, he'd barely attended to her desperate exhortations that she had no one else to call upon, though he had put a comforting hand upon her shoulder before he'd departed.

The sensation that passed through her at the touch was with her still, and her heartbeat increased just at the anticipation of their reunion.

But what if he wasn't coming to Lady Brigalow's ball after all?

What if she really was as friendless as she feared?

It was in this mood of uncertainty that she stopped upon the threshold of one of the withdrawing annexes and beheld someone she immediately knew would aid and abet her.

"Vanessa!" she cried, hurrying towards her old bosom friend who was standing obediently by the side of a stout, talkative young man to whom Charlotte was introduced as her husband.

And as the talkative young man seemed more interested in discourse with a distinguished rear admiral, the two young women were soon enjoying a modicum of privacy in a corner, each with a glass of orange punch.

To Charlotte's surprise, however, there a sense of wariness on Vanessa's part.

She'd expected to be greeted with vociferous delight.

Now, Vanessa sent her a somewhat beady look over the rim of her glass and said, "Why, I thought you were dead, Charlotte. You did not reply to any of my letters."

Ah, so that was it. Of course, Mrs Henley had overseen any correspondence with Charlotte's old friends and naturally prevented contact if she'd even suspected Vanessa's part in her thwarted elopement.

Charlotte sent a furtive look over her shoulder and, ascertaining Mrs Henley was speaking to Lord Collingwood, whispered, "Vanessa, you've got to help me! I've been guarded day and night by a woman whose mission in life is to make me a slave to her whimsies. She kept your letters from reaching me, and mine from you, and now she's marrying me against my will to Lord Collingwood."

"Perhaps you have loftier standards than the rest of us, Charlotte," Vanessa said with a sniff. She didn't look the least bit sympathetic. "Lord Collingwood has an even grander estate and no doubt even more money in the bank than Gilray. And if you don't want to marry Lord Collingwood, just do what you did to Gilray."

This stopped Charlotte in her tracks, and for a moment, she just blinked at her friend.

Former friend?

Vanessa sounded as if Charlotte had caused her the greatest degree of offence by not following through with her elopement with her cousin.

Well, if Vanessa only knew the things Gilray had done, thinking that pleasure was only to be had by him when Charlotte now knew—

She stopped, mid reflection, as a tall gentleman in elegant evening wear crossed her vision.

Dear Lord, how could she not reveal to her stony-faced the effect on her evoked by the sudden arrival of this wonderful stranger?

Jasper.

Breathe, she exhorted herself, as her heartbeat ratcheted up alarmingly, though she managed to keep her poise, nodding coolly in response to Jasper's casual greeting as he passed her by, while her hopes became gilt-edged at the knowledge of what this could mean.

Jasper Creighton *had* come.

Against all odds, he had found a means to attend Lady Brigalow's's house party. He was here. He'd not been on the invitation list, and had had no desire to attend, but because Charlotte had pleaded that he help her, he had not failed her in her hour of need.

Suddenly Vanessa wasn't her last and only hope, though Charlotte might well need assistance from her; meaning it wasn't sensible to take umbrage which she might well have if she'd been seventeen and in the habit of having a tiff with her highly strung friend. Highly strung was how her papa had described Vanessa who'd spent a week with them in France.

So, taking a sustaining breath, Charlotte smiled, and said, with a satisfying waver in her voice, "Oh Vanessa! I was thwarted. Did you not learn the truth of what happened? No? Well, I suppose everything had to be hushed up. But you see, Gilray and I were nearly at the border when… the man papa sent to stop us burst into the inn and threatened Gilray and me with terrible repercussions if we continued. We had no hope at all of achieving our aims—"

"You and Gilray were parted? *Violently?* And you were banished to the country and kept a *prisoner?*" Vanessa's plump, pretty face seemed to dissolve into a blur of compassion as she gripped Charlotte's wrist.

Charlotte nodded, instinct telling her she had to make the

most of the agonies both she and Gilray suffered, while she hoped Gilray had not apprised his cousin of too much contradictory detail.

"I was manhandled all the way back to Miss Prism's Seminary, but as I was about to cross the threshold, Mrs Henley appeared and took custody of me. I've literally spent three years under lock and key with her as my guardian." With her fan, she indicated Mrs Henley, still in deep conversation with Lord Collingwood, whom Charlotte now saw was watching her with an unsettling interest.

Catching his eye, she bobbed a curtsy, feeling the heat of her discomfort burn her cheeks, before turning back to Vanessa.

No, she would not encourage him. She'd not smile or indicate any gratitude in the knowledge that her sumptuous new wardrobe was courtesy of his generosity.

He was merely buying her. Buying her gratitude and her—

A sudden image of what else his lordship was buying made her squirm.

"Charlotte! What is it?" Vanessa's hand shot out to steady Charlotte, who had splashed orange punch onto her lovely ballgown as she realised how close she was to unmitigated disaster. For in just two weeks, Lord Collingwood would be her husband, expecting husbandly pleasures, and there really could be no greater motivation for escaping her marriage contract than that reality.

No, Charlotte needed Vanessa as a friend—and another ten friends who would vow to aid her when the moment was right.

Closing her eyes briefly, Charlotte whispered, "My husband-to-be is over there. Lord Collingwood is speaking to my guardian, Mrs Henley. Do you see him? I cannot marry him. I truly cannot!"

Vanessa frowned as she transferred her troubled gaze between Charlotte and somewhere over Charlotte's shoulder. Slowly she said, as she nodded, "And now Lord Collingwood is talking to my husband. Why, I don't know what objection you could have. Lord Collingwood is handsome if you like dark, intense looking gentlemen. And goodness, Charlotte, with the size of his—"

Charlotte didn't want to think of the size of anything belonging to Lord Collingwood, as she rapidly fanned herself and Vanessa went on, "Of his pocket book. Really, Charlotte, it's a failing to be *so* particular."

Charlotte shook her head vigorously. "How can I wed Lord Collingwood—or anyone else, for that matter—if my heart is elsewhere engaged? Oh Vanessa, you must help me. Only you are clever enough to help me find a way out of this. If I have to marry Lord Collingwood, why, I'll just die!"

Charlotte added this judicious flourish in the knowledge that Vanessa was very receptive to the theatrical. Nor did her erstwhile friend disappoint when she gripped Charlotte's wrist once more and whispered, "Oh, Charlotte, you are in love with someone else?" Her dark eyes grew large and her expression concerned.

"I can't sleep at night for dreaming of him. You must help me to escape Lord Collingwood so that I might return to—"

"Gilray?!"

Charlotte had been on the point of saying "my papa" but Vanessa appeared so enthralled by the idea of a thwarted love affair between Charlotte and Gilray that it seemed best to simply nod and allow her the happy reflection that her original matchmaking plans had been sound all along.

Especially when Vanessa went on with great sagacity and solemnity, "Upon my very life, Charlotte, I shall ensure that you will escape the clutches of Lord Collingwood so that you and Gilray can be joined in holy matrimony."

CHAPTER 14

I t had taken Jasper a couple of moments before he could reconcile the poised beauty in the corner of the room with the nunnish creature he'd last seen in the dank and dark Marshalsea Prison.

And on that occasion, it had been almost impossible to reconcile *that* iteration of Miss Charlotte Treloar with the wickedly desirable—no, wickedly irresponsible—young woman whose rescue had become his duty.

As Jasper had been crossing the rich Aubusson carpet on the way to Lady Brigalow's saloon, he'd checked himself in order to see if his eyes were deceiving him.

But no, it truly was Miss Treloar—Charlotte, as he was entitled to call her, and had been exhorted to call her in view of their past... intimacy. He swallowed down the recollection and anything else to do with those heady couple of days three years ago.

No, he was here because she'd begged him to...

Rescue her?

Jasper raked the stylishly garbed Miss Treloar with a long,

considering, and appreciative look. Her gown was the height of fashion. He knew that. Her skin glowed with good health and her lustrous hair was dressed in ringlets and woven through with pearls. She was speaking with animation with her friend and, though her expression might suggest the subject matter was intense, there was nothing else to suggest that Miss Treloar was a prisoner.

Jasper glanced about the room. Several gentlemen in conversation in various clusters showed surreptitious signs of being equally interested in the young lady.

Jasper's gaze slid across to Collingwood. Ah. He was in conversation with Mrs Henley. Jasper paused. Would the woman recognise him?

He picked up pace once more, nodding briefly to Charlotte, betraying nothing of the jolt he experienced when she registered his cool greeting with a slight widening of her eyes and a barely perceptible inclination of her head.

Concealing himself amidst a group of acquaintances, he glanced once more across at Collingwood to ascertain whether his arrival stirred any response in the young man for whom he'd formed such a dislike.

Collingwood disregarded him. Even when Jasper crossed his line of vision to greet an attractive matron with whom he'd once enjoyed a brief *amour*, Collingwood's cold fish stare indicated he was interested only in what Mrs Henley had to say.

Which, Jasper soon realised, was a ploy that enabled Collingwood to drink in the pure beauty of the woman he'd deemed collectible enough to marry, for Charlotte was positioned just behind Mrs Henley in Collingwood's line of vision.

Collingwood was strategic. A hunter. Even now, in a ballroom, he must have his prey in his sights.

Contempt rose up in Jasper's breast. Collingwood presumed too much. He presumed it was enough that he would shower the woman he deemed worthy to be his wife with riches in order to claim her as his own.

But he would not have Miss Treloar.

No, Jasper would play the knight errant, this time proving he was as noble as he'd set out to be the first time. It would be his way of atoning to Miss Treloar, and of showing himself true to the ideals of his beloved Mariah, who would have expected him to behave the gentleman…

With every chivalrous, gentlemanly instinct delivered as intended. Just as he'd behaved with Mariah.

"Mrs March," he greeted Charlotte's companion in as urbane a tone as he could manage. It was a boon that Jasper had already been introduced to the pretty young wife of a fellow from his club at a ball some months prior.

For now she could introduce Charlotte as if it were only natural.

And she would be doing so in front of Lord Collingwood and Mrs Henley.

"Mr Creighton. How delightful to see you again. I wonder if you have seen my cousin, Lord Gilray, this evening?"

Jasper crinkled his forehead a moment and then exclaimed, "Lord Gilray is your cousin? And he is here?" He flicked a glance at Charlotte and was relieved that she appeared unruffled. Or was it only pretence since she could not show her true feelings in public?

"Vanessa and I were schoolgirls together at Miss Prism's Seminary," said Charlotte. "I last saw her three years ago and never had an opportunity to say a proper farewell." She gave a tinkling laugh which Jasper recognised for its falsity for he'd heard it before when Charlotte was doing her best to hide the fact she was discomposed. "I thought my step-mama or guardian had passed on a letter to tell Vanessa I was leaving the school and that I hoped she'd visit me one day. But Vanessa never received it." She gave a heartful sigh. "Now, after such a long and regrettable absence, we have just pledged to atone for the past, haven't we?" She smiled at her friend who inclined her head and repeated, "Atone for the past. I like the way you phrased that, Charlotte. Yes, I think that's exactly what we must do."

Jasper saw Charlotte looked relieved, but he didn't quite like the look in her friend Vanessa's eye.

$\sim$

"I DON'T QUITE like the look in your eye, Miss Treloar," Jasper now said, snatching a moment to speak to Charlotte in the midst of a set.

Tempted though he'd been, he had not had the temerity to ask for the first dance, although many others had.

For Lord Collingwood had not even shown that regard for his betrothed. As far as Jasper could tell, he was playing a game. He'd heard so many quiz him on the identity of the woman he was to wed, but for a young man seemingly devoid in social understanding, he'd known how to up the ante when it came to anticipation.

The most beautiful woman in all England.

Jasper had heard the term bandied about by some at his club as if they were all too ready to refute the possibility. Collingwood, after all, was hardly a lady's man.

There had however been a collective gasp when the music had begun and, as if in front of everyone's noses, Miss Treloar's hand had been whisked up to Collingwood's blood-less lips before being caged upon his arm as he led her onto the dance floor.

The hunter was blooding his prey before all those who'd

shown any degree of scepticism that he couldn't indeed snare himself England's greatest beauty in addition to the hunting feats for which he was renowned.

Unlike the firebrand hunters of Jasper's set, stealth and patience had got Collingwood what he wanted.

Now, finding himself at Charlotte's side, and ensuring they could not be overheard, Jasper added in a whisper, "You look content enough with your lot, Miss Treloar. I wonder if this is not the ideal match for you since this is a marriage that will ensure you will forever be garbed like royalty, if only to remind the rest of us mortals that Collingwood has bagged a beauty for a wife."

"So charmingly put," Charlotte said with the faintest tug at her lips. Jasper understood that it was important she deport herself with gravitas. Collingwood was not a man who indulged free spiritedness and Jasper understood enough to realise that the young lord assumed that beauty symbolised not just the purity of which he spoke, but demure restraint.

How little he knew his future wife.

And how unsurprising was Charlotte's answer. "Anyone who wanted to make me their prisoner would be wise to feel your concern, Mr Creighton," she whispered. "Promise me you'll be on hand to facilitate my escape plans this weekend."

Before Jasper had the opportunity to respond, she'd been whisked into a different waltz hold for the next steps, however her look had held a warning.

And Jasper was not a man who would renege on his word.

He had promised to help Charlotte and by God he would.

Only this time he would do it in the spirit with which he would have aided Mariah if she had asked him.

With honour and gentlemanly restraint.

~

CHARLOTTE KNEW how to behave so it wasn't difficult to give Mrs Henley the impression that she'd become reconciled to her future.

It was to be expected that she'd have to share a bedchamber with Mrs Henley but to her surprise her whispered exhortation that Mrs Henley's snoring was likely to reduce her to a bundle of sleepless nerves had seen her accommodated in a suite of rooms that had her bedchamber adjoining the loftier appointments of her guardian.

So there was at least some privacy.

Not that Mrs Henley was likely to observe it. No, she kept the adjoining door open and for the full fifty-five minutes that Charlotte's coiffure was being arranged, she reenforced every tiresome admonition that Charlotte had heard a thousand times before.

"Appear interested and engaged at all times."

"Don't allow your gaze to slide to anyone else."

"He has spent a small fortune on ensuring that you do him justice by appearing as he would wish you to comport yourself. Honour him accordingly."

It really was quite a pompously ridiculous collection of exhortations, but Charlotte had grown in wisdom sufficiently to know that the more she appeared to take heed, the less likely Mrs Henly was to do something underhand like lace her milk to make her dull-witted.

Oh, Charlotte had trodden that path and it had taken a good couple of years before she'd become wise enough to realise what was happening to her and then a good few months more to know what to do about it.

The hardest had been fighting the urge to drink that milk, even knowing what it contained. She'd come to like the dull lethargy that would overtake her. Lord, there was little enough to look forward to everyday.

But now, with her future about to become hostage to a man she didn't know, and the more she did, the less she liked him, the more invested she became in ensuring she had as much control over her future as was possible.

As for how she behaved towards Lord Collingwood, she would not pretend that she was thrilled to become his wife. She would not smile and preen for his benefit, nor flatter or cajole.

She'd thought this would disturb him. What man, after all, did not want a wife who would flatter and cajole?

Disturbingly, however, she discovered over the course of that evening, and during her walk with her betrothed the following morning as they traversed the lake, that he seemed to *like* her barely veiled hostility.

So when she remarked with a disdainful sniff that she had no intention of dirtying her hands in anything related to food preparation, he'd raised an eyebrow, smiled, and said, "Bravo, Miss Treloar. I am not disappointed in your character. I shall have great enjoyment smoothing the rough edges. You will indeed grace Emsley Manor with that attitude."

Charlotte ended the walk more discomposed than ever so that when she encountered Vanessa on her way to the drawing room upon her return, she seized her friend by the arm and propelled her to the conservatory, where they could speak in private.

"I will die if I have to marry him. Vanessa, do I have your promise to aid my escape?"

For she'd had no contact with Jasper since their unsatisfactory encounter on the dance floor the previous night and now, with the entertainment nearly at an end, and her marriage so imminent, Charlotte realised how quickly time was running out with no proper plan in place.

Charlotte was also canny enough to know that Vanessa was more likely to respond if she appeared desperate, whereas Jasper would be more receptive if she approached the matter in a more level-headed manner.

In truth, though, Charlotte was beginning to wonder if salvation really would be forthcoming.

CHAPTER 15

It came in the most unexpected of sources.

Of course, it wasn't salvation in its final and finished form. Nothing came that easily, Charlotte had come to realise.

Rather, it was a chance discovery that sparked the beginnings of a coherent plan—something she'd been sorely lacking. Ingenuity was her strong point. She knew that. But the tools can be sparse when one is a prisoner.

These were the thoughts running round her head as she sat on her bed, staring into the distance through the open sash window at the group in the garden playing at lawn billiards. She was reluctant to join them mostly because Mrs Henley had unexpectedly encouraged her to do so. And Charlotte was opposed to doing anything Mrs Henley encouraged.

But Mrs Henley was, for the moment, out of their shared chamber. Only a minor modification ensured a little privacy. Charlotte's bed was in an alcove, such as might have been occupied by a servant to perhaps an invalid. Someone who would be called upon to assist at the slightest noise, she thought, for rather than a door separating them, there was just part of a wall.

So as Charlotte sat on her bed, she could see Mrs Henley's bed.

And the drawers in which her belongings had been unpacked.

Charlotte stood up suddenly, cocking her head for any sound of approach. She and Mrs Henley had been returning to their chamber, together, just a few minutes before, when her guardian had been detained by garrulous Mrs Feehan. In fact, Charlotte could hear the two of them in discussion from where she stood.

Moving quickly upon sudden inspiration, Charlotte went to the drawers and opened the first one. She knew exactly what she was looking for since she'd been thwarted in previous searches back in London.

But when both were guests at a different location, Mrs Henley would have few options to hide the powders which Charlotte was sure she administered to her when she needed to ensure calm obedience.

Sometimes Charlotte pretended to drink her milk and then pretended to suffer the consequences, only to lull her guardian into the false complacency that Charlotte was always controllable.

Kitty usually delivered the milk and Charlotte wasn't entirely certain if Kitty was also responsible for spooning in the requisite dose. But there was a high likelihood that Mrs Henley kept the powder with her.

Hastily she rummaged through the top drawer and to her surprise, found exactly what she was looking for within a minute, which was just as well since she could hear the sound of approaching footsteps while the conversation of the two women outside had ceased.

She knew she couldn't take the entire packet as its

absence would, of course, be discovered by Mrs Henley. But with the door squeaking open, Charlotte took a small handful—perhaps a teaspoon's worth—and had time only to close the drawer and walk to the window, the loose powder in her closed up hand as she pretended to stand at the window admiring the view.

Mrs Henley entered with a maid at her heels. Clearly, the girl had been detained in the passage to attend to the fire that burned feebly in their grate, for with barely a glance at Charlotte, Mrs Henley ordered her to stoke up the embers and encourage more warmth.

"And Lord Collingwood has requested you join him for another walk if your delicate constitution isn't up to the rigours of a game of lawn billiards," added Mrs Henley.

It was just the encouragement Charlotte needed to decide to participate in a game after all which required a change of clothing and, therefore, the aid of the maid, she decided quickly, stopping the girl as she was about to leave the room.

"What is your name?" Charlotte asked as she turned her back, carefully concealing in a cambric handkerchief the small amount of powder she'd purloined.

"Emma," the maid replied, waiting obediently as Charlotte withdrew a walking dress and a pair of half kid boots to replace the slippers she was wearing.

The admiration in the girl's eyes was unmistakeable as she gazed at Charlotte's accoutrements and Charlotte had to hold her tongue for it would not do for Mrs Henley to hear any suggestion that Charlotte didn't value what she had.

Charlotte had been bought. She'd have liked to tell the girl that. She'd have liked to tell anyone who would listen in case they could illuminate some way in which they could assist her to escape.

She thought of Lord Collingwood, who wanted to walk with her, dance with her, converse with her. All on his terms, of course. She could see the future stretching endlessly before her, in a series of ghastly vignettes, as she obediently tended to his husbandly needs.

But she was silent, for there was nothing to be said.

The maid might think Charlotte was the luckier of the two of them, but she was wrong.

Turning back to face the girl who had just done up the buttons of her walking dress, Charlotte saw the way her eyes were drawn to the necklace Charlotte wore about her neck.

Another gift from Lord Collingwood. Another token of possession.

A bold idea suddenly took hold. Charlotte's hand went to her throat as the girl bobbed a curtsey and left the room.

What was her name? Emma?

Would Charlotte recognise her if she saw her again?

Could Charlotte trust her?

"If you see Lord Collingwood, please pass on my apologies as I have decided to play lawn billiards after all," Charlotte said amidst a hasty leave-taking of her guardian.

And then she was hurrying down the corridor, fortunately empty, in pursuit of Emma whom she stopped as the girl was about to take the servant's entrance.

"Emma, there is something I want to speak to you about," she said, fingering her necklace as she sent a furtive glance back up the corridor before adding in a hasty whisper, "Are you able to come to my room tonight?"

So now Charlotte had a plan. An almost fully formed plan.

So pleased with herself was she that when Lord Collingwood intercepted her as she was about to join the garden party, and suggested they walk by the lake together, she was able to smile and appear quite daintily agreeable.

Light-hearted charm was easy when she knew she now had the means to escape the man who intended to make her the jewel in his collection. He'd talked about his hunting exploits to the extent that Charlotte wondered if she was to grace his trophy room like Mahmoud. Oh yes, he'd told her about his two hundred pound lion and his elephant tusks that weighed three hundred pounds apiece.

But rather than voicing her suspicions, she tipped her chin at the artful angle she and Vanessa had often practised and, smiling at his lordship as she gripped his forearm so he could lead her around the lake on the narrow gravel path, said, "The weather is shining upon us, Lord Collingwood. Let us hope it will shine on our wedding day."

This was the first time Charlotte had been anything other than serious and quiet, bordering on morose. She had never brought up the subject of their wedding on the two occasions since accepting his proposal. It was, after all, very hard to play-act when she was feeling so cornered.

But now she was no longer cornered. She had a jolly good plan and it was going to work. She was sure of it.

"Let us hope so, Miss Treloar."

Did he feel uncomfortable calling her by her Christian name in view of their limited acquaintance? Charlotte wondered how dangerous it would be to encourage him and then decided her plan would work better if he was disarmed.

"You may call me Charlotte, since we are to be married," she said, running her hand along his coat sleeve in an almost flirtatious manner.

He looked scandalised and immediately she sobered. Clearly, he preferred her docile and serious.

She pressed her lips together. "Do you intend calling me Lady Collingwood as if I had no Christian name? I would prefer less formality." No, but she would make the effort to draw him out. "Surely I should be Charlotte to you alone, and Lady Collingwood to everyone else?" It took an effort to maintain the light-heartedness in her tone. He really was a hard nut to crack. With no smile, there was no thawing in his demeanour as he continued his purposeful steps while Charlotte struggled to keep up.

Just when she was about to give up and lapse back into silence, he said, "I am honoured by the invitation." He nodded, as if contemplating what she'd said. "Charlotte. Yes, you will be Charlotte to me, and Lady Collingwood to everyone else." And then he gripped her hand, which rested on his forearm, and sent her a look of quiet intensity before he added, "I trust the sun will shine on our wedding day. I would like it to honour you as much as me."

RATHER THAN BE RELIEVED by their encounter, Charlotte felt unaccountably unsettled when she returned to her bedchamber later that day where Mrs Henley was waiting.

"You need an afternoon sleep, my girl. Your beauty sleep for it was a late night last night and there are two more nights of dancing. Ridiculous! Such flagrant waste."

"Then why do you indulge it, Mrs Henley?" Charlotte asked as she sank onto the bed and began to unlace her boots.

"Because there are larger matters at play."

"Such as my marriage? But that is organised." She raised her head. "Why did you agree to come here? She skimmed the skirt of her fashionable walking gown with one gloved hand. This is *all* flagrant waste. Well, I don't think so, of course. But you've never indulged me with anything remotely—"

"Come now, girl. You suggest that I decide your future when, of course, your papa and step mama advise me as to what is and isn't allowed."

Charlotte took a deep breath. "Papa's last letter—" She wasn't sure how to go on? No, she could not make any accusations now, even if she was desperate to learn the truth.

"Your papa was delighted to hear that you were so happy and that you embraced your future with all the felicity that could be desired as your nuptials approach." Mrs Henley's thin lips turned up slightly. "His last letter was indeed kind, was it not? A letter any proud papa would write when his beloved daughter is behaving as he would wish."

Charlotte held her guardian's look. But Mrs Henley did not flinch even though Charlotte was almost certain that Mrs Henley never sent most of the letters Charlotte wrote to her papa.

As an experiment this last month, Charlotte had written a missive laden with fulsome praise of her guardian, and delight at her forthcoming marriage. She'd laced it with several specific questions, for it had been a test.

If her papa answered, then he was still interested in her welfare. And it would prove that he had never received those letters that Mrs Henley deemed unsuitable: the ones in which Charlotte had begged for her papa to take her home. There had been too many of those to count.

All unanswered.

So now Charlotte knew the truth. Mrs Henley only sent on Charlotte's letters when Charlotte evinced pleasure, obedience and satisfaction with her circumstances.

Mrs Henley had no conscience.

Now she merely smiled at Charlotte and said, "We must all accept our place in God's world. It is he who decides our lot in life, and yours, Charlotte, is to be a good wife to a man who has the means to make important changes in our world.

Now, drink your milk and enjoy a good rest. You have everything that a venal girl like you could wish for."

~

EVERYTHING AND NOTHING.

Charlotte pretended to drink the milk. She pretended to sleep.

Oh, but she had got good at this little ploy. And Mrs Henley had become complacent, no longer training her beady eyes on Charlotte to ensure she drank every last drop.

Instead, Charlotte merely withdrew the baudelaire she'd packed in her carpet bag, a receptacle used in extreme circumstances to relieve herself during long carriage rides, into which she poured the milk.

Then she pretended to sleep.

Heavily. For two hours.

That was the hardest part as Mrs Henley occupied herself in their shared chamber, writing her letters of complaint and admonition to anyone who'd listen in the furtherance of her cause.

Seeking funds for the acquisition of bibles for missionaries in Africa.

But at least a small partition provided a modicum of separation, enabling Charlotte to stare at the wall as she contemplated her next move.

Surely Emma wouldn't let her down?

Surely Charlotte could dance at Lady Brigalow's second ball and enjoy the adulation before returning to her room and—

Tomorrow she would leave this hated place.

She would leave behind her life with Mrs Henley and her life as a prisoner because she—and not Mrs Henley—would be in charge of her life.

~

THIS TIME CHARLOTTE did play ground billiards, a new game, she was told, involving sticks and hoops.

Lord Collingwood decreed that she must, and, apparently, that was good enough for Mrs Henley, who was surprisingly interested in the gown Charlotte was to wear. When she settled upon an afternoon gown that was more embellished than the plainer blue which Charlotte had assumed she'd wear, Charlotte was only too happy be laced into it.

Today and tonight she'd enjoy the novelty of being beautifully presented—just as she'd always dreamed of given her love of clothes—but tomorrow she would have to sacrifice her wardrobe if she was to execute her plan for freedom.

When she was out in the fresh air and being induced to try her hand at the game, Charlotte saw Lord Collingwood advancing and was certain he'd take the opportunity to tutor her in the right handling of the strange stick shaped like a mallet, to play this unusual sport.

Instead, Gilray, perhaps not seeing Collingwood, stepped forward to volunteer his services, standing a little to Charlotte's side as he placed her hands upon the stick.

She could feel his breath on her neck and shifted a little, conscious now, not only of Collingwood on the sidelines, but Jasper.

Oh, but she wanted to make him jealous. Jasper had danced with her, flirted with her, promised to help her escape.

He would be her choice if she really were to ride into a golden-limned future but he'd shown no signs of being lovelorn.

Not like Gilray who, to her horror, muttered into her ear, "I'm here to rescue you at a moment's notice, my lovely Miss

Treloar. Surely you've rued the day you cast me aside if you're now to endure Collingwood for the rest of your life. He's not the right man for you."

She was aghast. To say such a thing to her, in public, when she was required to show her composure.

"And if he's not, what is that to you? We didn't exactly part on the best of terms last time," she whispered, before saying in a louder voice for the benefit of those watching, "It's much more comfortable if I position my hands this way." Then she lowered her voice and shot back at Gilray, "And beware, for my future husband has you in his sights. Enough of this talk."

Gilray raised his voice to match Charlotte's, clearly for the benefit of the onlookers. "But you'll get a more successful shot at it if you place them here," before he whispered, "Might I remind you that you're not married yet, Charlotte." And then, in a softer voice, "Have no fear, my dear, you will never marry Collingwood if I have any say in it."

When Gilray stepped back and Charlotte played her first shot, getting the ball right through the first hoop to a smattering of applause, it was Collingwood's breath, cold on her neck as he remarked, "I knew you'd not disgrace me, my love. Well played."

Charlotte tried not to show her distaste as he put a hand around her waist before dropping it, as if he'd exceeded the proprieties.

The thought of what the intimacies of darkness might bring made her shudder.

"There, my dear." His tone was playful, but the twist to his lips looked contrived. "It was Miss Treloar yesterday morning, Charlotte by the afternoon, and now I am so confident in the rightness of my choice of wife that I've gravitated to a term of affection I expected would feel natural only after many years of marriage. And now for my turn." He stepped back with a short nod, indicating to all to be watching, for he was to follow with his first shot.

And, indeed, he played ground billiards like Charlotte presumed he hunted.

With deadly precision.

CHAPTER 16

Tonight was the main event, with additional guests arriving from all over the county, and Charlotte's most lavish gown had been selected. Now, if there were any possibility that she could make her escape with just this one gown, she'd feel she really had made the best of her situation.

However, it would all depend on how Jasper planned to manage matters.

And when he arrived at the entrance to the ballroom at the same time as Charlotte, and whispered, "By Gad, Miss Treloar, you are a beauty tonight," Charlotte's heart nearly burst with happiness as she responded—for Mrs Henley was in conversation with a dowager a few feet away—"That's the first time you've volunteered such kind words."

He raised his eyebrows. "Really? Perhaps I don't want to turn your head since it is so obvious you're the most beautiful woman in the room."

"Collingwood likes to think I'm the most beautiful woman in all England. It's the only reason he's marrying me, of course. He likes the best of everything. Am I more beautiful than your Mariah? That's the question I'm most interested in having you answer."

She didn't mind that she'd discomposed him and he couldn't immediately answer. His obsession over his dead Mariah was unhealthy when he should be concentrating on the living. And she didn't mind saying that, either—or words to that effect—as she stood upon the threshold, waiting to be announced while staring into the middle distance and catching the eye of, first, Gilray, and then Collingwood.

Collingwood looked deeply appreciative, and, a little ruefully, Charlotte had to admit that her vanity was fed by the slavish want that was quite clear on his face.

Mrs Henley joined them at that moment, saying, "Why Charlotte, you have made quite the impression," as Lord Collingwood walked smoothly across the room and took Charlotte's hand to kiss.

Charlotte curtsied, angling her face as she rose, to see Jasper watching her carefully. He was standing silent, and alone, as she passed by on Collingwood's arm. And as Collingwood had paused to respond to congratulations and compliments from rear Admiral Dashwood, Charlotte took the opportunity to incline her head with a clearly provocative smile at Jasper, and to whisper, "I hope you will dance with me. We are living in the present, not the past."

For Mariah was dead, and Charlotte was alive.

And she needed to remind him of that.

HE DIDN'T DANCE with her and while she was disappointed, Charlotte also realised that the least suspicion Collingwood felt towards Jasper, the better. She certainly caught him looking askance at Gilray, who made no secret of his interest and who did engage Charlotte to dance during the earlier part of the evening. But Jasper kept well away.

Nevertheless, she felt a small stab of devastation when she saw him bow to their hostess before quitting the ballroom.

So, he had gone to bed without a word.

What did this mean? That he had no intention of helping her?

Or would he make contact with her later?

Charlotte felt positively forlorn. And if it showed, it didn't matter to Collingwood who remarked, softly, "I can't decide whether you are more beautiful when in a pensive mood, or when rare gaiety strikes you." He squeezed her hand and added, "But I shall demand that your gaiety be reserved for your future husband alone. I do not like the way every man in this room follows you with their eyes."

But Charlotte suspected he did. And that was exactly why he was marrying her.

He enjoyed having what other men wanted.

~

IT WAS WELL before midnight that Charlotte declared to Mrs Henley that she felt it was time to turn in for the night. She'd danced for hours, and enjoyed the activity which helped allay her growing nerves for she was about to take a tremendous risk. And she wasn't at all sure it was going to pay off.

In fact, her hands were shaking as she turned the door-knob so that she and her guardian could enter their chamber.

"I'm glad you had the good sense not to parade yourself like a butterfly when Lord Collingwood so clearly admires restraint." Mrs Henley sat on her bed and began to unpin her hair. It fell in lank, grey waves upon her shoulders, making her face appear thinner and more pinched than usual.

Charlotte sat quietly on a stool by the dressing table and began to do the same, carefully removing the strand of pearls that had been incorporated into her stylish coiffure. She'd hide these in her boots, she decided, and bolster her meagre resources for her flight back home.

Once she was safely with her papa, he would not force her to marry against her wishes, or send her back to Mrs Henley. If he was finally acquainted with Charlotte's real desires, he would be the kind, loving papa he had always been.

The kernel of worry that had lodged in her chest was growing larger all the time. What if she didn't escape in time? Would she really marry Lord Collingwood? Surely no one could force her?

But a glance at Mrs Henley's sharp chin and bloodless lips defied all hope. Mrs Henley had received something from Mr Collingwood to ensure the marriage went ahead. Of course she had. And Mrs Henley was a fearful adversary.

A short rap at the door had Charlotte sagging in relief.

For here was Mrs Henley's warm milk before bed and little did she know that Charlotte was an equally fearsome adversary. She had tutored the girl well.

Charlotte slanted a glance at the girl and, to her relief, she saw that it was Emma.

Furthermore, the maid indicated with the merest glance towards Charlotte's partitioned-off bed that she had done as requested. Was that not what her look implied?

The maid left without a word and Charlotte excused herself to put on her nightrail, perceiving with joy the bundle half protruding from beneath the bed. Kneeling to ensure everything was there, she reached into the drawer to retrieve the tiny twist of paper which held the powder with which Mrs Henley liked to dose Charlotte's warm milk.

When she returned to bid Mrs Henley goodnight, she was

delighted that the woman had taken herself off to use the chamber pot, which meant her back was to Charlotte for the mere seconds it took to tip the powder into her drink. It wasn't much, but surely if it meant she slept just a little longer and a little more deeply than usual, it would be sufficient for Charlotte to carry out her desperate ploy.

"And Charlotte—"

Charlotte halted halfway across the carpet as she looked enquiringly at Mrs Henley, who was now sipping her milk.

"Yes, ma'am."

"Don't think it escaped my notice that Lord Gilray was particularly attentive." Mrs Henley's lips pursed and her nostrils flared.

Charlotte bowed her head. "I've learned from my sins, Mrs Henley," she whispered.

"Have you, my girl?" Mrs Henley put her head on one side and just when Charlotte feared she may insist that Charlotte remain where she could see her, she shrugged. "Time will tell but you will not encourage his attentions, do you hear me?"

Charlotte knew better than to say she didn't think she had. "No, Mrs Henley," she said tonelessly.

"Now off to bed. I'm weary, but I think I will read a little. The lighting here is better than it is at home."

Charlotte's spirits plummeted. She felt her desperation rise. Time was running out. She had had no proper discussions with Jasper, or indeed, anyone who could help her.

Now Mrs Henley was keeping an even more vigilant eye on her as she perceived Lord Gilray's interest as a dangerous thing.

CHARLOTTE TRAILED off to her own bed. Sitting down, she reached for the parcel Emma had left, not even feeling the jolt of the anticipation she'd expected when she saw it was as she'd requested: a serviceable maid's gown with a white cap. Unflattering, of course, it would render her unnoticeable. Not unrecognisable, but who looked too closely at the servants?

Yes, the necklace she'd left beneath the bed had gone. Emma knew a good bargain and was sensible enough to avail herself of Charlotte's generosity. Charlotte wasn't afraid she'd talk because Charlotte would be gone.

Well, that had been the plan. Now Mrs Henley was going to keep vigil over her and Charlotte would never escape.

But a noise made her ears prick up. She straightened, tiptoed a few steps into Mrs Henley's side of the room and saw the woman's book had slipped out of her hands and that, slack-jawed, she was snoring loudly.

Charlotte hurried back to her bed, tore off her night rail and within barely a minute was out in the passage, the unflattering white cap upon her head, the plain gown and white apron proclaiming her as beneath the regard of the couple whom she passed.

The couple whose lack of interest declared her ploy sufficiently believable.

She didn't have long, but then Mrs Henley was a deep sleeper. Charlotte knew that and so a few minutes longer to ensure that Mr Creighton understood the gravity of her situation and promised to act accordingly was all she needed.

Lord Gilray had promised to help her flee but Charlotte was not going to make that mistake twice.

She wanted to return to her papa, but Jasper would take her there.

Yet his early exit from the ballroom confused her.

She was not surprised at the look of horror on his face when he discerned beneath the servant's guise that it was indeed Charlotte.

"Gad's teeth, you're taking a risk," he hissed as she seized her wrist and hauled her into his bedchamber. "What are you about, Charlotte? Yes, I know you don't want to marry Collingwood, and I've agreed to help you if you really need it. I received an invitation here in any case. But you are old enough and wise enough to be able to simply state it yourself. It's not the dark ages. No one can force you to wed against your will."

He seemed a little gloomy and Charlotte, whipping off her cap and tossing her dark hair so that it rippled over her shoulders, ran her fingers through it and smiled up at him as he stepped back, warily.

"In fact, this is outrageous," he went on. "Why, if we were discovered, Collingwood would run me right through with a rapier and lord knows what Mrs Henley would do."

"That's a charming welcome from the gentleman who ought to have stepped up and made an honourable offer of marriage after he ruined me three years ago."

"I didn't ruin you," he muttered, turning his back on her and walking back to the bed.

"Well, you did, rather," she said, following him. "You ruined me a second time. Or, if not in the technical sense of the word, you ensured I could never wed Collingwood, knowing what I would miss out on for the rest of my life if I went through with this hateful wedding. Which I will not, and which I am here to talk to you about. You came here because you were prepared to help me. You would not have come here at all if it was an empty promise you made at the Marshalsea. You are a man of your word. But now you are here and I have only another few nights in this house before I am all but leg-shackled—I believe that's the term you gentlemen use – to Lord Collingwood. As you can see, I am resourceful—"

"You've always been resourceful. It's one of the things I admire about you."

"*One* of them? Pray tell me, what are some of the others?" Charlotte invited as she settled herself beside him on the bed. "Maybe if you can think up enough, you'll decide that I really would make an appealing bride."

"Oh, you wouldn't want to marry me," Jasper muttered.

Charlotte shrugged. "I think I might if you tried to persuade me. But you're in such a blue-devilish mood, so against the idea of marriage that I promise I'm not here to push you into anything other than arranging to spirit me away to my darling papa who has not received a single letter of entreaty I've written these long three years. It's true!" she added with spirit when he looked about to interject. "I tested Mrs Henley and after three abjectly miserable ones to which he didn't respond, I wrote one letter containing fulsome praise of Mrs Henley and my delight at my marriage to Lord Colling-wood, and within three days I had an answer from papa."

"That doesn't prove Mrs Henley was keeping your letters from your papa, but that he wants to be assured of your happiness."

Charlotte made a noise of disgust. "Do try to put yourself in my shoes, Mr Creighton, if you would," she said in tones of heavy irony. "*You* are not a beleaguered debutante with no say in her future. I thought you conceded that when you saw me at the Marshalsea. You knew I could not be happy being wed to the man Mrs Henley wishes me to marry for her dark reasons which I believe are to buy her a ticket to heaven once she's donated to her special cause the money she'll receive for her devil's bargain with Lord Collingwood."

The furrow between his eyes deepened and Charlotte thought she'd made him understand. Then he replied, cautiously, "Charlotte, that is dramatic—"

To Charlotte's great surprise, she began to cry. She hadn't at all been intending to use tears as a ruse to garner his compassion, but when it actually worked, she wasn't about to squander her opportunity.

"I'm sorry," he said, allowing her to nuzzle against him, and when his arms went about her, she found that, surprisingly, her body was doing very strange things. Things she couldn't remember feeling since the last time he'd held her.

She twined her arms about his neck and kissed his throat. To her delight, instead of rejecting her, his hold on her tightened, and she swung her legs over his lap, straining up to kiss his lips as she straddled him.

He kissed her back for a good few seconds and she felt his arousal, which only made her respond with greater ardour, before he scooped her up.

But instead of placing her on the bed as she'd hoped, he put her away from him and, although he was still kissing her from a slight distance, his words were not ones she wished to entertain.

"No, no, no, Charlotte. Impossible! We can't do this."

"Please, please, please, please, Jasper!" she begged, feeling the vibration of each word between their lips, for she was not going to let him go easily. "I'm not asking anything so very much from you. I'm not asking for marriage. I just want to feel what only you can make me feel. Like you did last time. Oh, please, just this one last time." She clambered back onto his lap and pushed him onto his back as she covered his eyes and throat with kisses. The strength of feeling she had for him threatened to engulf her. He really was the most delicious, wonderful man she had ever encountered. "And then you can help me escape to papa."

CHAPTER 17

Of course Jasper knew he shouldn't let her hold sway over him. A brief kernel of cognisance flashed through his consciousness and then was consumed by the astonishing feelings this young woman aroused in his breast.

Well, more than just his breast.

It wasn't just the pure, unadulterated wanton want of it all, but the delicious familiarity, and yearning that accompanied his lustful desires.

She didn't give him a chance to articulate any of the cautions he might have. And he didn't really entertain any either.

The sensations were unexpected, his feelings surprisingly overwhelming, for he had bedded more than a few married society matrons who had set upon him with similar enthusiasm.

He was a practised lover.

And practised in the necessary restraint that would enable him to withhold offering matrimony for the sins he committed against a young woman who might reasonably expect such an offer for the risks they'd taken.

But Jasper wasn't thinking about that, for all that he acted on instinct. His instinct was to kiss Charlotte back with all the enthusiasm and ardour she was showing.

And by god, his enthusiasm was unparalleled by the time she wriggled on top of him, kissing his lips, his eyes, his throat.

Every time she came near him she offered what he knew he should resist.

Offered what he wanted and tried to resist, not because he didn't feel she obviously did, but out of respect for Mariah.

Charlotte was an unmarried young woman, not a society matron, or a lightskirt. He was honour bound to make her a proper offer, except that she explicitly withheld that requirement through the way she offered herself to him.

She'd marry him if he asked, but she wanted him physically, whether he asked, or not.

He wanted her physically, too.

In fact, he'd never wanted a woman more. When his hand crept up her skirts to skim her soft, smooth thighs, the fire of desire was well and truly lit and there was no turning back.

Not when she was kissing him with such passion and she knew where this would lead.

MAKING love to her was so exquisite a sensation, and clearly her enjoyment matched his own, that when they rolled apart after a sensational climax, laughing breathlessly as her hand crept into his, he couldn't think straight.

Then a second of remorse and horror had him sitting up before she pushed him back down saying, "Enough of that. I have to go soon but perhaps we can do it again a little later, this time with no clothes on. I might never see you again after you deposit me with papa. There. Did that make you want me more?"

She laughed softly as she kissed his cheek and Jasper felt a wave of some strange emotion he'd never felt before she said, "Tell me again why you don't want to make me your wife? Gilray offered to elope with me and I'd have him before Collingwood any day. But Jasper—" Her look became forlorn – "we would do so well together. Please don't tell me it's about this silliness with your Mariah who can't come back from the dead, you know."

Jasper sat up, his mood somewhat deflated by her words, for he really did feel strongly about Charlotte and wasn't quite sure what to say except that only honesty would do since he couldn't have her holding out hope when there was none.

He stared about the gloom, the candle flickering on the chest of drawers. "I just am not in the market for marriage right now. I know Mariah can't come back but she was –" He struggled for the right words, finishing lamely, "She was quite perfect. A goddess of purity and—" He stopped himself suddenly, seeing her face fall and realising the wounding he'd caused.

"Please, Charlotte, I didn't mean to cause offence. I like you more than I like any other female I've ever encountered – except Mariah, of course. But I'm not ready to take a wife and when I do—"

He broke off and she whispered, "But when you do, it'll be a young woman who is as untarnished as Mariah ever was. Because looking at me will remind you that I was spoiled before you had me. That's what gentlemen think, isn't it? And maybe that's why Gilray is offering. He's arrogantly confident in the fact that he had me first. That I was a virgin before he had the privilege of ruining me."

Jasper got to his feet. He put his hands on her shoulders and tried to soothe her. "You're right. My sentiments do me no justice, whatsoever. I'm an entitled male and you have every right to be angry. But I will help you, Charlotte. I came here with one objective which was to help you escape to your papa in France. I will not let you down, for my word is sound. Much more so than my morals."

He felt her shoulders slump but when she raised her face she was smiling, albeit, waveringly. A surge of admiration made him want to cradle her to his chest once more. Not to let her go, in fact.

But then she turned and, smoothing her skirts, walked to the door with grace and dignity. "I know you're not enjoying it here, so perhaps tomorrow you might wish to leave?" She smiled. "And I will go with you. That's why you came, isn't it? Because you promised to help me."

Jasper nodded.

CHAPTER 18

Charlotte didn't sleep well.

And it wasn't that Mrs Henley was snoring loud enough to wake the dead after Charlotte had made a successful return with no one the wiser.

It wasn't that her body continued to pulse with longing and the uncomfortable observation that she was in love.

It was the realisation that Jasper never would love her as she would wish a future husband to love her.

He simply couldn't with that ideal stuck in his head as to what constituted the perfect wife. She'd lost all claim to that status before she'd even met Jasper and he'd now made that quite clear.

But he was still going to help her. She had to bolster herself with that thought.

So really, she would do well to brighten her spirits and make the best of things. She had, after all, made great strides in the past six months since she'd discovered what Mrs Henley was doing to keep her submissive; and especially since Lord Collingwood's offer. Charlotte had been exploiting the relative freedom that gave her because she knew she'd have even less freedom in the future if she married Collingwood.

Which she would not.

"Why the long face?" asked Mrs Henley when Charlotte emerged and sat at the dressing table to attend to her morning toilette. "Lord Collingwood doesn't want a po-faced misery of a wife. Did you see how he responded to a little gaiety yesterday. Who'd have thought it? Use it to your advantage, Charlotte." Charlotte had been surprised to think that, for once, Mrs Henley might be thinking of what might aid Charlotte's happiness until she added, "We will need to remind him from time to time that there are others less fortunate who will benefit from his largesse."

No, Mrs Henley never considered that Charlotte might be classified as an unfortunate.

Only, Charlotte was resourceful, and Jasper had complimented her on the fact which prompted a pleasant glow as she reflected how she might trade on that during the journey home to her papa tonight which Jasper had promised he'd organise immediately after the ball.

Butterflies coursed through her ribcage and brought a smile to her face which Mrs Henley's motivation for liveliness had failed to do.

Marriage to Lord Collingwood? No. Many women were forced to wed against their inclination. It was the way of the world, she knew that.

But Charlotte was resourceful.

And being resourceful meant putting on a wonderful act. She would charm Lord Collingwood during their post-breakfast stroll around the lake. And she'd delight Lord Gilray with her witticisms as they loitered on the riverbank before lunch.

Mostly because Charlotte knew Jasper was enjoying a game of ground billiards nearby and that it would not escape his notice that Gilray found Charlotte entertaining company.

But might she marry Gilray since it was clear Jasper was not in the market?

"You dance better than you play ground billiards, Gilray," Charlotte teased her companion. "Is that why you've withdrawn from the competition?"

He grimaced as he stopped to look at the play in the distance. "I can't bear being in competition with your future husband. He turns everything into the most tedious battle which he takes deadly seriously. Do you see? I think Creighton is determined to best him but it will not augur well if he does. Colllingwood will find some way to exact a petty revenge."

"You are not very charitable towards my betrothed," Charlotte remarked, which prompted Gilray to respond with startling passion, "I cannot believe you agreed to marry Collingwood when you could have had me."

Charlotte glanced about her to ensure they were not being overheard – or observed by Collingwood. She'd left the play in company with Vanessa who had disappeared when her cousin appeared. They'd been out of sight and she knew she should step out of view but for the moment she hesitated as she glanced at the cluster of players in the distance, which included Collingwood and Jasper.

And then she glanced at Gilray who looked handsomer and less dissolute than she remembered.

But her knowledge of Gilray was sufficiently off-putting.

She'd marry Gilray as readily as she'd marry Collingwood.

Meaning that she'd not marry anyone if she couldn't marry Jasper.

Again, her body pulsed with the most mind-altering want and she had to close her eyes a moment after focussing her gaze on that beautiful man who was swinging the stick as if it were an extension of himself.

What an athlete.

What a consummate athlete, as adept with a mallet as he was in—

Charlotte's face burned, and she was glad of the gentle, cooling breeze. Jasper was her ideal in so many ways but she would not delude herself.

Nor would she chastise herself. She'd taken pleasure which no young woman would get away with in their society, but no one was going to know.

Gilray would not. She slanted a cynical smile up at him. "My dear Gilray, you didn't fight very hard to have me, if you recall."

He made a face. "I don't remember very much of anything that night, to be quite honest. Except that you were marvellous." He raked her with a lascivious look before sobering at her withering response.

"But you were not."

"I was in my cups, you know that. And when Creighton dragged you from my bedchamber, I knew he'd have reported back to your family that I really had not acquitted myself in a very gentlemanly way. But I've changed, Charlotte." There was a pleading note to his voice, and he gripped her hand. "You are the only woman I've truly loved. The months since that time have only made this clearer to me. Please, Charlotte, if I could go down on bended knee and do it properly this time, would you have me?"

Charlotte withdrew her hand. "Really, Gilray, you're embarrassing both of us. No, I will not marry you. I don't know what possessed me to think it was a remotely good idea in the first place."

"You're surely not going to tell me that you prefer

Collingwood over me? Why, at least I have *some* sense of humour."

Charlotte smiled as she began to walk.

She supposed she would marry in time, but she was in no hurry. The only hurry she was in was to escape to her darling papa.

To escape from Collingwood.

How had she found herself in such a situation?

What foolish woman would agree to commit themselves to a lifelong union if their heart was not in it?

She answered her own question.

Someone who had been ground down for three years by a guardian who forced them to toil and subsume themselves to an ideal that was beyond earthly salvation – in between being drugged when not sufficiently biddable.

When Charlotte's papa realised the gravity of her situation he would protect her like a good father. Mrs Henley claimed he had happily signed the marriage contract upon Mrs Henley's advice that Charlotte was eager.

Well, he'd not sought her advice. And why not? He'd been as deceived by Mrs Henley as Charlotte had been, and Mrs Henley had clearly misrepresented Charlotte's feelings.

"What do you and Gilray find so amusing?" It was Vanessa who had returned, her face flushed with the cold. She smiled between them before hooking her arm through Charlotte's. "I hope my cousin is behaving like a gentleman and not putting wicked thoughts into your head, Charlotte. He can be very persuasive, and I should know, being his cousin."

"I think, Vanessa that you are very well aware of how persuasive your cousin can be but I will not fall for his charm a second time."

It was good to be with her old friend and the camaraderie of the old days lightened Charlotte's spirits. "Run along, now,

Gilray, for Vanessa and I want a quiet coze which would only bore you."

"I don't think it would," Gilray said quite earnestly, until Vanessa flicked him with the end of her shawl and he rolled his eyes before reluctantly obeying.

"Do tell me that you were exhorting Gilray to rescue you from the biggest mistake you've ever made?" Vanessa sounded breathless as if it really were a matter of the greatest gravity. "You surely aren't going to marry Collingwood, are you? Oh, Charlotte, I don't know how you could ever have agreed. He won't make you happy. Don't you know that?"

They were in the apple orchard now and Charlotte stopped beneath a gnarled old tree. Resting her back against the trunk, she sighed. "I do know that, and you're right." She hesitated, weighing up her words. "My guardian, Mrs Henley, pressured me to agree when I was at my lowest ebb. Even now I don't know quite why I accepted him. I just wanted to escape Mrs Henley's guardianship and didn't know of another way."

"You obviously haven't refused Collingwood yet."

"No, and I don't have the courage to do so."

"But... you'll have to, won't you?" Vanessa sounded rightly concerned.

"I won't if I run away."

The crease between Vanessa's eyes deepened and then her face lit up. "Why, Charlotte! I'm so glad! You're so brave. You've made the only decision—"

She broke off, her large, mobile face revealing her fear as Collingwood stepped into their orbit, seemingly from nowhere.

"And what decision is this, ladies?" he asked, offering both an arm.

"Why, that..that..." Vanessa said haltingly as she allowed him to escort her back down the hill.

But Charlotte managed with a smoothness that came surprisingly easily and which made her a little proud, also. "Why, the decision to wed you, of course, Lord Collingwood," she said with just the right degree of coyness and determination that she felt would appeal to him.

And clearly it did, for he squeezed her hand, smiled warmly at her, and said, "You have indeed made the only decision that would make me happy, Charlotte. And I commend you for it."

Charlotte' smile broadened.

He really had no idea when she was sincere and pliant, and wasn't that just as well?

And soon that wouldn't matter for Charlotte would be free.

The thought gave her a warm sense of pleasurable excitement that began at her toes and seeped through her despite the chilly wind.

Buoyed with excited confidence, she allowed her supposedly future husband to set their course for his cold, impressive showpiece of a home.

CHAPTER 19

But Charlotte was feeling far from excited confidence as she danced a reel with Collingwood later that night.

She wished she was wearing the exquisite ballgown from the previous night. This one was lovely, but it was not quite as magnificent, though she knew it was foolish to be worrying over little things like the fact that tonight's ballgown only had one row of bows around the hem, and was pale green which was not her favourite colour.

But she supposed she was simply trying to keep her mind off how Jasper would orchestrate their departure into the dark night.

He'd told her to have a small bag stowed in the bushes that she could snatch after she'd made her excuses to go to the ladies' mending room.

Jasper would be waiting with a post chaise on the road beyond the park.

Everything was in place. The maid's dress and cap were stuffed in the bag in case she needed to evade detection at any later stage.

Jasper had counselled her to change into the maid's clothing before she made her way across the park, but Charlotte was not going to do that. It was much more romantic to escape from Lord and Lady Brigalow's grand estate dressed in a fine ballgown than some down-at-heel servant's costume.

And the more she twirled about the room wearing this lovely pale green gown, the more Charlotte decided she liked it. Perhaps, even more than the pink.

"And what are you thinking about that brings such a faraway look into your eyes?"

Charlotte was astonished Collingwood had the ability to notice such things. He seemed completely consumed with himself.

"Why, the thought of marrying you, Lord Collingwood."

Charlotte was conscious that he faltered as he twirled her about the floor, and she glanced up to see him gazing at her, first with a frown that cleared when he said, "Why, Charlotte, I... I am a lucky man. I did not think—" He cleared his throat and said, with the first sign of diffidence he'd ever shown her, "I could not imagine you would come to care for me...so fast." His hand about her waist tightened and his breath was warm against her ear as he murmured, "I am the luckiest man in the whole of England."

Charlotte managed a smile that wasn't as robust as it ought to have been. Might he keep a closer eye on her now? Would he follow her movements more watchfully?

Or would he reduce his vigilance through complacence?

Whatever happened, she just had to make her escape before midnight. The night was dark and Jasper had been reluctant to make their journey but she'd been forceful.

It was, she truly believed, her only chance.

If she returned with Mrs Henley, she'd be under even greater surveillance.

"I do have the most pounding megrim," she murmured as Collingwood led her off the dance floor at the end of the next set. "It really has set upon me with quite a vengeance. If you'll excuse me, I will retire for the evening." With an apologetic look, she turned in search of Mrs Henley while Collingwood murmured his sympathies.

"My dear, I shall escort you to her. Yes, an early night will do you good. Too much gaiety must be dangerous for a delicate constitution like yours." He brought her hand to his lips. "You have acquitted yourself well. You are robust when you need to be, Charlotte, but you are commendably frail. I would not like a wife who was altogether too vibrantly healthy."

Charlotte accepted this equably as she joined Mrs Henley, telling her of her intention to take to her bed. Mr Collingwood's concerned endorsement that this would be a good thing seemed to satisfy the older woman, who nodded and said, "Perhaps I ought to come with you, for it is late."

This was the difficulty. If Charlotte agreed, she'd have to wait until Mrs Henley was asleep. This, perhaps, was the safest option.

But not the most ideal given the weather.

Charlotte needed to gauge just how much Mrs Henley was enjoying herself and hope that it was enough to keep her occupied for at least another half an hour. Preferably more.

"I did hear Lady Fairway mention her interest in Mrs Fry when we were playing lawn billiards," Charlotte said artfully. She pretended to admire the gown of a passing debutante, adding offhandedly, "Why, there she is. She mentioned she'd like to talk to you about your good causes."

Charlotte was astonished that her lie should be so successful. As soon as she saw Mrs Henley talking animatedly to Lady Fairley who had, fortuitously, made some vague mention of something related to charitable works, Charlotte made her way leisurely through the double doors, then hurried as fast as she could to the stairs. But instead of going up to the bedrooms, she deviated to the servants' stairs. They were behind the main staircase and immediately Charlotte had transcended the main areas of the house she was engulfed in gloom.

Charlotte thought she had a good gauge on the house and how to find her way unobtrusively outdoors, but having descended two staircases she was thoroughly disoriented.

And frightened.

"Miss? You shouldn't be here."

A timid voice made her stand rigid in fright for she'd been cowering in the shadows near the end of a corridor, trying to tell from the sounds, and smells, of the house where the kitchens lay, for if she could sneak into the scullery she'd be able to leave via the courtyard, then make her way to the shrubbery and then through the back gardens to the park.

"No, I… I know I shouldn't," Charlotte said.

"'Ere, miss, let me lead you to the main stairs. I ain't supposed to go into the main 'ouse but I can take you to where you need to go, at least."

In the gloom, Charlotte saw the little servant was no more than thirteen, at most. One of the most junior twee-nies, she supposed. So, on a burst of inspiration, she said, "I wanted to find Emma. I didn't realise I'd plunged myself into the servant's quarters. Do you think you could find Emma for me?"

The tweeny didn't blink, if she thought it an odd request, and within a surprisingly short time she was joined by the young maid who had already been so helpful.

"Oh, miss, but you should be dancin' with the rest of them upstairs. Janey shouldn't have brought me down 'ere when she should a' taken you directly to where you belong."

"But, you see, I don't belong there," Charlotte said in a

rush. "Please Emma I'm meeting someone in the park and I have to go there as quickly as possible. I thought I knew the way and now I'm hopelessly lost. I don't even know which direction the park is. Please, won't you help me?"

Emma looked dubious. "In this dark, miss? Why, there's no moon. It ain't a night for horses. That's why all the guest are staying."

"And why it makes it a perfect night for me to be leaving without anyone the wiser." Charlotte was removing the ribbons from her hair as she spoke. "You'd like these, wouldn't you, Emma?" she asked, handing them to her. "They're yours if you just take the few minutes to help me navigate my way through the dark. "

She really didn't know what else to do, now, except place her trust in Emma who had not let her down the first time.

"Please?"

~

IT SEEMED Emma was ripe for adventure, for she didn't need asking twice.

And within a few minutes, Charlotte was making her way over the dew-covered lawn, wishing she'd heeded Jasper's advice, for her dancing slippers were quite ruined by the time she reached the edge of the gardens, and her hem was sodden.

But there was the carriage a little distance away, and her heart leapt.

She'd made it.

CHAPTER 20

THREE HOURS EARLIER

"It's not ready? When will it be ready?" Jasper glared at the ostler, who'd promised to supply him with the requisite vehicle for following through with his promise to Charlotte.

"Sir, I can't provide something that ain't here. In the present, that is," the ostler pleaded. "It was due in this morning and... well, it ain't arrived yet. Yer'll have to wait a little longer."

Jasper glanced up at the sky. The afternoon was drawing on and he needed to secure the transport and have it safely ensconced amongst the trees at the requisite time.

He glanced at his timepiece. At best, he had one hour to lay claim to the post chaise, leave it with the postilion in a hiding place about a mile from the estate, dress for dinner, and the meeting he was to have with Sir Maxwell which he hoped would not go too late, then make his way from the ball to the post chaise by ten o'clock.

"Mr Creighton! How are you, sir?"

Jasper turned to see Charlotte's friend Vanessa hailing him from across the village green as she set her steps towards him, clinging to her cousin's arm.

He bowed in greeting before saying, "Gilray, should you not be hurrying back so your cousin has time to dress? It is growing late."

"You're returning to Brigalow House? Would you like to join us? Let bygones be bygones, as Miss Treloar has done? Three years is a long time to realise the folly of youth, if you don't mind my being blunt."

Jasper frowned and glanced at Miss Vanessa. Their past dealings were not for her ears, but she said guilelessly, "I heard you asking after a post chaise. Are you planning a long journey, Mr Creighton?"

Jasper's cheeks burned. How indiscreet he'd been.

"I, er, was planning to take a long journey, yes," he agreed cautiously.

"It must be a very long journey if you are hiring such an expensive vehicle. Could you possibly be going so far as the coast? And after that, perhaps to France?"

Jasper narrowed his eyes as she went on, "Miss Treloar told me." She lowered her voice. "She asked Gilray to take her but he said he didn't have the ready funds to hire a suitable equipage. A good thing, then, that she has secured you to return her to her father."

Jasper chose his words carefully. "Marriage to Collingwood will not make her happy and Lord Dewhurst has been kept ill-informed about his daughter by Mrs Henley, who is no friend of his. Or poor Charlotte's."

"And time is of the essence," Vanessa agreed. "We both know Mrs Henley will keep an eagle eye on Charlotte, though the news of Mr Rupert Everington's release means she is anxious to return home early and has her mind on other things."

She nodded, indicating her intention to move on, but the name that was had just spilled from her lips was like an incendiary device and Jasper couldn't let her go.

"Rupert Everington? How do you know he's been released?"

"Mrs Henley has long campaigned for his release on the basis of his unjust sentence, and this evening she received news she has been successful."

"Everington has been released! When?"

Miss Vanessa and Gilray looked shocked at his outburst. They weren't to know the finer details and he could not explain to them when time was of the essence.

"In the past couple of days." Miss Vanessa glanced at her cousin then went on, "I heard Mrs Henley say that he is taking a boat bound for the Cape of Good Hope at the earliest."

"He's been released, and he's leaving the country?" Jasper could not contain the extent of his rage. The man who had hastened his lovely Mariah to her death was a free man only three years later? And now he was to escape to foreign lands without a proper accounting for his crimes?

His conversation with him in the Marshalsea had only hardened Jasper's feelings. Everingham was a murderer *and* a liar.

"Yes, Mr Creighton. You seem upset. Did you know Mr Everingham?"

"I did, and I need to speak to him before he leaves the country. When did you say he departs?"

Vanessa shrugged. "Mrs Henley said he was going to take the next boat from Southampton, but of course he would have to make arrangements." She looked over his shoulder at the stables and the ostler, who had disappeared to attend to the needs of another gentleman. "Perhaps you'll see him at the docks when you take Charlotte to her papa." She bit her lip. "I do worry about the fact Charlotte will not be properly chaperoned, though. Have you secured the company of a respectable female for the journey?"

Miss Vanessa's concerns only added fuel to Jasper's concern. Of course, Lord Leeson had asked Jasper, discreetly, to aid and abet his niece's safe transport. He'd left the minor details to Jasper's good judgment.

But was it good judgment to snatch Charlotte in the middle of the night and disappear with her on a journey that would take more than twenty-four hours?

When he took too long before answering, Miss Vanessa turned to her cousin. "Gilray, I think we must rethink our denial of my friend's request. I will go with you. Really, I don't mind missing tonight's ball. If we hurry back and offer our excuses, Charlotte's departure will be less remarked upon, and less likely to cause a scandal if it's discovered; for I will be with you, and furthermore, I'll have my luggage so that Charlotte has a fellow female to lean on and from whom to borrow the necessary clothing."

She smiled at Jasper, adding, "If you are in a hurry, we could take responsibility for the post chaise, enabling you to go about your business. Charlotte is our collective concern, but as a fellow female, I'd feel happier providing her with the necessary chaperone."

Jasper hesitated. He was not in the habit of shirking his duty or relinquishing a promise, but Miss Vanessa spoke the truth. It would be safer if Charlotte travelled in her company.

The knowledge that Rupert Everington had just been released and might soon be beyond contact, thus denying Jasper the catharsis of hearing from his own lips his remorse and finally a confession was, he had to confess, almost unendurable.

Still doubtful, he glanced at Gilray but when that young gentleman considered the matter for but a second, then said,

"Why, I do believe you've hit upon the very best plan, Vanessa," Jasper felt the matter was settled.

He could, in all conscience, rescind his obligation to Charlotte and leave her in the hands of the man she'd suggested she'd now happily marry as a substitute for Collingwood.

"Then I thank you for your timely intervention," he said with a bow. "I shall, in that case, make all haste to return to London."

❧

CHARLOTTE WAS NEARLY in tears by the time she reached the carriage door which was flung open as she was about to collapse against it.

The night was dark, her dress was all but ruined, and the hoot of an owl just above her head had been the final straw.

She'd never been so terrified.

But with the welcoming arm that protruded from the carriage, hauling her onto the seat, she felt that her trials had all been worth it.

She'd escaped from the watchful eye of her guardian and she'd escaped marriage to Collingworth.

Jasper might not want to marry her, but she had the prospect of many enjoyable hours in his company.

And who knew? She might persuade him yet.

But it was a different masculine voice that greeted her and made her shriek, "Gilray! What are *you* doing here? Are you planning an elopement? Not with me, I hope! Mr Creighton was supposed to be waiting for me."

"I know, I know, and I promise I won't force you to run away with me this time, though I will do my best to persuade you of the merits of marriage to me over Collingwood. I'm very sorry I behaved in such a caddish way the last time. Vanessa said I went about things all wrong—"

It was at this point Charlotte realised her old friend was seated in the darkness.

"Vanessa! What is the meaning of all this? Why are you and Gilray here and not Mr Creighton, as arranged?"

Vanessa leaned forward to clasp Charlotte's hands. "Darling Charlotte, Mr Creighton had urgent business in London and as you weren't planning on eloping with him, Gilray and I decided we couldn't let you down." Her voice warmed. "Gilray has even undertaken the expense of your grand escape but you must know it's because you are so dear to both of us."

Charlotte reached for the door. This was not at all what she'd expected.

But when the owl hooted again, and she heard in the distance, the sounds of guests on the point of departure, the lights of Brigalow House that glittered through the trees were a reminder of her need to elude discovery for a cumbersome equipage like theirs would be noticed by anyone the moment they turned out of the park gates.

With a sigh, she indicated the postilion astride the left of the pair of horses that pulled their coach, enabling its passengers a good view of the road ahead.

"Tell the man to start riding. I suppose we should make what time we can. But you surely cannot intend travelling all the way to France with me? I need to see my papa as soon as possible because he can't see me in England or else—"

She clapped a hand to her mouth, but Vanessa said soothingly, "No need to be embarrassed on our account when we are such friends, Charlotte. Gilray told me about the long-ago scandal that prevents your dear papa from returning to his homeland yet despite that Gilray still wishes to honour you with his name."

Charlotte wasn't sure she liked the way this was phrased, though conceded there was some comfort in being amongst friends who knew her history.

Nevertheless, she sent Gilray a narrow look and said, "I believe I made it quite clear that my last foray with you to the border was a terrible mistake I do not wish to repeat. I thank you and Vanessa for your kindness, but I will not change my mind. I have as little wish to marry you, Gilray, as I do Collingwood."

"Why Charlotte, how can you say such a thing?" Vanessa burst out, which caused Charlotte to offer some concession as she added with a shrug of her shoulders, "Well, I did tell Creighton I'd prefer marriage to Gilray over Lord Colling-wood any day but that doesn't mean I *want* it."

"Then what are you going to do?" Vanessa demanded. "Why Charlotte, you are twenty! All but on the shelf and with a papa who is mired in scandal—"

"But who has provided me with a very handsome dowry, which makes me quite a catch," Charlotte said with a pointed look at Gilray.

Gilray looked scandalised. "If you are suggesting that pecuniary interests are behind my marriage proposal, you are shockingly mistaken, Charlotte."

"Then what *is* behind your marriage proposal?" Charlotte challenged.

Gilray regarded her a few moments then touched his heart. "Passion. Love. Admiration."

Charlotte put her nose in the air and tried to remain immune to his compliments.

"You have grown far more interesting than I remembered you, Charlotte. Why, you were such a schoolgirl out for adventure and quite self absorbed. Now you are determined and daring and so magnificent —"

This was going too far.

"And you want to snuff all that out so as to make me your wife? No, Gilray, I have endured three years of captivity at the hands of Mrs Henley. I will not subjugate myself to either you or Collingwood."

"Since no one can possibly force you to marry Collingwood, why this grand adventure?" Vanessa asked. "I thought it could only be because you wanted Mr Creighton to propose, but he was very eager to hand over responsibility for your flight to Gilray," her friend said unkindly.

For a moment, Charlotte had nothing to say to this. The fact that Mr Jasper had relinquished all involvement so very readily pained her more than she liked to concede.

To cauterize the pain, she flung back at Vanessa, "How do you suppose your reputation will survive a midnight flight, leaving your husband at Brigalow House while you aid and abet your cousin in his attempts to kidnap me for the second time?"

Instead of a prickly defence, Vanessa smiled pityingly as she reached forward once more to grasp Charlotte's hand.

"Dear Charlotte, I don't wonder you're upset. Like you, my heart was not Reggie's when I agreed to marry him, but he has proved so receptive to my whims and fancies that I positively adore him now. Gilray will be the same. Won't you, Gilray?" She flung a sharp look at her cousin who obliged her with a sober corroboration, saying, "My dear Charlotte—for I think our past acquaintance was of sufficient depth to allow me to call you that."

The wave of revulsion at the memory his words dredged up must have registered on Charlotte's face for he quickly changed tack, adding, "I believe the way forward is to start again and for you to direct me in all the ways I can facilitate your happiness." He cleared his voice, adding, sombrely, "Darling girl."

"See, Charlotte, it's finding the right husband that is the

path to true happiness. A husband willing to indulge one, like my Reggie, who knows exactly where I am and who is making all the necessary excuses for the reason neither of us is at Brigalow House. I impressed upon him the urgency of my duty towards my best bosom friend in all the world and he is helping cover our footsteps this very minute."

"So your husband knows about me and what I'm doing?"

"You're not ashamed of what you're doing, are you, Charlotte? You told me Mrs Henley drugged you and made you agree to things you didn't want to do, and that's why you had to run away. Of course Reggie is very worried about you, as are we all. Ah, now, Gilray, tell the postilion to stop for I see the lights of an inn and I do wish for some refreshment."

"No, Gilray, it is too soon to stop," Charlotte protested with a frown at Vanessa. "We must press on."

"No, Gilray, can't you hear my stomach positively growling? Charlotte, you'll have my death upon your conscience and a skeleton for all the world to find if we don't stop."

Accordingly, the horses slowed and the post chaise came to a halt in the stables behind the inn. Gilray helped his cousin to the cobbled courtyard, and then Charlotte, who felt suddenly all at sea.

She'd never get to France if Vanessa kept stopping their progress. They'd not been on the road for more than half an hour and now Vanessa was ordering a glass of Madeira and a slice of gammon pie.

Charlotte had completely lost her appetite; even when the tantalising aroma of the meat pie put in front of her was not sufficient for her to eat more than one mouthful.

"We must go direct to the coast when we are finished," Charlotte said, biting her lip. "Papa doesn't know I'm coming, but he will be my staunchest advocate. You know Mrs Henley will keep me locked up as securely as any of the prisoners at the Marshalsea."

"Indeed, Mrs Henley was quite spirited earlier this afternoon at news of the release of a wrongfully convicted prisoner whose case has been of special concern to her. It was also, I believe, the reason Mr Creighton left in such a hurry."

Charlotte stared at her friend, trying to gauge her expression through the gloom. "What do you mean? Who was released? Why would Mr Creighton be so interested in a prisoner at the Marshalsea?"

"Because, my dear Charlotte," said Vanessa with great sympathy, "Mr Everingham is the man who killed the brother of his former betrothed, Miss Mariah. He's vowed vengeance, you know."

"So, he rushed all the way to London to confront this man… instead of accompanying me home?" Now she really did feel like crying. Mariah would ever be his obsession.

"Ah, Charlotte, you know the depths of a passionate heart. Mr Creighton is a well-known rake. A philanderer. But everyone knows the reason why he only ever gets involved with married women."

"They do?" Charlotte hoped Vanessa wasn't alluding to Mariah.

"Of course. He was so pained by the death of his pure, sweet betrothed that simply no one can ever match." Vanessa sighed. "But he is a good man, and that is why he's helping you. I believe your uncle asked it of him."

"My uncle? Lord Leeson? Why should he do that?"

Vanessa shrugged. "I do not know the reason. I just know that he did." She paused, then leaned forward with a frown, adding, "And you do realise that Lady Leeson is Mrs Henley's daughter, though they are estranged."

Charlotte reared back as if bitten by an adder. "Lady Leeson is Mrs Henley's *daughter*?" Her mouth felt dry. Beautiful Lady Leeson, whose portrait she had admired, and whose husband—Charlotte's uncle—she thought was helping her, was the child of the woman who'd made Charlotte's life such torment?

Charlotte shuddered. Did Lord and Lady Leeson perhaps have some interest in seeing her married to…

Collingwood?

Her mind began to work.

Why, Mr Creighton had rescued her three years ago at the request of Lord Leeson.

Only to be delivered into the hands of Mrs Henley, who had kept her all but prisoner while she forced upon Charlotte a match she did not wish for.

"I have never met Lord Leeson," Charlotte whispered. "But Lady Leeson is Mrs Henley's daughter, you say? It cannot be true. Why would either of them be interested in me?"

"Lord Leeson is very interested in universal suffrage and seeing the poor are raised up."

"Like Mrs Henley." Charlotte swallowed. As time slipped by and she watched Vanessa eat her pie, she'd grown increasingly nervous. But knowledge of Lord and Lady Leeson's relationship to Mrs Henley put an even more frightening complexion on matters. "Lord Leeson was once my papa's dearest friend, but now they are estranged. Mr Creighton said they had some terrible argument over—" She put her hands to her mouth to hide her agitation and Vanessa stroked her shoulder, supplying, "A woman, yes. But that was long ago, Charlotte. And you still have your dowry, and Lord Collingwood wants to marry you, but Gilray wants to marry you more. Isn't that all that matters? That you will be free?"

Charlotte shook her head. "No, there is something strange and terrible at the heart of all this. At the heart of why Mrs Henley was allowed custody of me, and arrange my marriage. Questions I need to ask my papa before I can be anyone's wife."

Gilray glowered into his claret and muttered, "You can ask your papa all these questions when we return from Scotland, Charlotte. Right now, you just need to escape Collingwood."

"That's right, Charlotte," said Vanessa, standing up. "Collingwood will pursue you the moment he learns you have gone. Do finish your food so we can be on the road."

CHAPTER 21

J asper was back in London by six. The journey had taken him a little over an hour's riding and it would not be dark for another four hours which gave him plenty of time to do what he needed to do in order to ease his conscience.

While the hard riding had been what his fevered brain had needed, and the exertion had helped clear some of his agitation, what remained when he dismounted at the stables behind his lodgings was a heavy dose of guilt.

He should have at least sought out Charlotte to explain to her why he could not accompany her to France.

But he knew she'd take a dim view of the reason behind his defection. She'd hardly endorse his decision to ride hell for leather for the docks to try to arrest the departure of the murderer of Mariah's brother.

Well, that was of no account.

Jasper would be unable to live with himself without a final accounting with Everingham. The fact that the fellow had been released from the Marshalsea and was now enjoying his freedom after such a short time, was intolerable.

There was only a short window of opportunity for Jasper to charge Everingham with his crimes. It was tonight or never.

The least Jasper could do, though, was make a quick visit, en route, to Lord and Lady Leeson's townhouse and inform them of Charlotte's health and situation.

"Mr Creighton, you have news for us?" Lady Leeson looked flushed and very lovely as she directed him to a seat in their elegantly appointed blue and silver drawing room. "How is Charlotte? Please tell me she is not marrying Collingwood. That is my main hope. But I thought she would be with you."

She sat down, looking anxiously between Jasper and the door until her husband entered the room and took a seat beside her.

"Mr Creighton has news of Charlotte," she said. "I know how worried about her you are."

She seemed unusually tense, and Jasper waited until Lord Leeson had settled himself for although his wife was good to take an interest, Charlotte was his niece, though of course, the rift between Leeson and his old friend, James Treloar, Charlotte's father, must make the relationship difficult.

Perhaps the two men were at loggerheads and Treloar had no wish for his once greatest friend, Leeson, to concern himself with his daughter's welfare.

He remembered what Charlotte had told him, and now said, "Charlotte claims her letters are not being forwarded to her father. I was going to escort her to France tonight but urgent business has called me to Southampton. I thought it only fair to tell you that while I am not personally escorting Charlotte to France, she will be leaving later tonight under the care of her friend from Miss Prism's Ladies Academy, Vanessa, and her cousin, Lord Gilray."

"Lord Gilray! The miscreant with whom she eloped three

years ago!" Lady Leeson put her hand to her throat and her eyes sought her husband's.

"Yes, but she is reconciled with Gilray who is doing this out of friendship, and is in company with his cousin, Vanessa," Jasper reassured her. "Charlotte will be comfortable with the situation." He was certain she would be. And Charlotte was no longer his business, he counselled himself.

Avenging his beloved Mariah was now his principal concern.

"What do you mean 'comfortable'?" Lady Leeson challenged.

"I mean that when I told her that I might not be able to be as obliging as she would like—"

"Would you speak more plainly, Mr Creighton?"

Lady Leeson leaned forward, her tone sharp, as if she had a vested interest in the matter.

He sighed. Lady Leeson might be a beauty still, but she was more exacting than her reputation painted her.

Surprising, also, was the manner in which Lord Leeson pandered to her, patting her hand as if she were to be soothed.

Jasper frowned. "I'm sorry, Lady Leeson, but your interest in Miss Treloar is obviously greater than I understood," he said crisply.

To his surprise, she gave a little gasp then, putting her hand to her throat, she relaxed back into her seat, relinquishing the conversation to her husband who asked, "Are you sure that Lord Gilray is not, in fact, spiriting Charlotte across the border, just as he tried three years ago? Are you telling me that this time she is a more willing participant?"

"She was a willing participant three years ago," Jasper reminded him.

"But by the time you arrived she'd seen the error of her

177

ways. You did not have to wrench her from Gilray? She went willingly?"

He now seemed anxious and Jasper, very anxious himself to be seen in the light of Charlotte's rescuer, said, "Of course she went willingly."

"I don't understand what you mean when you say Charlotte has mended her quarrel with Gilray and that the pair are quite comfortable. Are you insinuating that Charlotte does in fact wish to marry Gilray? Is that what you are saying?"

Jasper looked at Lady Leeson and tried to remain calm. The truth was, all this talk about Charlotte and her preferences were making him uncomfortable. He could hardly tell Lady Leeson that Charlotte had said quite plainly she would prefer to wed Jasper above all others. So he settled for, "She said she'd marry Gilray before she'd marry Collingwood."

"I told you she was coerced into the marriage!" Lady Leeson leaned forward, gripping her husband's arm. "Oh, how could it have been kept from us for so long that Charlotte was with that ... that dreadful woman?" She turned to Jasper. "You knew, of course. But you didn't know who she was or to what dreadful fate you were consigning her!"

Jasper swallowed. Her distress was alarming him. "When I delivered Charlotte to Miss Prism's Academy, Mrs Henley said she'd been sent by Charlotte's father."

"*Why* would he do that?" Lady Leeson turned to her husband. "Was he trying to punish me?" She clapped her hand to her mouth and then said quickly, "I cannot know the reason why Mrs Henley was appointed Charlotte's guardian but I can tell you she is a cruel woman."

Jasper frowned. What did he know of Lady Leeson other than that she had married her husband at about the same age as Charlotte having just returned from living abroad. Her late father had been a diplomat in Vienna. He did remember that. And her mother? No, the wisp of memory eluded him.

Nevertheless, she had taken Charlotte's welfare to heart and somehow Jasper felt he had failed both of them by handing over Charlotte's responsibility this evening to Gilray though at the time he'd felt fully justified and had only stopped by Lord and Lady Leeson's townhouse as a formality to let them know that Charlotte was being conveyed to her father by someone whom she had indicated she would willingly marry ahead of the man to whom she was currently betrothed.

"I am very sorry that Charlotte went to live with Mrs Henley," he said with suitable gravitas. "But now she is being conveyed to her father as we speak. I'm sure she will not be judged harshly for her flight. Many brides get cold feet on the eve of their nuptials. When she's safely with her papa, he can sort out the matrimonial mess in which she has found herself."

Lady Leeson stiffened. "Where is she *now*?" There was a new intensity to her tone as she leaned forward. "You left at what time? The ride is a little over an hour, you say? Therefore … my husband could intercept her on the road." She turned to Lord Leeson. "You could do that, my love. Couldn't you?"

This made Jasper feel worse. He cleared his throat. "Indeed you could, Lord Leeson. But if you both would excuse me, I must go for I came to London in some haste, myself."

"Ah yes, and why was that?" Lord Leeson asked as he caged his wife's hand though he did not appear to be too invested in the answer.

"I have heard that the man who killed my late betrothed's brother has been released from prison and is about to leave the country."

"And you wish to call him to account?"

Jasper knew he looked a trifle defensive as he said, "Would you not?"

Lord Leeson smiled. "I would just remind you that the reason Charlotte's father was stripped of his title and is unable to return to England is for what is known in his adopted country as a *crime passionnel*. He too felt justified in taking to task someone who had wronged—" he hesitated, glanced at his wife, then added— "the woman he loved."

"Do you mean... caution me?" Jasper challenged, with more brittleness than he'd intended.

Lord Leeson inclined his head. "I would not presume. You are clearly not as passionate as Charlotte's father, Lord Dewhurst. His reputation precedes him, even though many years have passed."

"Seventeen," murmured Lady Leeson to Jasper's surprise.

"But vengeance," Lord Leeson went on, "often leads to unforeseen consequences. That is all I would remind you. And if you have a grudge against this man, would it not be better to seek him out and state your case with words rather than provocation?"

Jasper tried to maintain his equilibrium but it was hard when his heart was in such turmoil. At this very moment Everingham might be eluding him.

"I thank you for your counsel, Lord and Lady Leeson and I bid you farewell."

With a bow, he quit the room.

BEFORE THE DOOR had closed behind him, his hostess was already gripping her husband's hand, whispering urgently, "Tristan, you know what I'm about to ask you—"

But Tristan was already eyeing the door, his look grave as he took Adelaide's hand and brought it to his lips.

"You mustn't blame young Creighton for misunderstanding the urgency of this matter. It would be one thing if his heart had been engaged by your darling girl but it is quite apparent he is still pining for his departed love and now he can think only of avenging her." He sighed. "I tried to tell him—"

"No one can reason with a man whose passionate heart won't be still. The worst has to happen. But Tristan—"

"Hush, my love. I am going." He went to the door. "I will find Charlotte. I will do whatever I can to keep her safe."

THE DARKNESS WAS unrelieved now for the moon was behind a cloud and the lights of the post chaise flickered and disappeared amidst the trees. Charlotte was too busy nibbling her fingernails to attend to Vanessa's chatter with her cousin.

It seemed unreal to be in the company of these two when her heart was so far away, a factor which Vanessa remarked upon when she said, "Dear me, Charlotte, can you pay attention! Gilray has gone to such expense to rescue you and you can't pay him any mind. He does love you madly!"

"I do," Gilray corroborated. "We could go to Scotland not France—"

"We could not!" Charlotte swung round from her contemplation of the passing blur and glared. "I might think you hatched this plan to make me agree to something that you know from past history is unpalatable to me."

"Charlotte! How can you say such a thing to poor Gilray?" asked Vanessa. "He's pined for you all these years. And clearly Mr Creighton wasn't going to wait around to look after you when he had matters much more important and pressing to attend to."

This stopped Charlotte from the rejoinder she'd been about to make. It was true.

Jasper hadn't waited. He'd been too wrapped up in his feelings for his dead beloved that it was as if Charlotte was now dead to him.

The thought brought her close to weeping.

Perhaps perceiving that Vanessa had struck a nerve, Gilray leaned forward and very tentatively put his hand over Charlotte's. "You know I do care about your happiness, Charlotte," he said. "And I am sorry that things worked out the way they did but I am motivated by the best of intentions. I do want to make you happy."

Charlotte managed a smile for his expression did hint at a degree of sincerity.

"I'm sorry. I'm very tired. It has all been quite dramatic and I am grateful to you for helping me."

This mollified Vanessa somewhat who suggested that they would all feel much better after some more refreshment when they stopped to change horses.

And although Charlotte remained anxious as they made their way into a modest hostelry, she also felt that nearly two hours of travel put sufficient ground between them and Collingwood to alleviate that anxiety sufficiently to in fact eat the food put before her this time.

They were part way through their repast in a private parlour when the innkeeper appeared in the doorway with a frown.

"Is there a Miss Treloar amongst your party?" he asked. "Lord Leeson hopes to find the young lady." He peered at Vanessa and then Charlotte. "Are either of you Miss Treloar?"

Charlotte kicked Vanessa sharply under the table as she

brought her napkin to her mouth, smiling weakly at the publican who, seeing her shake of the head, disappeared.

"But that is your uncle, Charlotte." Gilray sent Charlotte a puzzled look.

"Mrs Henley has sent him to look for me." Charlotte tried to hide her panic. "Do you not see? Last time I left with you, the same thing happened and I was returned to Mrs Henley at Lord Leeson's behest. I've been thinking about it ever since you told me. I'm sure he was behind my three years' incarceration. And he's working with her because it's in their interests for Collingwood to make me his wife. Lady Ogilvy mentioned that Lord Leeson goes hunting with Collingwood."

Gilray looked satisfied. "So, you have chosen to remain with me."

"You, at least, won't return me to Mrs Henley," said Charlotte with a grimace. "And we're not going to Scotland. We're going to France—"

Her sentence was cut short as the door was thrust open and a familiar voice muttered, "You're going nowhere except Emsley Manor with me. Stand up, Charlotte."

The two women gasped. Gilray looked distinctly green around the gills but he didn't say anything to champion Charlotte when Collingwood took a menacing step forward and put his hand on Charlotte's shoulder.

"If we leave now we will make it back to Brigalow House before your disappearance is noticed. Mrs Henley is waiting for you. She is making whatever excuses necessary. I understand you are suffering wedding nerves. Perfectly natural." His smile did not reach his eyes.

Gilray moved forward but then relaxed back in his chair at a look from Collingwood. And why would he champion Charlotte when she'd shown him such luke warm regard?

Besides, Collingwood was the best shot in the country.

Dry-mouthed, Charlotte considered her options. She could resist and make herself a public spectacle. Their so-called private parlour was infiltrated by another table of gentleman of the country-solicitor breed, judging by their clothing.

Any hint of scandal would imperil Charlotte's future more than it was already imperilled. And yet she truly had thought that if she could only return to her papa then all would be well.

Slowly she rose, accepting Collingwood's hand.

"Yes, wedding nerves," she said with a weak smile. Nodding to Vanessa and Gilray, who'd risen to pull back her chair, earning him a cold but meaningful nod from Colling-wood, she prepared to quit the room.

CHAPTER 22

The speed of travel as Charlotte was returned to Brigalow House seemed much faster than her escape, even though there was little conversation to divert her.

Charlotte spent most of the journey ensconced in Mr Collingwood's carriage staring out of the window and into the darkness while she contemplated her miserable options.

At first, she'd been defiant.

Well, mildly defiant because she didn't quite know what to expect from Mr Collingwood now that she was alone with him.

But after he'd remained stonily silent, she'd grown a little afraid.

Now, as the road improved, and she wasn't being thrown all over the place, she clasped her hands together to stop them shaking and, screwing her courage to the sticking point, as Lady Macbeth was wont to say, said, "So, what do you intend to do now, Mr Collingwood? Now that I have disgraced and embarrassed you?"

She supposed it was best to tackle the matter head on. He'd surely not want to marry her now.

At least, she hoped he wouldn't.

And, at least he couldn't force her.

She was quite determined on that. No matter how hard Mrs Henley tried to pressure Charlotte, she would not give in.

"You have neither disgraced nor embarrassed me."

She was surprised at how calm he looked.

"I haven't? But I left in the middle of Lady Brigalow's ball. What would people think?"

"Over excitement. That's what I told them. That's what Mrs Henley told them."

Charlotte put her hands to her face. "Mrs Henley will vent her rage on me, you can be certain of that."

"Charlotte, why did you wish to escape from me?"

Charlotte glanced up at his tone. He looked perplexed. Forlorn, even.

"I have given you all I thought a young woman could possibly wish to have. New clothes in the latest stare. I've decorated my home so that you will be surrounded by all the comfort and beauty you could wish for."

To Charlotte's surprise and not a little alarm, he leaned across the small space and took Charlotte's hand. "I thought you liked me. You gave me every reason to think so when we walked together yesterday. And when we danced this evening."

Charlotte pressed her lips together. "I don't dislike you," she said softly.

"But you… like Mr Gilray more?"

"Goodness, no!" Charlotte cried. "He is the cousin of my friend Vanessa and… as they were leaving today I asked them to take me."

"Why, Charlotte?"

"I… I was afraid." She supposed it was the truth. "I barely know you, Mr Collingwood."

"But we shall have a lifetime for you to overcome that." He sounded surprised as he squeezed her hand. "So there is no one else you wish to marry?"

Charlotte thought of Mr Creighton as she shook her head.

Lovely Mr Creighton with his lopsided smile and his easy manner. Yet she knew how to overcome that. She knew how to excite his passions.

She really did—

Charlotte stopped herself.

She swallowed. Swallowed her daydreams and her disappointment.

Mr Creighton. Yes, she might admire him above all others. How could she entertain thoughts of that gentleman when he'd made it so abundantly clear he did not wish to have her for his wife?

"That is all right then." He leaned back satisfied. "We can start afresh, anew, and we can start tonight." He smiled at her. "Can we do that, Charlotte?"

Charlotte thought of Lord Gilray and Vanessa churning up the miles, no doubt talking ill of her for breaking Gilray's heart a second time.

And again she thought of Jasper. Mr Creighton. Somewhere far away and chasing the man who'd wronged his beloved, or however the story went.

She thought of her papa who had done absolutely nothing to check with her that her wishes were being accommodated.

And she thought of Mrs Henley into whose care she would be returned if she didn't marry Mr Collingwood.

So, when he repeated the question, there really wasn't any other answer than…

Yes.

CHAPTER 23

The wind tore through Jasper's hair as he rested against the stern and stared across the frothing sea.

He'd not expected to have left England in such a hurry. But nor had he expected to have been offered the chance to find his purpose.

Since he could remember he'd felt at a loss. As a youngest son, his older brothers had done as duty required. His oldest brother had taken up the mantle of custodian of the family estate, his second brother had gone into the army. The third had obediently, and happily, it seemed, entered the church.

But there was nothing for Jasper. No goal, no purpose.

Mariah had given him purpose.

She'd been young and vibrant and her lower station in life had energised him to fight for their love against family opposition.

She was like a hothouse bloom living in a dank environment from which he'd intended to pluck her so as to replant her in the rich and fertile soil of a new world he imagined they'd both joyfully inhabit.

Her death had cheated him of both the possibility of love,

and a means of following through with his ideals of championing need and neglect.

For many years he'd been rudderless. He'd enjoyed flirtations with silly debutantes, full-boiled affairs with eager matrons and widows.

The one time he'd come close to properly losing his heart was in the arms of Miss Charlotte Treloar.

He thought about her now as he stared across the sea, into the grey nothingness of his future. A land, faraway, beckoned, for the England of his past was a place of disappointment and disillusionment.

He had not the heart to be the husband Charlotte needed.

And while many would call it pure folly to embark on a long sea voyage to frontier lands, he'd felt England offered him nothing.

Everingham had escaped him. And by a whisker. At first he'd cursed his luck, blaming Charlotte for his inability to make it to the docks in time.

Charlotte.

He wanted to cast her from his mind for always her image intruded.

It was Charlotte who needled him with her wicked flirtatiousness, demanding that he provide her with what she wanted.

Charlotte who made him act against his better instincts.

He might be a rake but he prided himself on being a man of principle when it mattered.

Hence this race across the sea to track down Everingham who was forging his own path across the African veldt; imagining he could bring the fellow down with a stare of recrimination so that Everingham was singed from the soles of his feet to the top of his head.

Jasper supposed he didn't need to hurt the fellow. Violence was not in his nature.

But just to hear Everingham finally admit to the crime he so vehemently denied, would be some catharsis. And to see guilt at least acknowledged in his faltering look.

That was worth the danger and ennui and illness of travelling over the high seas.

Jasper stared into the glare of the setting sun and reminded himself of all that. And that the reason for his mad, impulsive dash across the globe was because this was the culmination of his dreams for finding peace.

For Mariah.

But now that he was on a course he could not change, instead of Everingham's fearful eyes, or Mariah's smile of beautiful innocence, Jasper could see only Charlotte's bright smile.

And then its transformation into dull acceptance as she'd danced with Collingwood.

It was a contrast that only whipped up memories of their incendiary moments between the sheets.

Lord, but that was unwise ruminating. Not at all what he needed or wanted to dwell on right now.

Or any other time.

Charlotte was not the girl for him. He'd know that *from the very start.*

And he'd made that plain to her *from the very start.*

And she'd accepted that *from the very start.*

So why did he continue to conjure up images of her dimples which popped out each time she told him some wicked titbit to cajole him into some semblance of good humour?

He frowned. He was a surly bastard, now he thought about how often she'd had to cajole him into a good humour.

And why was that? He was generally the best humoured of fellows.

It was only with Charlotte that he was churlish.

The thought made him uncomfortable for he realised he liked her to cajole him because he liked seeing those dimples pop out in her cheeks.

And he liked the feeling of her arms hugging him close, and her unashamed enjoyment of being with him. There were no shows of coyness.

Charlotte was exactly as she appeared on the surface.

"Land ahoy!"

And just as well, Jasper thought. For he didn't want any more time to dwell on Charlotte when his chief priority was running Everingham to ground.

He owed Mariah at least that.

CHAPTER 24

8 MONTHS LATER

"Does it pain you?"

Surprised, Jasper looked up at the stranger who had questioned him over his bandaged leg.

It was a young boy, leaning across the space in the carriage that was transporting them across the veldt.

Or rather, a youth for he had the peach fuzz about his cheeks that suggested he had just begun to shave.

Jasper smiled. "A graze, that's all. Completely my fault so I'll concede victory to the elephant that bested me. Still roaming the plains, I hope, for it was a skirmish in which I showed my inexperience."

The lad smoothed back his neatly oiled hair and nodded sagely. Like Jasper, he spoke with a British accent that suggested a similar background.

However, his clothes had seen better days, despite their fashionable cut.

"Henry Jones." The young man extended his hand. "From

Wales, though you'd know that." He smiled. "What brings you to these parts? Lured by adventure? I've turned professional hunter." He glanced self consciously at his faded coat though the waistcoat looked new—garish, in fact—and shrugged. "It'll soon pay the bills." He hesitated. "I know where the best game roams the plains. I've been here more than a year. Green I was at first but I've done my apprenticeship. I could send you home with a fortune in ivory if you just say the word."

Jasper shrugged. "Elephants and I are not on speaking terms at the moment. I'm heading off to the coast, so no more deviations for me, thank you, all the same. Going home. Had my adventure and it wasn't all it was cracked up to be."

"And what adventure were you seeking, sir?" The lad shifted in his seat, his eyes eager as he leaned forward. "I too came here seeking adventure. I found it, and it is a lot more alluring than the grey skies of England—or Wales—I can tell you. You just need to know what you want."

Jasper considered this.

What *did* he want?

He'd almost forgotten. Eight months ago he'd boarded a boat bound for Cape Town on a whim. Mostly because he was too afraid of the diversions England held when he knew how important it was to follow through on his pledge.

What else did he have to prove he was a man of integrity? A man of his word?

Mariah's image was fading and he needed to bring her back into sharp relief. He needed to prove he was the knight in shining armour she'd always believed.

Everingham's name had provided the impetus to abandon the alternative path that had sprung up so suddenly and unexpectedly.

And dangerously.

But Everingham had been as elusive after his conviction as he had before. He'd fled to the Cape Colony, and still Jasper had failed to pin him down.

He thought back to their encounter at the Marshalsea. He'd been in the same cell, for God's sake. Jasper had used this as a ruse to speak to Miss Treloar. Charlotte.

His heart did a small leap at this memory before it resumed the default emotion. He was unmoved. She had the power to make him feel as any red-blooded man would feel if his manliness was complimented—assaulted.

She was a beautiful woman with lustful feelings.

Unwomanly feelings.

Mariah would never have acted as brazenly as Charlotte.

Jasper blinked a couple of times as he reflected upon this. What would Marish have done if she'd been alone with Jasper and circumstances had allowed?

Well, they wouldn't. Mariah had been carefully kept and nurtured by her brother and her father. Jasper and she were betrothed. They had held hands. They had kissed, all while a chaperone had been within yards of them.

But the idea of anything more physical was unthinkable.

As was right and proper. Mariah was a respectable, virtuous young woman.

A goddess of the utmost integrity. No wonder Jasper shuddered when he thought of how degraded she'd have felt if Jasper's hands had roamed over her as...

They had roamed over Charlotte.

No wonder he shuddered to think that Mariah might have been as free with her emotions as Charlotte had been.

No, Mariah was an angel. A goddess.

And that was the reason Jasper was right here.

In the middle of the African veldt, his mission not yet accomplished.

Yet he had received a tipoff that Everingham was still in

the country. The fellow had, like Jasper, been lured by the thrill of diamonds or gold or the abundant game.

Little did it matter. He was an adventurer following danger, excitement.

And freedom.

And that freedom had been too easily won for Everingham had killed Mariah's brother and served only three short years.

Three short years that had taken no account of the reduction in years Archie's death had cost Mariah.

"Might I surmise that you will be heading home soon, then?" Jones asked.

Jasper considered this. Would he head home?

What awaited him there?

His elder brothers were fulfilling their requisite roles in the family hierarchy. Jasper was untethered to anything. He had a reasonable allowance but nothing was required of him.

Nobody wanted him. Needed him.

Loved him.

This last caused a frisson of pain that was quickly cauterised as first he thought of Charlotte but then extinguished all memories of their playful, lustful encounters.

She needed a rescuer.

She hadn't needed Jasper. Jasper's role could have been fulfilled by anyone.

But who did love Jasper enough to make him want to stay and pledge more than just his physicality in a couple of meaningless encounters.

No woman came to mind.

Which galvanised his thinking. There really was nothing that could motivate him sufficiently to return home.

"Where are these elephants of which you speak? And if not elephants, what else can you suggest to take a man's mind off the interminable that England offers?"

~

FOUR MONTHS LATER

"Sir Bertram will be seated on your left, my dear. He likes a pretty face, and he appreciates levity." Collingwood, leaning over Charlotte's right shoulder as she finished her breakfast, pointed to the table seating he had placed in front of her.

"By contrast, Sir Roger, who will be seated on your left, is of a sober temperament. He will not appreciate a woman who voices her opinions. Women should agree with him, no matter how outlandish his ideas. Do you understand?"

"Yes." Charlotte managed to draw in a deep breath as she nodded. She'd been feeling light-headed and vague these past few days and put it down to the onerous social demands placed on her by Collingwood.

Far from being the recluse she had originally believed, she had come to realise that he was a man laser focused on social advancement.

And pecuniary aggrandisement.

She hadn't realised the generosity of her dowry until Mrs Henley had let slip an indication during another of their heated exchanges.

For there had been many of those during the past few months since Collingwood had retained the woman on staff for her 'unique capacity to temper the whims and fancies of Lady Collingwood who otherwise would do her husband proud.'

To think that Charlotte had chosen marriage with Collingwood to escape Mrs Henley.

"So I am to be a chameleon?" Charlotte smiled up at her husband, pretending the levity he required of her with regard to Sir John.

But when he merely looked dark, she sighed, and

retreated to the usual calm acceptance which was her lot. Life was easier if she simply acceded to his whims, allowed him the use of her body, and didn't complain ... at anything really.

In return, he made no demur at the outrageous nature of her milliner, furrier and dressmaker's bills. Charlotte had a keen eye for fashion and, as Collingwood's show pony, she needed to reflect the size of his pocketbook. Augmented by her dowry, of course.

For with money, came power.

And that was what Collingwood sought.

Charlotte hadn't decided if her husband enjoyed power for power's sake. She supposed it didn't matter for his motivation didn't change the role she had to play.

She was like a puppet and he played the strings.

"You are to be a good and proper wife," he said between gritted teeth.

"I am always a good and proper wife," Charlotte responded sweetly, before grimacing as a strange light-headedness overtook her and her womb convulsed in a momentary spasm that had her gasping despite herself.

"My dear, what is it?"

Immediately Collingwood was the concerned husband, taking a seat by her side and gripping her hands. "I've noticed you've been off your food these past couple of days. And you complained of stomach gripes yesterday. And your courses are late." He brought her hand up to his lips and kissed her palm, his eyes shining as he said, "Could it be that finally we can welcome an heir into the household?"

ONE YEAR LATER

It had been a while since Jasper had felt such satisfaction but he felt it now as he stared at the rough piece of rock in his hand.

Only it wasn't just rock. It contained a magnificent diamond.

He might not have found Everingham, but he had found a stone sufficient to cement his fortune.

Or his future, as he'd been told; only that word still landed strangely.

His future.

Where was the satisfaction in cementing his future when he had no one with whom to share it?

Yet, he'd felt a certain freedom in this wild, beautiful country.

He'd hunted, caroused, womanised.

Jasper supposed he'd be the envy of his compatriots.

However, he felt strangely unfulfilled.

Was it that Everingham continued to elude him?

He told himself this was the reason yet as time went by he wasn't entirely sure.

For, increasingly, he thought of Charlotte.

He reminded himself that he was not the man for her.

Or, not, at least, until he had found Everingham.

So when in a saloon in the Cape, he heard the familiar name trip off the tongue of a fellow drinker, his senses went into freefall.

"Rupert Everingham was in these parts?" He pushed himself across the bar, past a fellow drinker, to enquire in tones that suggested a very special interest.

And he got the answer he was after.

It should have filled him with renewed purpose but it

only thrust him into the roiling void that seemed to accompany any thought of his past disappointment.

"The fellow breeds ostriches in some God-forsaken part about a hundred miles from here with a wife he picked up along the way. He believes it's the future, though what would he know? Women adorn their bonnets with wildflowers and bows and the like. Not ostrich feathers."

The fellow across from Jasper laughed scornfully before asking, "You're acquainted with him?"

"In a manner of speaking," Jasper replied. "So as far as your information has it, Rupert Everingham is there still? It's not the first time I've followed a trail only to find he has moved on."

"Everingham has, by all accounts, settled his heart in the darkest part of Africa. Let's hope his new lady wife is a little less arid," the other fellow added with a drunken laugh.

Jasper thought back to what he knew of Everingham. That he was a murderer. Not that he had a softer side. He supposed the lady involved had no idea of his treacherous heart.

Well, maybe it was time Jasper let her know.

Maybe it was one way of avenging Mariah. To let any other innocent, unsuspecting damsel know the evil that lurked in Everingham's black heart.

Jasper's drinking companion raised his third bourbon to toast "new challenges" before asking, "And where are you bound, my friend?"

There was no hesitation as Jasper said, "To find Everingham."

CHAPTER 25

FIFTEEN MONTHS LATER

"I do love watching the baby ducks, don't you?"

Charlotte's sister-in-law, Genevieve, smiled as they stopped at the edge of the lake and watched a mother duck shepherd her ducklings across the smooth surface of the lake. "When he was a little boy, Collingwood used to try and cause mayhem by throwing stones amidst them." She sighed as she rocked the baby chariot to calm the sleeping child. "He said he wanted to test the mother duck's ability to do what was required under fire."

"And what did you do?" Charlotte asked.

"I cried." Genevieve looked into the pram. "Like I always did, to mama and papa's irritation. And Collingwood's." She sighed. "But he is much calmer now. You have wrought a great improvement in Collingwood and as a result I am much more inclined to seek his company. Or tolerate it." She frowned. "Or accept it."

"Genevieve, you are speaking in riddles. You sound like you do not know your own brother."

"I don't." Genevieve blinked, her light, slightly bulbous eyes looking a trifle concerned. "When he was unkind to me, I feared and loathed him. But when he was indulgent and kind, I adored him." She shrugged. "I don't know how you find him, Charlotte, and I would never seek a confidence, but the truth is, I have no idea what drives my brother. Finchley, on the other hand," she said, referring to her husband with a coy smile, "is as transparent as a gossamer spider's web on a crisp autumn day. He's made a home that ensconces me with all the insulated protection I could wish for and he keeps vigil. Not in an intimidating way, but he's just... there. Guarding me and keeping me safe." She hugged herself. "I could never have imagined such happiness. Isn't that right, little Leo?" she added, bending to reach into the baby chariot to touch the cheek of the stirring infant... Straightening, she turned to Charlotte and said, "I do hope that is what you've found with Collingwood. He was never an easy brother growing up but I believe you have softened his baser impulses. And perhaps little Lucy has, too. What a shame she was not well enough to come on our walk."

Charlotte managed a smile though she offered no rejoinder.

No, Charlotte had not found anything like the calm and happiness that Genevieve had clearly found with her Finchley. As for Lucy, she wished with all her heart that the child had been allowed out with her.

Collingwood was as demanding, unpredictable and exacting, as his sister had painted him.

Sometimes he was kind.

Occasionally he was affectionate.

But mostly he was exacting.

Yet it was Mrs Henley who pulled the strings in this household. She was forever to be found with Collingwood, poring over some chart with an invitation list, a seating plan, a series of entertainments.

Entertainments?

The only entertainments Collingwood enjoyed were those which highlighted his prowess in the sporting arena. Collingwood lived to surpass. To suppress and surpass, Charlotte supposed, since his weekly ritual seemed to be to illustrate to Charlotte just how dominant a marriage and bedroom partner he was.

"I can't believe you've been married nearly two years and this is only the third time we've been together," Genevieve marvelled as they continued along the path by the lake. "Collingwood said you were quiet and that I would make up for both of us. Mama and papa said it was difficult to believe we were siblings for I was the sun to his moon. But he was, of course, so much older, so I really didn't have too many dealings with him growing up. But I do hope he has been a good husband to you."

Charlotte nearly reared back in surprise at such a remark.

I do hope he has been a good husband to you.

Wouldn't it have been nice if Mrs Henley had voiced such sentiments?

Instead, Mrs Henley kept to her rooms, making her lists of good works to be achieved, prisoners whose causes needed to be petitioned.

Or, when she didn't keep to her room, she was with Charlotte, reminding her of this duty or that.

It was exhausting.

But Genevieve appeared to be waiting for her answer.

Charlotte turned her gaze from the baby ducklings and considered her sister-in-law a moment. The young girl was just a couple of years older than Charlotte with a sunny, empathetic nature that invited confidences.

But could Charlotte have told her the truth of what was

in her heart any more than she could, her brother? Or anyone else who cared to know it?

No, she could not.

Collingwood had trained her well.

Charlotte's heart, once vibrant and full of love, had become a closed, carefully guarded place.

It was the only way to survive.

CHAPTER 26

The African veldt. A desert and as good as place as any for a murderer to spend his remaining days.

Jasper felt he had travelled to the ends of the earth.

He'd made the most of his time in the Cape Colony doing what a young man with money and vigour would do.

As he occupied himself in a series of exploits around hunting, gold and diamonds, he told himself he was not driven by vengeance.

But what else could it be when his lonely, empty heart responded to nothing but the promise of satisfaction; when satisfaction had failed to be found in any woman's arms? Any useful employment? Any occupation and activity for any length of time?

He was forever restless. Forever searching for something.

He just didn't know what. Which suggested that he really was as bitter hearted as Charlotte had once claimed he must be.

Again, he put her out of his mind. He didn't need her bright smile to intrude.

He stared at his worldly goods at his feet. Was this what his life amounted to? Three rifles and an assortment of canvas rolls?

When he was given the information that a man by the name of Everingham did still reside near the town his drinking companion had named, he was surprised he didn't feel a greater jolt of satisfaction.

Was the moment not nearly upon him? Had he not been heading towards this for the past four years?

"Where, exactly, will I find him?" Jasper asked as a couple of local lads took his trunk and boxes to his rooms.

"Fellow keeps ostriches, of all things. Tends the creatures as if they had feelings." The publican and a couple of patrons laughed but there was no malice.

"Keeps to himself mostly but sociable when he's here," the publican's wife supplied, coming into the room with a steaming plate of what Jasper recognised as Kudu steaks. The smell made his stomach growl with desire for it had been days since he'd enjoyed something as substantial.

"Not the same since his wife died, though. Follow that road east and you can't miss it," she said, pointing out of the window. "But have something to eat first."

Jasper accepted the invitation and joined the other patrons.

Once not even the most succulent roast on an empty stomach, or the most alluring woman with the most enticing proposition would have been sufficient inducement to have delayed him.

But now, suddenly, with the end in sight, and satisfaction to be had, he was consumed by a strange hesitancy.

He ate a plate of kudu and vegetables washed down with a fine bottle of red from the cape region. He was familiar with their wine and their ways now. He could adopt them as his own, he supposed, and stay in this great continent, pulsing with opportunity, that had been so good to him and made him rich.

Yet something about England was calling to him.

Homesickness?

Whatever it was, he realised it was time to return to those he loved and who loved him.

His parents and his sister.

He didn't suppose anyone else would particularly care, and he was careful to cast out Charlotte in that consideration.

He had missed his chance for she was, no doubt, suitably married by now.

Though not, thank God, to Collingwood.

No, once he received satisfaction from Everingham—an admission of guilt, a cringing fearfulness in his manner that testified to his guilt—Jasper would go.

The years had smoothed the edge off his rage but he needed this final accounting with Everingham as the catharsis that would enable him to seek happiness for happiness' sake.

Finally, he would be ready to settle down and do justice to whatever hopes some worthy future bride would place in him.

AFTER PASSING a simple grave bearing a cross and the inscription 'Beloved Susannah', he found the man within minutes of being pointed in the direction of his house. It was a modest thatched dwelling surrounded by what Jasper recognised as mealies, the corn that was a primary source of subsistence. The arid land, brown and dry stretched into a long, low mountain range.

Everingham was in a pen at the rear surrounded by ostriches.

He was speaking to one of them as Jasper approached from around the corner, facing him full on.

"Creighton." There was no surprise in Everingham's tone. After the initial glance, a flare of something difficult to identify but which wasn't fear or remorse, Everingham returned his attention to the ostrich.

The ugly bird with its flat, triangular beak and sharp black eyes made a violent peck at the corn in Everingham's hand. Jasper was familiar with them. Spiteful, bad tempered creatures, he thought them, motivated by who knew what. They reminded him of someone back in England.

Mrs Henley, however, had more strategy in her brain that was at least larger than the pea-sized brain of the ostrich with whom Everingham was communing.

"Everingham." Jasper greeted him with a civility at odds to that which he'd assumed would be the case when he'd dreamed so often of this moment.

"I've been expecting you."

"You have?" Jasper leaned on the fence post a yard away and waited. How many times he had contemplated this moment? In his mind, Everingham was taller and more formidable. Everingham was a vain and hard-hearted villain who had wrought destruction without compunction.

Now he seemed feeble and ineffectual, his wiry hair a fading shade of carrot, his eyes blue and watery in the harsh sun. Jasper supposed his health had suffered in the Marshalsea but any feelings of sympathy were cast away by memories of Everingham's role in Mariah's death.

Everingham produced a corn husk from his pocket for the ostrich, then said, "I was in the Cape about a year ago when I heard your name mentioned. It was in relation to hunting but I knew there was only one reason you'd come to this God-forsaken part of this great, dark continent."

"What reason was that?"

Everingham straightened for the bird had departed in its proud, haughty manner now that there was no more corn to be had.

"You do know that I was exonerated."

"You were released early. That is not the same."

"I had a champion who had the ear of those in high places. Mrs Henley whom I had come to know from her many visits to the Marshalsea. The evidence in my case was revisited and found to be non-existent. Circumstantial and too flimsy."

"Your guilt was based on Mariah's sworn testimony."

Everingham stiffened. His watery eyes flashed and for a moment Jasper wondered if he would strike him for he flexed his fists.

"Miss Banning's testimony sent me to the Marshalsea though I had an alibi that would have exonerated me. She knew it, too. But she knew my alibi would likely consign me to the gallows or transportation. Oh, she knew how to use a man's weaknesses against him."

Jasper winced and clenched his fist at his side. "You seem to know a great deal about the inner thoughts of the woman you malign. The sister of the man you killed. The woman I loved."

"That is why I see no point in repeating the truth to you. Love is blind. You loved Miss Banning and you want to retain the idea of her purity until the bitter end. Regardless of the fact that it was *she* who ruined *my* life. No, Creighton, it was not the other way round." His voice had gathered strength and he pushed himself back from the fence post to face Jasper squarely. "Miss Banning's brother and I were together at the same place the night she claimed *I* stole from the Exchequer. Her brother didn't know what she'd done. That t was she who took the money. She intended to return the funds without discovery as soon as she'd shored up a short-term loan. Oh, I know exactly what happened. But I could not say where I had been. Where I and her brother had been."

"Why not? Isn't the truth the best defence?" Jasper's anger few. "Your attempts at evading responsibility are a sop but worse is how you deflect blame onto an innocent woman who cannot defend herself—" he drew in a laboured breath, adding—"because she is dead."

Everingham shook his head sadly. "The trouble with people like you, Creighton, is that you go on a mission believing yourselves holier than thou. Believing that the purity which motivates you can transcend the tawdry truth." His nostrils flared. "You remind me of the woman who got me out of that hellhole. Mrs Henley. You must already have known the kind of woman she was otherwise you'd not have had to hide in a cell that auspicious day of our last reunion. You wanted to speak to sweet Miss Treloar and no wonder, for not a kinder soul existed. If you seek purity, there was no one purer than the Angel of the Marshalsea. Miss Treloar fed me hot bread and words of succour for the two years of my confinement. She was kind without judgement. She had a lively, wicked sense of humour that brightened the days of so many of us. Her guardian, on the other hand, was one of those whose kindness is overlaid by judgement. I was one of the faceless rabble whose cause Mrs Henley championed because she worshipped that champion of prison reform Mrs Fry and wanted to be recognised for her own part in reforming the deplorable system."

His words pained Jasper at the same time as igniting some tiny flame just to hear Charlotte spoken of so glowingly.

Yet he said, "You have no gratitude, have you, Everingham? You malign the woman I was to have married and now you malign the woman who got you out of the Marshalsea. You should have been found guilty of murder, Everingham. You struck Mariah's brother the blow that killed him." At one time Jasper would have flown at him with fists flailing. Now he satisfied himself with a stony look and a curled lip.

"I defended myself, having been falsely accused by Banning—and his sister—of theft. I have never stolen anything in my life. But Archie Banning came after me like a hellcat, though he *knew* I was not guilty. We'd been at the same house, for God's sake. A place neither of us could name. He was my alibi."

"Then why didn't he stand up and defend you?"

"Because doing so would have implicated his sister."

"By God—"

Everingham put up his hand to stem Jasper's response. "You came all this way to find me. Don't you want to hear the truth?"

"I expected nothing but lies," muttered Jasper. In fact, he hadn't known what to expect, though he certainly hadn't expected to feel as conflicted as he did.

Everingham went on, "He had to double down on her lies because someone had to take the blame. Miss Banning's brother had a choice to make. One of us would go to jail and it would not be his sister. I took a proper hiding from him before I defended myself with one blow. I had no intention of causing injury. I was trying to save my life. One blow to deflect his upper cut. He threw the first punch. I defended myself. And I nearly hanged for it. Instead, I spent two years amidst the stench and the wails and the rats at the Marshalsea as much because of that one unfortunate blow as because of the lies spouted by your beloved." Everingham's voice rose and his eyes flashed.

Just as Jasper's did as he contemplated countering Everingham's lies with violence.

"You accuse Mariah of being untruthful under oath? By God, that's rich coming from you."

Everingham lurched around and the ostrich reared back before its hoary head intruded into their conversation, resembling, for a moment, an adder with its vacant, stony eyes.

"So you are accusing Mariah," said Jasper. "I have a mind to demand satisfaction here and now."

Everingham looked pained. He transferred his gaze from Jasper's face to the endless dry veldt that surrounded them, then he glanced at the rifle leaning against the fence. "You could. In England it would be illegal for us to blow each other's brains out. Here there are not many who would care. So, if you've come all this way seeking revenge, I daresay this is our final destiny. Mine, that is, for I am not going to fight you, Creighton. I've told you the truth. If you want to know what might have motivated your Mariah to blame me for something I didn't do, then I suggest you seek out that little maid who served your Mariah so loyally."

Jasper frowned. He did recall the girl, vaguely.

"She was slavishly attentive and knew your Mariah better than anyone, I daresay."

Everingham thrust his hand into his pocket and withdrew some small stones which he offered the ostrich. It pecked at his open palm, swallowing them down until the stones were gone. Then it turned and sashayed across the dirt, a strange, ungainly yet regal silhouette against the arid earth.

"I had hoped to find my fortune in this country," Everingham said on a sigh. "But what I thought were diamonds are nothing but pebbles. And I have no means of making a trade with the ostrich feathers I hoped the ladies might favour over their heron and peacock plumes. My heart is as barren as this place. You might as well do what you came here to do, Creighton, and kill me. Even though you'll have an innocent man's murder on your hands."

Jasper shook his head. "You know I won't kill you. I wanted only to understand and to gain some small satisfaction. And I have it. You came here with nothing, and because you have nothing, you will never return to England. At least I have that satisfaction."

"You're wrong. I was well-funded to come to this country. It's where I'm supposed to stay, but my heart is not here."

Jasper raised his brows. "You were paid? By Mrs Henley. I didn't expect her do-gooding to extend that far."

"No. Lord Collingwood paid me. He even had his spies on the docks to make sure I boarded the vessel. A handsome cabin I had, too."

Like the ostrich, Jasper jerked at his words.

"Collingwood? Good God, why would Lord Collingwood interest himself in you?"

"Because I was dangerous. I knew too much."

"Lord Collingwood? He has an estate in Hampshire and a hunting lodge in Scotland. Young man similar in age to me?"

Everingham nodded.

Again, Jasper asked, "Why would he interest himself in you?"

Everingham pondered his reply. Finally he said, "You don't need to know."

Jasper remained perplexed, waiting until finally Everingham said, "He needed me out of the country after Mrs Henley took it upon herself to emulate Mrs Fry's efforts at getting the prisoner John Harris a retrial. He was afraid too much prying into the night I supposedly stole would make public his proclivities."

"His proclivities were such that he would pay to get you out of the country? What are you suggesting?"

"I'm not suggesting anything." Everingham seemed to lose patience suddenly. "Lord Collingwood was at the same Molly House as I was the night I was supposedly was helping myself to the ill-gotten gains that sent me to the Marshalsea."

Jasper reared back. "You... and Collingwood—?"

"You really have no idea, do you, Creighton?" He sighed. "No one does. Collingwood was an occasional visitor to an establishment where gentlemen liked to deport themselves in finery... befitting a beautiful woman." He glanced down at his patched, faded shirt and trousers. "Collingwood was a dilettante. He loved beauty and finery. He loved the best of everything. The finest of everything. I saw him at this particular establishment on only a handful of occasions but when he learned I was imprisoned for a crime that had supposedly taken place within a few hours of the two of us being at Mother Dobbs, where many gathered in women's clothing by a gin shop, he was afraid I might talk. He visited me at the Marshalsea to say he would do what he could to get me out if I kept my mouth shut. And that he would pay me well for my silence. That was when he met Mrs Henley and our angel, the lovely Miss Treloar. I hope to God he didn't marry her."

Jasper pressed his lips together. "They were betrothed, but they didn't wed," he said as a wave of remorse swamped him. He should have been there for Charlotte.

Everingham looked about him, then sighed. "If you don't want to kill me, you'd better come inside and slake you thirst before you make your long journey home. That's where I long to return. Home. If you don't kill me, I'll take my chances with Collingwood. I've served enough time in one prison. I'll be damned if I'm going to be consigned to another any longer."

The ostrich had returned, its feathers blowing in the breeze. It pecked mindlessly at Everingham's open hand.

Jasper stared at it. He stared at Everingham.

"Come," said Everingham, beginning to walk back towards the thatched, whitewashed dwelling. "Let me offer you what I have before you begin your journey home."

Home.

For so long, Jasper had not known where home was.

Now he listened to his head and his heart.

Home was back in England. He wasn't sure what awaited him there, but he hoped it would be the truth.

CHAPTER 27

"I'm going away for a couple of months, Charlotte. I hope you will not miss me too much."

Collingwood had come into her room when she'd just finished dressing for dinner. Ellen, her maid, discreetly left while Charlotte glanced up to see if there was any irony in his tone.

It was hard to tell with Collingwood.

"Of course, I'll miss you." Charlotte leaned into the mirror to smooth an eyebrow. She hoped the gesture would hide her delight, though she remained grave. "Where are you going?"

"To the Cape Colony. A few fellows who've hunted there are coming to dinner next week. I'm joining a little expedition next month with the earl of Altmore."

"You were there six years ago. Why would you want to go back?" She was genuinely curious. Collingwood suffered dreadfully from seasickness. He'd said several times he never intended travelling by sea again.

"Sir Stithian bagged a pair of tusks and a lion considerably larger than two, and three hundred pounds."

"So this is purely competitive. You want to add to your collection."

He nodded as if that was a perfectly good reason to leave home for up to six months, while inwardly Charlotte rejoiced. Not that she revealed that. It had become a game to keep her emotions in check.

"I want you to speak to cook and the servants regarding a house party I intend to have for Altmore and Sir Stithian and their wives."

"How many guests?"

"Six. They'll be here from Saturday until Monday. Cook and you can discuss the menu and see to the sleeping arrangements. I will organise everything else."

"Who is the third gentlemen?"

"Mr Jasper Creighton. He recently returned from the Cape. I believe you've met him. He was at Lord and Lady Brigalow's house party." Collingwood held her gaze and Charlotte dropped her eyes first, though there was nothing in his expression to indicate he knew of her association with Jasper.

She put her hands on the polished wood of her dressing table to steady herself.

Jasper Creighton was a name that had the power to send the blood rushing to her extremities, making her feel lightheaded…

With despair.

For Jasper Creighton had never loved her as she had him, try though she had to make him.

And now he had married someone else.

For three days, therefore, during this house party, Charlotte was going to have to try to keep her feelings in check, both from her husband and from Jasper as she responded to him with bland civility.

Collingwood hesitated. "I think you should wear the lilac

for the first evening. The colour brings out the delicacy of your pale skin and the cut is demure while up to the mark with fashion."

Charlotte nodded as if his directive were perfectly reasonable. As a bride-to-be, Collingwood's generosity in funding such an extensive new wardrobe had tilted the balance when deciding whether to go ahead with the marriage. Not that she'd had much of an alternative. She'd received no support from her father who, she realised later, had been experiencing some personal crisis which precluded him from fully realising the extent of Charlotte's unhappiness. When he had, it was too late.

She looked down at the earring in her hand. She'd been toying with it when Collingwood had entered the room. One of the pair she'd been wearing when she'd first met Jasper Creighton.

She remembered everything about that evening.

About him.

But he had not wanted her then and, she had to accept, he never would.

If Jasper Creighton had married, he'd no doubt found the pure virgin he'd been looking for to replace the unsullied Mariah Banning.

CHAPTER 28

J asper shivered in the cool spring air, a not altogether refreshing contrast to the dry African heat to which he'd grown accustomed. Even when he'd boarded the boat, he'd not been sure that returning to England was a good idea.

Mariah was no longer the reason she had been.

He tried not to think of any other to draw him back for Miss Treloar was not a contender. He wished he'd been kinder to her. She'd certainly deserved more but Jasper had not been kind to anyone back then.

Still, if he wanted memories that stirred him, in which he could lose himself in feelings of awareness and admiration coupled with a piquancy of desire, he had only to think of Charlotte.

He rapped sharply on the blue door and stepped back, wondering if his third attempt to contact Kitty Cooper, Mariah's former maid, would be successful.

He was astonished when the housekeeper, arching her brows as she regarded Jasper with suspicion, said she'd fetch the girl.

Jasper had no idea what she looked like and whether he'd even remember her but when the saucer-eyed lass arrived, the memories of the past flooded him with painful nostalgia. How could he have forgotten the carrot-haired maid who fussed about Mariah, sponging her mistress's brow as Mariah's health declined?

She had been loyal then and no doubt she'd be loyal now as she corroborated Jasper's recollection of the events surrounding the tragic death of Mariah's brother.

Instead, she took one look at Jasper, and crumpled to her knees as she wailed, "I ain't no thief, Mr Creighton. I didn't know what to do with it. Honest. I still 'as if it you want to take it wiv you now."

Jasper blinked in surprised consternation, then signalled to the interested housekeeper to leave, murmuring, "I have no idea what the girl is saying but I'll get to the bottom of it."

Turning back to Kitty, he said, "Stand up, Kitty, and tell me what you are talking about. I came here to ask you about Mariah. Not about something you did or did not take."

"It weren't me what took it but I was supposed to get rid of it, only when Miss Mariah died, I couldn't just take the necklace back to the pawnbroker and get money what wasn't due to me. First, I thought I'd just leave it where it was. Underneath the floorboard. But when I got me new position, I took it wiv me and hid it here. I coulda sold it and made me fortune but I never have. See, it proves I ain't no thief, don't it, Mr Creighton?"

She was trembling and on the verge of another bout of tears. Jasper realised he needed to take care if she was to remain coherent.

And he very much wanted to understand her story of a valuable necklace that belonged to Mariah, yet obviously wasn't distributed as part of Mariah's estate.

"It's all right, Kitty, I'm not here to lambast you or

demand you hand over Miss Banning's necklace. No doubt she gave it to you as a token of her appreciation of your care of her. You were so very good to her. Especially towards the end. I never saw a maid look after her mistress with such tender care. She valued your services and I've no doubt she wanted you to have her necklace." He hoped he sounded sufficiently reassuring.

Kitty shook her head wildly. "She didn't give it to me as a gift. She giv'd me it to take back to the pawnbroker. She wanted to make sure the money from the necklace went back to the place where her bruvver worked, so no one would get in any trouble. Course they did. And after that... after Mr Archie died and then me mistress got so very sick... I just kept the necklace where Miss Mariah had hidden it. I only took it when I moved to me next position."

An odd sensation had lodged in Jasper's gullet. This havey cavey talk was not in line with the image he had of Mariah, although of course he remembered her wearing the necklace. She'd said it had been a birthday gift from a wealthy uncle, and Jasper had complimented her, saying how the large sapphire in the centre of a circlet of tiny diamonds matched her eyes.

It was surprising enough that she'd bought it from a pawnbroker, but more surprising was the reference to her brother's employment. Something was distinctly off but he couldn't frighten Kitty too much, for the girl was spluttering even more as she tried to stem her tears with her apron.

"Calm yourself, Kitty, and take a seat here." He indicated the chair by the housekeeper's desk in the small, spartan room they occupied. "Would you like a glass of water? You have nothing to fear from me. All I want is the truth. Can you give me that?"

"If you promise I won't lose me position, Mr Creighton." The girl nodded warily, seating herself. "I'll tell you anything if only I won't be turned off. I ain't got nowhere else to go. It's why I said I'd 'elp Miss Mariah, even though I knew it were wrong, for *she* said she'd turn me off if I didn't. But a girl like me won't be believed over a fine lady like Miss Mariah. Not that she were a fine lady, though she wanted ever so much to be one. That's why she got the sapphire necklace. So that you'd think her fine enough for the likes of you."

Jasper, who'd been about to take a seat opposite Kitty, began to pace. His mind was churning, but he had no idea how to phrase his next question. He didn't want to lead Kitty in the direction his thoughts were going.

Carefully, he said, "Kitty, I think you are the only person who knows anything about the events surrounding the death of Mariah's brother and the money he stole. Miss Mariah left this world some years ago now. Now all that is important is the truth. If the necklace is not hers, I want you to tell me how," he hesitated, "and why, she got it. If you can put your hand on your heart and promise me to tell me the absolute truth, I will make sure that the housekeeper values you for your honesty. If you leave out details, or misrepresent matters, I will know. And neither I, nor your current house-keeper, will look kindly upon the matter. So, please, Kitty, the truth only. And from the beginning."

Two large tears rolled down Kitty's cheeks. She blew her nose loudly and then she took a deep breath and began.

"It were cos of you, sir, that me mistress needed so badly to impress. You were a fine gentleman. She reckoned she were beneath you."

Jasper nodded. Slowly, he said, "It did not matter to me that Miss Banning came from humbler stock. Her brother had a job at the Exchequer and was supporting her, she said, until her ailing uncle died. She said her rich uncle had made provision for her in his will. Not that it mattered to me." For he'd loved Mariah, though he wasn't going to sound mawkish in front of the little maid. She'd have surely remembered the depth of Jasper's adoration through his many visits.

From the moment Jasper had been introduced to Mariah at a music recital, he'd been entranced. Mariah had been similarly struck, he remembered, for her eyes had sparkled and he'd told her, then, that they resembled sapphires.

When he'd sent a note around to her lodgings the following day requesting her company for a visit to the National Museum, during which she'd been chaperoned by her brother, he'd set in train a whirlwind courtship that had culminated in his offer of marriage a scant month after meeting her.

And whether her uncle had indeed made provision for her in his will, or not, was of no importance. Jasper wanted Mariah as his wife with an intensity that defied reason.

With her lilywhite skin and her lustrous dark hair, she resembled a fairytale heroine from his favourite storybook.

She'd become his obsession.

"But the necklace, Kitty? I don't understand the importance of the necklace. She said her uncle gave it to her. Is that not true?" He fixed her with a steely stare. Jasper wasn't in the habit of intimidating the staff, but if that was the only way he could be reasonably assured of the truth he'd do it.

Kitty shook her head. "No, sir. Her uncle didn't give it to her. Miss Mariah bought it from a pawnshop to go to the Winter ball wiv yer. You'd invited her and she wanted you to see her as … a proper lady. It were the night you made her an offer, and both she and I reckoned it were the necklace wot did it." Her gaze grew misty. "My mistress had never looked such a lady."

"But you say she bought the necklace from a pawnshop,

Kitty? How did she manage that if she had not come into funds from her uncle?"

"It were wiv..." The maid trailed off, staring at the wall behind Jasper.

"With what, Kitty?"

She sighed, then said with more determination, "Wiv funds borrowed from her bruvver."

It was more the way Kitty said the words than the words themselves that sent the short hairs spiking on the back of Jasper's neck.

"Archie gave Mariah the money?" Jasper made sure he asked the question in the most serious and intense manner he could contrive. He did not want to lead her, though how desperately he wanted the answer to that question to be a categorical endorsement.

Only that would exonerate Mariah.

Kitty shook her head and said softly, "Miss Mariah asked him if he could lend her the money, but he said no."

"As he would if he was a lowly clerk working at the exchequer. He'd not have money to spend on a sapphire necklace for his sister."

Kitty nodded slowly. "She wanted him to borrow the money so she could get the necklace from the pawnbroker, wear it for the night of the ball, and then return it."

Alarm bells began ringing in Jasper's head.

"So if Mr Archie didn't borrow the money, how did Miss Mariah find the funds for the necklace?"

"She knew where the money were kept at the Exchequer. She went there to ask her brother to walk her home and when he got up to fetch his hat and coat, she... borrowed the funds." Kitty's voice, which had dropped very low, rose suddenly. "It were only for a day and a night. She wanted the money to buy the necklace and then she were going to return it as soon as she returned the necklace to the pawnbroker."

"But that's not what happened, was it, Kitty?"

Kitty shook her head, and the tears flowed freely.

"Do you remember what happened next?"

"Her brother were accused of theft and when he said it weren't him, and could only have been the other clerk, Everingham, Miss Mariah testified that she had seen Mr Everingham take the money."

"That's right, Kitty. And when Everingham protested his innocence as he was being led away, he got into a scuffle with Miss Mariah's brother. Everingham struck a blow that caused Archie Banning's death."

"Miss Mariah never meant such harm!" Kitty wailed. "She had the necklace in her reticule ready to take back to the pawnbroker but after her brother died she lost the will to do that... or anything, really."

"Miss Mariah was insistent that I avenge Archie's death," Jasper recalled bitterly. "I don't know if I believe you, Kitty. Perhaps *you* stole the money and the necklace."

"No, sir, on my honour. I can prove it, too. For Miss Mariah wrote saying how sorry she was. But then... she died."

Her claim checked his agitation. Jasper so wanted Mariah to be blameless. Or at least as uncompromised as possible. She was his angel of purity and Kitty's words were intolerable.

"And this letter? To whom did she write it?"

"To nobody, sir. It weren't a letter, it were her diary. She wrote it in her diary and she asked that it be buried with her for she became so very ill so suddenly and she knew that she'd soon be joining her brother."

"Was it?"

"Was it what, sir?"

"Was it buried with her?"

Kitty shook her head. "No, sir." She coloured. "If I ever

did wrong, it were the only wrong I ever did. Not doing as Miss Mariah asked. No, sir, I hid the diary."

"Why would you do that, Kitty?"

"In case I had to prove that I was telling the truth. About all this." She waved her hand vaguely about the room, then burst into tears.

CHAPTER 29

One hour.

Charlotte's heart thundered.

In one hour, Jasper Creighton and his wife would join the company for the three days they would enjoy Lord and Lady Collingwood's hospitality.

But word had been sent ahead that bad weather had hindered their progress. A rider, on horseback, had craved pardon and begged that the party should please sit down to dinner and to not wait.

Charlotte had made small talk to the other guests as they'd waited. Sir John was older than Collingwood by at least a decade, Lord Altmore more of a contemporary, as was Lady Altmore. Their wives were both younger yet considerably older than Charlotte who felt diminished by the two women's condescension and their smug, cosy mutual friendship with each other.

Two rooms had been prepared for the Creightons and although Charlotte had not surmised the reason, she'd overheard the parlour maids speculation as to whether it was due to the fact Mr Creighton snored or if Mrs Creighton was with child.

Charlotte was not about to volunteer the information that she could verify that Mr Creighton did not snore, but the alternative dragged heavily upon her.

She'd hoped to be deep in conversation with her guests when Jasper and his wife arrived. That might help disguise any uncomfortable giveaway signs of Charlotte's feelings when the late arrivals were announced.

Alas, Charlotte was temporarily unengaged in conversation and feeling at a loss as the rest of her guests discussed the politics and hunting in the Cape, for both wives had heard much about the daring exploits that would soon engage their husbands.

Charlotte was glad Collingwood hadn't spoken to her at length about such unpleasant pastimes but knew it was important that she did appear the dutiful and devoted wife he expected during social gatherings.

"My dear, Sir John was just admiring your ruby necklace. Tell him where that came from."

Charlotte's smile was in place as she glanced across the table at her husband whose expression managed to convey the utmost felicity.

How did he manage to craft such a mask in public? Charlotte wondered as she worked on disciplining her own features.

"My generous husband bought this for me when he was last in London," said Charlotte putting her hand to the gemstones at her neck. "He does have good taste, do you not think?"

"He certainly does," Lord Altmore replied with a wink that made Charlotte blush and creased Lady Altmore's forehead.

His lordship had had a little to drink but Sir John had

clearly had more when he added, laughingly, "Word was that Collingwood's competitive nature led him to contract a marriage with England's greatest beauty so it's good to see that marital felicity underpins his collecting instincts."

There was a slight hush at this, the tension broken, to not just Charlotte's relief, she was sure, as the door was opened to admit the man she had been awaiting with such anticipation and trepidation.

And his wife.

One look at the pretty young woman's swollen belly and Charlotte felt about to swoon with disappointment.

Of course she rose and glided across the room, appearing gracious and welcoming as she enquired after Mrs Creighton's health and their journey while the other guests murmured their welcome.

"I've kept dinner warming for you so let me show you to your rooms," she said when she learned that the butler had conducted them directly to the dining room to pay their respects while their trunks had been delivered to their respective chambers. "Please excuse me," she added over her shoulder, wishing she could remain within the safety of the dining room which she'd wanted to escape not ten minutes before.

"Mrs Creighton, we've prepared this room for you," Charlotte said, opening the door to the rose chamber which adjoined Jasper's. Not that it was likely he'd be sneaking through the interlinking door this evening given his wife's advanced pregnancy. No, he'd done all that some months before. The reflection made Charlotte's cheeks sting and her heart burn.

Yet she managed the cool poise required, earning herself a warm and grateful smile from pretty Mrs Creighton before the door closed behind her and Charlotte was leading Jasper towards his chamber.

Of course she hadn't planned on saying anything. She wasn't the hoyden she'd been during the two occasions she'd hurled herself at Jasper. She had to remind herself that he'd been very resistant to both her seductions before he'd obviously overcome his scruples to enjoy each event as much as she.

But he was a red-blooded male. He enjoyed sexual congress as much as any man and why would he spurn the offer of Charlotte's favours presented to him on a platter?

Charlotte burned at the remembered indignity which helped her retain her icy demeanour as she indicated the room's accoutrements. "Your dressing table, Mr Creighton. I've had the maids supply you with warm water if you'd like to wash before joining us. Your wife has similar though if you would like to attend to her before—"

"Charlotte!" He stopped her, putting both his hands on her shoulders. "What is the matter? I hoped you'd be pleased to see me. We are old friends, are we not? And Jane is not my wife. She's my cousin. I said this in the letter I wrote to Collingwood when I explained that I was escorting her from our parents' home to be reunited with her husband – who is a cousin who bears the name Creighton – and Collingwood obligingly welcomed her as his guest. Why are you so stony-faced? Are you—?"

But his words were cut short as Charlotte hurled herself into his arms and began to cry, loud gulping sobs against his chest.

"Hush, my dear girl," Jasper whispered, wrapping his arms about her and drawing her to the bed where he sat down and held her against him. He felt dry-throated for neither response from Charlotte had been what he'd expected.

Her icy demeanour cut deep when he'd hoped to be

welcomed; and now her obvious emotion made him curse his wrong-footedness for the hundredth time in a week.

"Why did you leave me?" she cried. "When you knew I loved you! Oh, I know you didn't love me back but could you not have let me down kindly instead of abandoning me?"

Her words were like daggers.

"Charlotte, I had urgent business. And the last thing I expected was for you to marry Collingwood. But as I knew no one could force you I assumed—"

"Yes, always you assume!" Charlotte cried. "And no, I was not forced as in my hand was not held to sign the wedding register but I had little alternative when papa was not in his right mind and Mrs Henley was determined to have her way."

Jasper held her closer, his concern deepening. Jane would be rapping on their door very soon and Charlotte needed to make her appearance in the dining room looking presentable at least.

"Charlotte, please forgive me. It was wrong of me to do what I did but at the time I felt I had no alternative."

"Just as I felt I had no alternative. And now—"

Jane's knock was followed by the opening of the door and her sweet smile faltered as she took in the scene.

"Oh, I did not mean to intrude," she said, retreating, but Jasper had risen and invited her in, saying, "Charlotte and I are old friends and she is a little upset. Perhaps you could settle her while I return to the dining room. I could tell the guests that Lady Collingwood was seeing to your comfort, Jane?"

His cousin looked nervous but relented. "Perhaps that would be best," she agreed as Jasper nodded. The urge to kiss Charlotte's hair in parting was very strong but he had lost the right to do that.

He'd lost the right to do anything to help Charlotte and

he was disgusted at himself. Not because he was leaving her to Jane's tender ministrations. That was, he'd decided, the best way of safeguarding Charlotte's distress from her husband.

But because Charlotte's distress was due to one terrible, incontrovertible truth: Jasper had squandered his greatest chance at love.

And there was not a damn thing he could do about it.

CHAPTER 30

Charlotte knew it was best that Jasper leave her so he could make excuses on her behalf. He was quick-witted to come up with such a plan and Charlotte could not stem the tears that seemed to have been built up and then released as if a dam wall had collapsed.

"Lady Collingwood, I'm not sure what has distressed you," Jane now said, nervously and ineffectually as she faced Charlotte. "Are you sure you'd not like me to fetch your husband?"

"Lord no, he's the last person in the entire world I want anywhere near me," Charlotte protested. "And I only tell you that because I trust that won't reach his ears. You don't look the sort and you are Jasper's cousin. He's a man of honour even if he did leave me when I had no alternative but to make the choice I did." Wearily Charlotte drew herself up. "Forgive me, Mrs Creighton, for I don't know what came over me. It is hardly dignified when I have tried so hard to cultivate the necessary glass veneer these past two years. Seeing your cousin again has shattered that." She shrugged, not caring what the young woman read into this, as she went to the looking glass to inspect the damage caused by the storm of her emotion.

"You and Jasper were…?" Jane pushed out the words with difficulty.

"I loved him. He left me." Charlotte smiled at her reflection. "As he had every right to do and I have no right to make an undignified scene. But seeing him again was harder than I'd expected. Now, let me see if I can make myself presentable with a splash of cool water."

"You look only more beautiful, Lady Collingwood. Jasper said you were the most beautiful woman he'd ever met. And the most determined. I was expecting to be daunted but—"

She stopped, and Charlotte sent her a wry smile. "But instead you were shocked."

So Jasper had thought her beautiful.

But now Charlotte was married and nothing Jasper thought was of any account.

For Charlotte had no choice but to continue her charade…

As Collingwood's perfect wife with the icy demeanour.

BY THE TIME Charlotte was ready to face her guests, they were eating dessert.

They looked up as she made her entrance and Charlotte recognised the usual interest in the men's faces and the envy of their wives.

It had ever been thus.

Though of course Jasper had been immune. The one man she had truly loved had seen in her nothing worth pursuing.

Yes, this evening he had evinced regret but nothing too passionate. It was Charlotte, as ever, whose feelings were out of control.

Not that anyone would guess it now. She inclined her head with regal grace, first at her husband, and then her guests, though she barely looked at Jasper.

She couldn't. It was too painful.

"Won't Mrs Creighton join us?" asked Collingwood.

"She is exhausted after her journey and begged me to offer her excuses." Charlotte smiled. She felt strangely calm. She was conscious of Collingwood's eyes upon her as she passed behind him to take her seat.

She was achingly conscious, also, of Jasper's gaze. What must he be thinking of her latest display of hysteria? Yet again she'd thrown herself at him, revealing her feelings with no transparency.

When would she learn?

Jasper had loved her – because she'd begged him – and then he'd left her.

Time, after time, after time.

Now he'd be sitting uncomfortably at the dinner table wondering when she was going to launch her next unprovoked and unwanted attack upon him; demanding from him feelings he did not have.

But of course this time would be different.

For she was a married woman now.

And what Charlotte did when she was not bound by duty and law didn't matter. She took her vows seriously.

She'd made her bed.

Now she must accept her fate.

For the rest of her life.

How Jasper maintained animated conversation with the gentlemen on the subject of hunting in the Cape Colony he could not have said if quizzed later.

Everything that came out of his mouth originated from a region of his brain completely remote from the focus of his concerns.

It had been one thing to have seen Charlotte as a happily married woman though, he realised, that would have been hard enough.

But to have seen her so moved by his arrival, only to witness the glass walls she erected around her when she was with her husband and the rest of the company was too painful.

He was so busy ruminating on this that he dropped his fork when Lady Bertram asked, "Remind me how old your little girl is, Lady Collingwood?"

"Little Lucy is two years old."

Apologising, Jasper picked up his fork and tried to continue to eat but his mind was whirling. So Charlotte was a mother. But of course she would be. He'd just seen no evidence of a child. Nor heard word of any progeny resulting from the union of Lord Collingwood and his bride.

He glanced at her. She looked barely older than the seventeen-year-old he'd first rescued.

If he'd known what he knew now, he would have made her his wife when he had the chance.

But he had been too caught up in vilifying the wrong people for their mistakes when he'd made more mistakes than anyone.

"I have not seen your little girl in the two days we have been here."

It was Lady Altmore, smiling at Charlotte as Charlotte responded, with a veiled glance at her husband, "Mrs Henley looks after Lucy."

As if that was an appropriate response from a mother.

And as Jasper intercepted the looks between Lord Collingwood, Mrs Henley, and Charlotte, suddenly...

He knew.

~

MORE WINE WAS IMBIBED and the spirit at the dinner table became more animated. Collingwood rarely drank but this evening it seemed he was caught up in his enthusiasm for his forthcoming hunting expedition.

He quizzed Jasper excessively, asking about the size of the herds, the size of the largest beast he'd bagged, the weight of the elephant tusks.

And all the while Jasper responded like an automaton as he tried to reconcile what he had thrown away. What he had given this man; this undeserving man, Collingwood, as a result of Jasper's idiocy.

"I want you to come with us. Yes, Creighton. You must come." Collingwood sounded determined, his smile confident as if he knew he'd not be refused.

NO ONE REFUSED HIM ANYTHING, Charlotte knew that.

Least of all, Charlotte.

Fortunately, his bedroom demands had not been onerous. Every Wednesday at 10pm for one hour, and then he'd leave. If Charlotte could survive that, then she supposed she could survive her marriage.

"I'm not long back from the Cape Colony. When do you plan to leave?" Jasper asked.

"In a month. Perhaps six weeks."

As her husband evinced similar enthusiasm, Lady Altone murmured, "That is very sudden and earlier than I had expected, Henry. I trust you'll take me to London for some entertainment before you abandon me?" She looked coquettishly at him, and he responded dutifully.

"We'll hold a farewell ball so you lovely ladies can have something to look forward to before we go adventuring. Eh wot, Collingwood?"

"Indeed. I'll take my lovely wife to the capital to outfit myself for the expedition, and she can visit the sights and indulge her fancies."

"And will you bring little Lucy?" asked Lady Grey.

"Lucy will stay here," Collingwood said before Charlotte could answer. "Now, gentlemen, who's for sherry while the ladies retire? We have much to discuss before we reconvene in London for final preparations."

CHAPTER 31

FIVE WEEKS LATER

J asper hoped he'd find Charlotte feeding the ducks in Hyde Park. It didn't escape him that while she was effectively alone, her maid sat on a bench a few yards away.

She and Collingwood had been in London a week, attending the theatre and various public and private engagements. Jasper had been to many of the same but this was the first time he felt it safe to approach Charlotte.

He'd watched from the periphery, noting the satisfaction on Collingwood's face to see his wife admired from the many gentlemen who paid her court, including the Prince of Wales.

Jasper supposed that if Collingwood's intention were to garner praise for his discernment, he wasn't disappointed. He received plenty of endorsement of his fine collector's eye for Charlotte was feted for her good looks wherever she went.

The most beautiful woman in London, *The Times* called her.

And it's what Jasper called her as he joined her by the edge of the pond.

She didn't look up but said, "I wish you'd been looking for beauty, not purity, when you met me three years ago."

"I wish I'd known what I know now, three years ago," he replied.

"Well, none of that matters anymore. I am married." She looked stonily ahead. "In a few weeks, I will be all alone in Norfolk with just Mrs Henley for company. You will find a wife. It'll be as if we never knew one another."

"You have a child."

She wouldn't look at him. "Why are you here, Jasper? After my stormy outburst the last time we were alone together, I'd said everything that needed to be said.I'm married now and there's no changing that. You are still young and free. You have your whole life ahead of you. I have obligations and a duty to my husband. My maid is watching. I think she's paid to report on my behaviour. I need to remind you that I'm now a respectable matron with a child."

"A child you do not spend a great deal of time with, I can't help noticing."

"Collingwood doesn't allow me to be alone with Lucy."

She angled her head at Jasper's gasp and gave a bitter smile. "It's my punishment. One of his many ways of ensuring I pay for not being the wife he thought he'd bought."

Concern battled with outrage. Guilt and suspicion needled him and although he'd not intended to bring it up now, he murmured, "I had no idea what harm I caused you, Charlotte. I wish I'd known." He swallowed his guilt and concern, with difficulty, struggling for the courage to ask, "Lucy is mine?"

"Well, Collingwood doesn't believe she is his. You'll have to go now, Jasper." She smiled, holding out her hand. "It was nice to see you again." He noticed that her eyes darted to the woman sitting on the bench. Although she pretended interest in her surroundings, the maid was watching them, it was clear.

"When will I see you again?"

"I don't expect you will." Her smile was bland. "I've been in London a week and our paths have not crossed. Clearly, we don't frequent the same places."

"I have seen you every night, Charlotte," he said under his breath. "I have followed your every step but I could not declare myself, obviously. Charlotte… I love you." He made to clasp her wrist but she just smiled and moved away, indicating to her maid that she wanted to continue walking.

"I expect you'll find my husband outfitting himself somewhere in Bond Street," she said over her shoulder. "He is very sorry you won't accompany him to the Cape next week. Do make sure to remind him how much I will miss him while he's away. Anything that shores up how much my husband is regarded, helps."

CHARLOTTE LEFT the lake feeling numb. In Jasper's conflicted look, she'd recognised a depth of feeling completely absent during their light-hearted exchanges over the years.

He loved her?

Well, that was a little too late.

"Charlotte, it's time for your dress fitting."

Charlotte glanced up at Mrs Henley who had taken Lucy's hand and was dragging her away from the maid, Lucy protesting loudly.

As usual, Mrs Henley ignored the child's distress. "Let us not be late for we don't want Madame Leville not to finish your gown before your husband's departure for the Cape. He has chosen it with great care. Who was that gentleman who spoke to you?"

"Mr Creighton."

"For a moment, I feared it was Lord Gilray. You know, Collingwood has promised to put a dagger right through his black heart if he sees him near you." Mrs Henley's tone hardened. "And I am duty bound to report on what I see."

Charlotte did not reply. Let her husband and Mrs Henley believe what they would. At least it offered some protection to Jasper if Collingwood believed that Lucy had been fathered by Gilray.

As they joined the foot traffic towards Bond street, Charlotte said, "How many bibles have been printed for transport to Africa, Mrs Henley? I am sure the heathens of the dark continent can't wait."

"I detect sarcasm in your tone, Charlotte. I'm sorry that the years you spent with me did not train you better in accepting your place on God's earth."

"And I'm surprised at how much you and my husband have in common. I thought that selling me to the highest bidder – Collingwood – was the pinnacle of your desire and so would have ended your association."

"The pinnacle of my desire?" Mrs Henley sent Charlotte a quizzical look. "My desire will never be reached, for I was placed on God's earth to do good. And there is always more good to be achieved."

"There will always be souls to save; yes, I realise that." Charlotte nodded. "And it is of far greater importance to save souls than to save the living." She gripped her reticule tighter to try to stem her outrage. "Your place in the afterlife depends upon it. We mere mortals are either an inconvenience or somehow to be exploited by you for what you perceive as the greater good. I was one of your sacrifices." She breathed deeply, looking straight ahead.

"You mistake the matter, my dear. I have saved prisoners from Newgate and the Marshalsea. Men, found to be innocent thanks to my intervention – and that of Mrs Fry –have walked free. Men who have gone on to live good, productive lives."

"Really. Name one, Mrs Henley. Who was your latest?"

"Mr Rupert Everingham. Yes, I see you remember him. The carrot-headed felon. You and he spoke often when you visited. He was falsely imprisoned for two years in the Marshalsea for theft and for causing grievous bodily harm to the man who, in fact, perpetrated the theft. This was revealed only due to my intervention. I believed his story, and I influenced those who could organise a retrial. And there were others."

Charlotte nodded. "No doubt Everingham had to offer his soul to Christ as a condition of his release."

"Of course. Now, Charlotte, we are at Madame Leville's and I'm sure you'll be anxious to return home to make the most of seeing your husband before he departs for such a long and arduous journey. Six or seven months, I believe he will be gone. I can understand the long face. What will you do with yourself without Lord Collingwood for so long? How fortunate that I shall be your companion while he is away. But Collingwood is concerned that you will be idle. He has decided that Lucy will stay at Emsley Manor while you and I involve ourselves with good works in London. He wants society to see you as a virtuous reflection of himself while he is gone."

Mrs Henley continued as if she didn't notice Charlotte's dismay. She had truly thought she might have more of an opportunity to spend time with her child.

"And after your fitting, we will visit the British and Foreign Bible Society regarding the shipment that Lord Collingwood will safeguard during his journey to the Dark

Continent for distribution to the missionaries who eagerly await."

After her visit to the dressmaker, Charlotte returned to their townhouse, walking into her bedchamber to find Collingwood.

"Collingwood? What are you doing here?" Collingwood only visited her here on Wednesday evenings at 10pm.

He turned, as if surprised at her entrance. "Merely deciding what you will wear tomorrow night."

Charlotte saw, then, that a number of gowns had been laid out on her bed and that her husband was holding up one of them before the looking glass.

"Has Madame Leville finished your new gown? I think this one will show you off to advantage."

The gown was had been finished the previous week. It was one of her favourites: a rose-coloured open robe gown with a double flounce of lace on the hem of the petticoat and a low, crossed bodice with a fall of blond lace from the short sleeves.

"If that is what you wish," Charlotte said.

"It is just one of the few things that I wish." Collingwood seated himself on the bed. "I wish that you would take your role as my ambassadress more seriously. I think that perhaps I have over-indulged you, Charlotte."

"Over-indulged me?" Charlotte bit back the sarcasm she'd not bothered to hide from Mrs Henley.

"Mrs Henley will, in the future, be more vigilant regarding your behaviour since you are to remain in the capital." His dark eyes followed her, and Charlotte was aware of his suspicion.

"I met Mrs Henley on the way here and she told me," Charlotte said, dully.

"Did she mention, also, that I have invited to tomorrow night's ball a couple of surprise visitors?"

"Oh?" Charlotte tried to hide her alarm. "May I ask who?"

"Ah, Charlotte, but that would spoil the surprise." Collingwood sounded almost indulgent but Charlotte knew that was when he was most dangerous. "Suffice to say that I have been watching you, Charlotte. You think I do not know the state of your heart?" He gave a short laugh. "I may surprise you, yet."

His nostrils flared, and he held up the pink gown again and stared into the mirror. At himself, and at Charlotte. "We have unfinished business, Charlotte, you see. For what I am about to do requires great bravery. A fellow who can bring down an elephant sporting tusks of more than two hundred and fifty pounds a piece courts great danger." He swung round, his face reddening with emotion though his voice rose only slightly, "A man who can do that is truly a brave man but there are risks and if I should not come home, then I need to have tidied my account book, if you will." He held the gown against himself, staring into the mirror, his expression distant as he added, "I need to have settled old scores, Charlotte." He breathed deeply, lowered his voice, and hissed, "To ensure that my honour and dignity are maintained."

CHARLOTTE SLIPPED OUT at the first opportunity, and made her way to Jasper's townhouse with fast beating heart, dry mouthed with fear.

Of course it was madness and she imagined his astonishment that should be here after their last meeting. But her fear for his safety was greater than anything.

"Jasper, my husband is planning great harm tomorrow night and I fear the consequences!" she cried once the door had closed behind them, running straight into Jasper's open arms the moment the butler closed the drawing room door behind her.

"Good Lord, Charlotte! What is it?" He blinked as if he could not believe his eyes, but his arms went about her as she threw herself into his embrace, the force loosening her bonnet which she cast aside.

"Has Collingwood hurt you?" There was outrage in his voice and at the touch of his lips upon the top of her head, she sagged with the joy of such closeness. How could she deny what was between them?

"He has never hurt me," she said, but I fear he has singled out someone—wrongly—for bearing the consequence of his unfounded suspicions."

"Hush, my darling! I am in no danger, if that is why you have come here." His tone lowered, and he added, gruffly, "Though I wish there *were* something for you to be alarmed about. You have been like an ice maiden, ignoring me at every turn until now. Perhaps you have run away, Charlotte? Are you going to come away with me?"

She stepped back, out of his embrace, shocked. "You cannot be serious? I would not ruin both of us."

"You, more than me," Jasper admitted, his hands still on her shoulders. "But if you were willing to make the sacrifice, I would make whatever sacrifices necessary, also."

Charlotte shook her head. "And leave Lucy?" she asked. "I could never abandon my child, even if I barely see her. One must have hope that will change. It's what keeps me going. But Jasper, Lucy has been consigned to the country and Mrs Henley is going to remain with me in London. To observe my every move."

"Then we must be careful, my love."

Charlotte blinked. "You mistake me if you think I would even try to see you when Collingwood is away. I cannot do that, Jasper. It's too late for us. But I had to come here to warn you, and to ask your advice."

"What's this? You come here and throw yourself into my arms only to tell me there can be nothing more between us?"

Charlotte nodded. "If my husband has guessed the true state of my heart I will not have your death upon my conscience."

"Because you're a godly woman or because you love me?"

"You know the answer to that," Charlotte said. "But… you also know our time has passed."

Jasper took her hands and drew her closer. "Tell me that's not true, Charlotte. I love you. I always have!"

"No, you haven't. You only say that because you know, now it's not possible for us to be together."

"That's not true!" He was breathing heavily as he put his lips to her hair and his arms tightened about her. "I was a fool when I threw away my chance at love two years ago, believing in a false narrative. The woman I thought so true was a thief and a liar. Mariah stole money from her brother's workplace and blamed this man, Rupert Everingham, who went to jail for the crime. I tracked Everingham down in Africa, intending to call him to account but he told me the truth which I had verified by Mariah's old maid. Oh, Charlotte, all those wasted years when I believed I could not be satisfied by anything other than someone of Mariah's purity —only to discover she was deceitful and without courage. But you, Charlotte. You don't pretend. What I see is everything you are. You speak the truth and you accept the consequences. I adore you. I want to be with you every minute of every day. Please don't tell me that when your husband is gone, we can't be together."

Charlotte closed her eyes. His words were both music to her ears, and intolerable. "Jasper, I'm sorry…" She pulled her hands from his. "I'm a married woman. I can't do what you want of me."

It was painful to look at him. Why now, when all these years she had pined for him, ultimately marrying Collingwood only because she believed Jasper was incapable of loving her?

"Charlotte, why did you not tell me about Lucy?"

"Where were you to tell?" Charlotte gave a bitter laugh. "Even if I'd known where to find you, it would have been too late. I was married to Collingwood before I even knew. Besides, I knew nothing about my... body. When the doctor declared me *enceinte* two months after I married Collingwood, my husband was overjoyed. I was too, for I hoped that providing him with an heir would satisfy him." She faltered. "But the baby was born early. And it was fair and slight."

"Was he unkind to you, Charlotte?"

Charlotte shook her head. She didn't add that his controlled anger was equally frightening. "But he found ways to... punish me."

"Oh Charlotte. I am... so sorry."

Charlotte smiled up at him. "You only ever did what I asked of you. Begged you to do, in fact, so do not blame yourself. I was a foolish, impulsive child." She sighed. "So different from my quiet, pious mama, as I have been told so many times by my step mama, as if it were a crime I should be this way." Charlotte shrugged. "I did try to be good, but it never lasted long."

She gave a rueful laugh and as Jasper continued to hold her, he said, "Your joy in life was what made you captivating. I wouldn't want you any other way."

"I wish you hadn't decided this so late."

"It was because I believed in a lie. You do not lie, Charlotte. Now I blame myself for the fact that your bright light has dimmed. But I beg of you, promise me you will see me while Collingwood is away. For six months at least we can enjoy what might have been."

But again, Charlotte shook her head. Pulling away, she went to the door. "Collingwood has made sure that cannot happen. I will not ruin us both and condemn little Lucy to be motherless."

He stared at her, his expression stricken. "Then don't deny me one last kiss."

Charlotte felt her defences crumble. Dropping her hand from the doorknob, she threw herself into his arms once more.

CHAPTER 32

The night of Collingwood's farewell ball was upon them. He had planned the entertainment in a small, replica castle on the banks of the Thames, with many of the two hundred guests being ferried up the river.

Charlotte spent several hours over her toilette in order to reflect well upon her husband.

The gathering was eclectic for not only were there men who took their hunting seriously, together with their wives, but there were missionaries and upstanding members of society and the church.

Mrs Henley had ensured Collingwood's expedition would also provide a means of proselytising so as to bring more of Africa's heathens to God.

"Charlotte!"

She was surprised to see Gilray looking cheerful and jaunty in flamboyant evening dress crossing the room towards her.

He took her hands and kissed them. "You're looking lovelier than I remember, even. Quite saintly. Ah, but you can't hide the truth from me, Charlotte. We'd have done well together."

He winked, and Charlotte couldn't help smiling. "We'd have done terribly together. I am always reading about your exploits in the gossip columns and you haven't changed. You're a ladies' man to the end, I suspect."

"Only because I let my true love get away."

Charlotte gave another smile, despite herself, for she saw how Gilray's eyes strayed when a pretty young lady crossed his line of vision. "You know I won't believe it for a moment. But enough of that. I'm surprised to see you here."

"I'm surprised to have been invited. You know I don't care for Collingwood and I thought the feeling was mutual."

"You are plump in the pocket." Charlotte shrugged. "If you can further either my husband's ambitions when it comes to Big Game hunting, or Mrs Henley's cause of saving souls, then you'll be invited."

"Mrs Henley is here?" Gilray looked about him and his eyes bulged. "Good lord, there she is, just as I remember and looking even more prune-faced. She looks like she's wearing a sack in that nun-like garb. Not a coloured ribbon or furbelow to be seen."

"And, of course, she's my companion for the duration of Collingwood's time away," Charlotte said on a sigh.

"Oh Charlotte, you should come away with me—or at least visit me. You're mighty unhappy, aren't you? I can mend that."

Charlotte's mouth turned up. "I can only presume you jest. No, Gilray, I would not go with you if my life depended upon it."

"That's very dampening to a fellow's sense of himself. Ah, what circus has your husband conjured up?" Gilray's eyes bulged even more, as did Charlotte's as they observed a massive, loose-limbed creature with an enormous mane being led on the end of a rope onto the dais at the end of the room.

"Good lord, it's a lion!" squeaked Charlotte. "Collingwood mentioned nothing of this."

"Surely it's dangerous?" Gilray sounded concerned. They both eyed the tall, heavyset man with a waxed moustache, wearing gold pantaloons and a red coat, leading the beast onto the raised platform. "The fellow looks like he's escaped from the circus."

For the gathering at the far end of the saloon, the spectacle had gone unnoticed but the lion's guttural roar had everyone in the room swinging their heads round to stare. Several ladies screamed and Charlotte, who stood only ten yards back, thought she'd faint, she'd never seen such a fearsome creature.

The lion's handler cracked his whip, and the sound reverberated around the room, just like the lion's protesting roar.

Now the room was silent. All chatter had ceased, and the lion sat, obediently facing the audience, between his handler and Collingwood, who appeared not afraid in the slightest.

Charlotte glanced at Gilray, her gaze travelling across the assembled guests as she searched for Jasper. But she could not see him.

Collingwood sent the crowd a lazy smile and stepped onto the podium.

"I promised a rare surprise and here we have Tangan, the greatest African lion in England, gifted to the Prince of Wales, but now on display for your entertainment." He signalled to the lion handler, clapping his hands as he said, "A short demonstration, if you will."

There was a burst of percussion from the orchestra, which had stopped playing when Collingwood began to speak. Then a small boy, also dressed in red and gold, darted forward, carrying a flaming torch in one hand and a large hoop in the other. He positioned the hoop on stage so that it was balanced, upright, between several bricks, lit it, then stepped back.

The audience gasped; then gasped louder as the lion tamer cracked his whip once more and the lion bounded through the burning hoop, came around, doubled back, then bounded through it once more.

For some minutes, the lion performed at the will of Collingwood and his handler while the crowd cheered the extraordinary spectacle.

Then Collingwood returned to the stage, clapping the performers off before holding up his hands for silence as the lion and his entourage disappeared behind a red and gold screen.

"Big game and bibles are the reason we're gathered here for tonight," he said. "In three days, I depart for the wilds of Africa to go hunting. I shall return bearing the biggest ivory tusks the world has seen." He paused and gestured towards Charlotte. "And my lovely wife, Lady Collingwood, will remain here to continue her good work with her former guardian, now her companion, the inimitable Mrs Henley." Now he gestured towards that lady who, with a show of modesty, made her way to the dais beside him.

"Please grant Mrs Henley a few moments of your time so she can tell you about her tireless efforts to bring to the heathens of the Wild Continent the celestial light."

Charlotte watched with her face frozen in a semblance of polite interest while Mrs Henley waxed lyrical about her good works, ending with a well-practised and compelling plea for the well-resourced crowd to lighten their pockets in the name of Christian Charity.

Charlotte's polite interest masked astonishment at how compelling Mrs Henley really was at spinning a tale that had the most cynical parting with their valuables.

"She is shrewder than she looks, eh, Charlotte?" Collingwood said as he tucked his wife's hand in the crook of his arm. "You will be well looked after for the time I'll be away. Such a long face, Charlotte? Our guests see how much you miss me already."

"There is not a Christian bone in that woman's body," Charlotte said under her breath. "Everything she does is for personal gain."

"Everything we all do is for personal gain, Charlotte. Some of us just have more power."

It was galling to see the smug look on Collingwood's face as he said this. Charlotte thought what satisfaction it would bring her to slap him in pubic.

Except that there was even greater satisfaction in watching her husband clearly discomposed as a gentleman joined them, introducing himself with a flourish.

He was of middle height, with reddish hair, mostly grey now, and slightly bulbous, watery blue eyes. Charlotte was sure she'd seen him somewhere but couldn't place him.

And he seemed to be someone Collingwood had not expected.

"Good evening, Lord Collingwood. It has been a while since we saw one another." He bowed for Charlotte. "Mr Rupert Everingham at your service. I don't know if you remember me?"

Collingwood pretended to think. Charlotte always knew when he was pretending. He would go very still, his eyes would glaze over for a fraction of a second, and then he'd jerk into renewed life.

"Everingham. Of course! Please remind me why you are here this evening?"

Charlotte was fascinated. It took a great deal to ruffle his feathers.

"I am from the British Bible Society. As you know, we've

funded the printing of many hundreds of bibles to be distributed. Mrs Henley is delighted by the turnout as we are looking for the funds to print many more."

"So many souls to be saved," intoned Collingwood. Charlotte nearly laughed. Collingwood wasn't interested in souls. He was interested in tusks. And lion skins. And having the biggest and the best of everything, including the most beautiful wife.

But he'd been persuaded of the benefits of showing a less self-centred side.

Now Collingwood was having to address someone he didn't want to address which was a rare thing for Collingwood never did anything he didn't want to do.

"That's right," said Mr Everingham. "Souls. We are determined to save as many souls as we can with the available resources. Mrs Henley is a saint."

Charlotte had been watching Everingham intently. The way his eyes warmed when he spoke with passion tugged at her memory. But it was when he said these last words that she realised the identity of the stranger before her.

He was the man in the prison cell at the Marshalsea. Often in company but often separated from the others, he was one of the few who'd addressed Charlotte with unfailing respect. And he'd always mistakenly referred to Mrs Henley as a saint.

"I know you!" Charlotte burst out before she could check herself.

The man blinked. "And I know you, of course, Lady Collingwood. I wasn't sure if it was right to reveal my identity tonight."

"If you are here, it's because you were exonerated." She felt a little swell of happiness. If Mr Everingham had made it out of the Marshalsea there was hope for others. Collingwood was wrong. Not everyone was concerned purely with self interest; though Collingwood certainly was.

"I am very glad you are here and not where you spent so many years. Obviously wrongly. And I'm glad Mrs Henley helped you." It was hard to believe that anyone thought Mrs Henley a blessed soul, though seeing the glow in the man's eyes when he spoke of his saviour, Charlotte supposed she could understand. She knew how foetid the Marshalsea was.

Charlotte turned to her husband. "Mrs Henley is indeed a Christian soldier if she helped release Mr Everingham. I was not aware you knew one another." She was astonished, in fact. Unless, of course, Mr Everingham was a former supplicant whom Collingwood had put in his place and now he was parading himself in front of Collingwood. Gloating. That was possible.

Maybe probable, judging by her husband's clear dislike.

"Ah, Creighton." Her husband was quick to greet the newcomer and turn his back on Everingham after a curt bow.

Charlotte felt suddenly chilled to the bone. Collingwood had intimated his intent to punish Charlotte's former lover. For so long Jasper had slipped beneath his notice, but could someone have said something?

She'd warned Jasper, at least.

But could Collingwood's informant have been Lord Leeson? When Charlotte had evaded him at the inn just before she'd been reclaimed by Collingwood, perhaps Lord Leeson had surmised where Charlotte's heart really lay.

She glanced about the room to see if perhaps Lord and Lady Leeson were amongst the crowd and intercepted the wary glance Everingham sent Jasper.

"Mr Everingham," Jasper greeted him. "And Lord Collingwood. After your exceptional performance with that fearsome lion, I hadn't thought the evening could get any better.

But it is good to see my old foe, Everingham, with whom I am now fully reconciled."

Charlotte blinked at her husband's response. Charlotte had never seen him look quite so cornered.

"To my shame, I played my part in helping put Everingham in the Marshalsea," said Jasper. "False evidence was manufactured." He sent a pointed look at Collingwood. "People who could have seen him exonerated did not step forward." He cleared his throat. "However, this is not the place to discuss the matter."

"No, it is not," said Collingwood abruptly, "Excuse me, gentlemen. I would like to ask my wife for this dance."

The ballroom was filled with people, the orchestra played a waltz and Charlotte had no choice but to put her hand on Collingwood's arm and allow him to lead her onto the dance floor.

"This has been a successful evening, Charlotte. I would be disappointed if you spoiled it, either tonight or while I am gone."

Charlotte gasped. "I would never do that, Collingwood. Besides, with Mrs Henley as my chaperone—"

"Companion," he interrupted. "You are a grown woman, Charlotte. It's time you behaved like one. It's time you were called to account."

Now he really was threatening her.

"Called to account? Pray, what have I done other than be the perfect wife? I have never defied you, never challenged your strictures on what is good for me. I have given you everything."

"Except your heart."

"I never had yours, Collingwood. You wanted only to possess me." She was careful not to display too much emotion as he danced her around another couple. "Ours was never a marriage based on love. You wanted me and you wanted my dowry."

"And I was given another man's child."

There was a moment of silence. Collingwood had never spoken so overtly of this. Everything he had done after Lucy's early arrival had implied this is what he thought. But her arrival was not so soon as to have caused gossip. Perhaps a raised eyebrow, but an eight months' child was not out of the realm of possibility for it to have been conceived within marriage.

"I want to know if that man is here tonight. Answer me, Charlotte."

Charlotte stared mutinously up at him. Of course, she wasn't going to answer. "You malign me, sir," she muttered.

"And you shame me, madam," he responded, taking her arm as the music came to an end and he led her off the floor.

Mrs Henley was making her way towards them, but took a step back when she saw the grim cast of Collingwood's expression. For once, Charlotte wished she had intervened.

"Where are you taking me?" Charlotte demanded as he hustled her out of the ballroom and along a short corridor.

"To see your lover, Charlotte. The man who has crept behind my back at every opportunity during this farce of a marriage."

"No, Collingwood. I have never been unfaithful to you," she protested as loudly as she dared. It was not a conversation to be had in company, but in this part of the castle, they were alone. After the warmth of the ballroom with its hundreds of bodies and bees wax chandeliers, the cold seeped through the stone floors, through her flimsy slippers and into her bones.

"Collingwood, please stop! You are hurting me! I don't want to go where you are taking me."

"But your lover is eagerly awaiting your arrival. Obviously, you and he have matters to discuss."

"I don't understand what you mean. How can there be anything to discuss when I don't know who you're talking about because there's never been anyone but you?"

But of course there had. And Jasper was in the ballroom, perhaps talking to Mrs Henley.

So she was surprised and dismayed when Collingwood thrust open the door of one of the tower rooms and Charlotte found herself face to face with Gilray.

A smile lit up his face when he saw her, but clouded over when he beheld Collingwood's angry visage.

"Together again. Does that make you happy?" Collingwood enquired with a sneer as he thrust Charlotte into the centre of the tower room.

Warily she looked at Gilray, then back at her husband.

When Charlotte turned back to Gilroy, she saw he now looked positively terrified.

As well he might.

For as Collingwood stepped back towards the open door, leaving them in the centre of the room, she heard a terrible, ground-rumbling, bone-chilling roar.

CHAPTER 33

Jasper had been waylaid by Mrs Henley for long enough. He'd been searching for Charlotte after he'd seen her dancing with her husband and had observed Collingwood's grim expression. Clearly it was not a harmonious evening, and he was worried for Charlotte.

She'd looked so breathtakingly beautiful when he'd laid eyes on her this evening but as the night had worn on, her smile had lost its brightness and her eyes had taken on a hunted look.

Now he wondered where Collingwood could have taken her in this great, crumbling castle. He didn't like the thought of them being alone.

"Have you seen my cousin, Lord Gilray?"

He turned to see Charlotte's school friend, Vanessa, smiling up at him.

She looked towards the door that led out of the ballroom, adding, "I overheard someone say there was a surprise awaiting Gilray in the tower. But this was some time ago."

Jasper raised his eyebrows.

Another waltz had come to an end. Jasper was aware of

the young ladies who sent him hopeful glances but could think only of Charlotte.

And where Jasper had taken her.

To the tower room?

He was assailed by a frisson of alarm. Could Collingwood have learned of Gilray's attempted elopement and was planning to have his revenge?

Did he mean to confront Gilray? With Charlotte?

Lady Henley had turned to converse with a dowager and her young companion. The girl was fresh faced and full of excitement at the sight of the lion.

"Will we see it again? Is that what Lord Collingwood is going to hunt when he's in Africa? It looked so fearsome and ferocious, I was afraid it would leap into the crowd and gobble someone up." She gave a girlish titter.

"The lion handler has taken the beast to the tower room," Mrs Henley informed them. "It is only kept in control with the lash of his whip. Otherwise it really would gobble someone up."

The grim twist to her mouth was not pleasant. Jasper could almost imagine she was savouring the idea.

And then he was needled by concern.

Collingwood had taken both Gilray and Charlotte to the tower.

The tower where the lion was kept on its tight leash.

Or was it?

"Excuse me!" he said abruptly, bowing himself out of the conversation and hurrying towards the double doors.

He was in unfamiliar territory but he knew he had simply to find the winding stairs that would lead to the battlements. There were various tower rooms at each level. He would find wherever Collingwood had taken Charlotte, and he'd put his mind at rest that no ill had come to her.

Collingwood was of a nervous, uncertain disposition.

But he surely wouldn't hurt Charlotte. She'd said he'd never touched her in anger.

This part of the castle was badly lit and twice he missed his footing on the worn stairs. Perhaps it was foolishness to come up here when Collingwood surely wouldn't lead his wife, in her flimsy dancing slippers, to such a place.

Yet something made him press onwards.

The walls were so thick no sound penetrated so that once he reached the next level he had to open each door as he came to it. Each room was musty, damp and empty.

At the end of this corridor were more winding stairs leading to the next level.

For a moment he was tempted to retrace his footsteps. This was a fool's errand and he was indulging in wild fancies if he thought Charlotte might be up here.

And if she were with her husband it would be embarrassing and possibly dangerous to reveal his concern.

But there was Charlotte's welfare at stake.

He tried another door, which opened into an empty room.

And then a little further along, he saw the door to the tower room open and Collingwood back out a few steps.

But before Collingwood closed the door, Jasper heard a cry from within. A desperate feminine cry at the same time that Collingwood looked up and saw Jasper advancing.

"What are you doing here?" Collingwood looked outraged. Or like a man with something to hide. "Following me?"

"Where is Charlotte?" Jasper demanded. "What have you done with her?"

Collingwood sent him a quizzical look. "What gives you the right to question me on what I do with my wife?" His voice was low and dangerous.

Pushing past him, Jasper thrust open the tower door, recoiling at what he saw inside.

Charlotte and Gilray were cowering by the window while the lion paced back and forth in front of them. Close up, its size was terrifying, its paws immense. Every few minutes a deep guttural growl resonated , bouncing off the walls, drowning the room in evil portent.

For the lion was without its master now. The lion handler was nowhere to be seen, and Collingwood, now outside the room, held the whip.

The lion turned at the intrusion, and Jasper braced himself. He'd take the lion on rather than see it injure the woman he loved. She looked so small and fragile in her ball-gown. So unlike the bold and jaunty Charlotte he knew.

And he knew in that moment he would do whatever was in his power to protect her, whether it was from Collingwood or a lion.

In the tense silence he heard Collingwood's rapid breathing. Jasper turned and saw his grip tighten on the whip as the lion uttered a low, guttural noise.

Trapped between Collingwood and the lion, and with Charlotte and Gilray pressed against the wall, Jasper weighed up his response.

There was a gleam of excited madness in Collingwood's eye. The man had the power to release them all with the crack of his whip which—Jasper had been led to believe—would guarantee instant subjugation from Tangan.

Clearly, however, Collingwood was not going to exercise this power.

His mouth had turned up ever so slightly as he murmured, "Torn between two lovers..." He cleared his throat, then added, softly, "And a lion."

And then suddenly Jasper felt Collingwood's hand in the

small of his back before he was shoved into the room, the door closing loudly behind him.

"Jasper!" Charlotte whispered, her eyes wide.

"Don't draw its attention," said Jasper, hoping to deflect Tangan's interest from Charlotte.

And interested, he certainly was, for the animal made a gesture like a grimace, revealing its enormous pointed teeth.

So this was it. This was how it would end?

He heard a commotion on the other side of the door. Heard the lion tamer's shout, a crack of the whip as the door opened.

Then Tangan leapt, not at Jasper but at the lion tamer, Jasper saw, as he spun around.

"Tangan!" shouted the tamer, the whoosh and snap of the whip cracking the air like a breaking tree branch.

"Tangan!" His voice rose again but whereas the first time it had sounded with authority, now it broke in fear as the lion leapt at him, knocking him backwards so that he fell onto the stone floor with a cry.

Jasper sought for a weapon, finding only the whip on the ground, cracking it loudly as he snatched it up.

The lion turned its head, leapt off the lion tamer whom Jasper saw was covered in lacerations, then went still, half crouched as it sent a considered look at Collingwood, who was backed against the wall.

If ever Jasper wished harm done to a man it was now, but honour reasserted itself and he advanced, cracking the whip as he shouted, "Off, Tangan, off!"

He wished he could close the door to protect Charlotte, whom he could see in the guttering candlelight staring with horror at the scene.

But now he had all the power, and he must use it wisely before the lion did any more damage. He was relieved to see the lion handler move, his eyes large and clearly taking in the scene, before he froze, no doubt in a move of self protection as the lion began to pace before Collingwood.

Jasper cracked the whip once more, and once again the lion hesitated. It raised its head, checked in its intent which clearly had been to launch itself at Collingwood who was backed into a corner, flat against the wall where the corridor ended in a narrow flight of steps.

Jasper could see the primal instinct to seek prey or avenge his human oppressors, and he cracked the whip again for it seemed the only way to keep the animal in check.

And now Jasper realised he held Collingwood's life in his hands.

That second of reprieve for Collingwood seemed to register with the man, too, for as his eyes locked with Jasper's, he muttered, "For God's sake, keep him off me. I'll give you whatever you want."

Jasper tightened his grip on the whip while his mind went through everything he wanted. Which amounted, in reality, to one thing. "I want to look after Charlotte. I want to make her my wife."

Collingwood's nostrils flared. "She's mine," he ground back. "My *legal* wife. I'm not giving up the most beautiful, exquisite piece in my collection."

"I don't want to be yours!" Charlotte cried from the far wall in the tower room, Gilray looking white beside her. "Please let me go, Collingwood! Let me be Jasper's wife, as I always wanted."

"Jasper Creighton?"

"It was always Jasper Creighton!"

And Jasper knew in that moment that she was right. Just as, for him, it had always been Miss Charlotte Treloar.

The lion growled again, restless and dangerous, dropping its head and sizing up Collingwood until Jasper cracked the whip once more.

Even so, Collingwood was adamant. "Divorce is out of the question."

"Then we'll find another way to save face. Or maybe a divorce would be preferable. Say you'll agree, Collingwood, or I'll not crack this whip again."

His words were cut short by another louder, more considered growl from the lion. Tangan was at the end of his patience.

Perhaps Collingwood expected Jasper to continue to hold the lion at bay, for he shook his head, angrily. "No one holds me to ransom!" he cried, his voice breaking in fear as the lion reared up, able to be contained no longer. And Collingwood realised it, for he'd barely uttered his final defiant denial of Jasper's demands before he was shrieking acceptance of all Jasper's terms.

But the lion had leapt, and now Collingwood was beneath it.

Jasper cracked the whip. He cracked it across the lion's back this time and the lion, feeling the scalding pain, was finally deterred, howling as it left Collingwood and turned towards Jasper.

Suddenly having possession of the whip seemed ineffectual as Jasper looked deep into the eyes of the massive creature, only feet away.

All it had to do was use one massive clawed paw to swipe at him, and Jasper could be dead in an instant.

The lion looked as if it were contemplating just that.

Jasper breathed deeply. Out of the corner of his eye, he saw the lion tamer's prone body surrounded by a pool of blood. It hadn't taken much force on Tangan's part to render him immobile.

Behind Jasper, Collingwood was groaning. By the dim light of the candle sconces Jasper could see one side of his face was shredded to a pulp, injuries sustained in a mere second.

Tangan had the power to do the same to Jasper and perhaps hated him in that moment all the more for wielding the whip that had clearly been the instrument of his subjection his whole life.

He was so close to Jasper that he could have stretched out a paw and drawn his claws like daggers across Jasper's face.

And although Jasper might hold the whip, he was powerless.

He held his breath. This was the moment. Then he bared his teeth, uttered a deep guttural growl from his lungs, and once more cracked the whip.

The crack broke the tension, the lion reared back, its eyes registering its fear.

And then it ran.

It bounded back down the corridor, and Jasper ran after it, catching a last glimpse of it as it disappeared, clattering down the curving staircase...

Heading towards the ballroom.

CHAPTER 34

The dancing had stopped, and the orchestra was on cue for Mrs Henley's latest pronouncement.

She was an effective orator, and she knew how to persuade those with money to ease their consciences by donating to her good causes.

Although she wasn't a Quaker, like her idol, the reformist Mrs Elizabeth Fry, her sober dark grey clothing and modest, matronly white cap painted her as devout and Christian.

"All of you here tonight, in your jewels and finery, know not what awaits you in the afterlife unless you have lived a life on earth that is wholly virtuous. Who here can declare such a thing? Even thoughts of envy and vice are enough to sway God into considering an alternative path as you enter the pearly gates. Remember this: donating to good and virtuous works such as saving the souls of the heathens in the dark continent can sway God from sending you on a journey in the afterlife you may not find to your liking." With her fan, she tapped the large silver epergne which stood upon a plinth beside her. It was decorated with grapes and ivy leaves and while it generally contained an elaborate display of cut flowers, tonight it was empty, evident by the hollow ringing sound as her ivory fan made contact.

"Ladies and gentlemen, I implore all of you tonight to think of your Christian duty and what your small contribution might be towards saving the souls of *all* of God's creatures, regardless of how deserving or otherwise they might be," she cried. "They will be forever grateful, and in directing the lives of others towards a more righteous path, you will be ensuring your own salvation."

She scoured the room with her icy gaze, convinced that her righteous path was the one and only path to salvation.

"Ladies and gentlemen, I implore you to give generously. Put your money, and your jewels, into God's vessel—" she tapped the epergne once more—"and consider it both a gift to God and to your own afterlife—"

Her words resonated, and the mood in the room was filled with energy. Women had begun pulling off their rings while men reached for their pocketbooks.

The orchestra had begun to play once more, a stirring piece to encourage the spirit of giving. The murmur of the crowd had become a more enthusiastic babble as people took to heart Mrs Henley's oblique directive.

"Tangan!"

The cry echoed from far down the corridor and was cut short by a fearsome growl. Eyes turned in terror towards the door where the creature that had been their entertainment reappeared, a great unrestrained predator in their midst.

Jasper, only yards behind it now, cracked the whip again, this time close enough to check its progress.

It turned its head, sizing up Jasper once more.

But then it looked back into the room, which was filled with sumptuously dressed men and women in ballgowns adorned with bows and furbelows. Men and women who cared more about their own pleasure but who had been sufficiently swayed by Mrs Henley's encouragement to buy their way to heaven.

And then it looked at Mrs Henley standing on the dais, bathed in light as she dominated proceedings.

Visually, she was the far less appealing of anyone there with her homely clothing, with her small eyes, sunken cheeks and thin bitter lips quivering as she cried, "What's that lion doing here? It's a menace to society and should be destroyed."

And perhaps the lion recognised in her shrewish words, the tone of a thousand injustices and petty tyrannies over its life in captivity.

For it ignored all the finely dressed men and women, better dressed and better fed, glittering with jewels, in its path.

With a roar, Tangan prepared himself for the final onslaught, ignoring the crack of the whip in his ear as his glittering eyes honed in on the woman standing on stage, posturing, shrieking, demanding his subjection, his demise.

Tangan had been oppressed his entire life and in Mrs Henley he recognised the greatest oppressor of all.

There was not a thing Jasper could do as the lion fixated upon his final prey.

With a mighty bound, Tangan launched himself from the doorway, clearing a path through the audience as it leapt towards the dais.

Hurling himself at Mrs Henley.

CHAPTER 35

TWO MONTHS LATER.

"Are you ready, my love?" Jasper's hand curled about Charlotte's wrist to give her the bolstering squeeze she needed.

He *always* knew what she needed, she thought as the carriage door closed upon them and the horses moved forwards, up the majestic driveway of Emsley House and towards the main road to London.

However, on this occasion, she wasn't so sure.

"Darling, this is our first journey out alone. It's scandalous as it is, with Collingwood in the Cape Colony—"

"He sanctioned it, Charlotte. Remember, he publicly recognised me as the man who saved his life and he publicly announced to everyone at the farewell ball that he trusted no man more than me to look after you while he was gone for six months."

"Which you have done, beautifully." She closed her eyes as she rested her cheek against his shoulder. "I'm just sorry I can't give you more." Her surge of affection had been truncated by the most acute concern for while Charlotte had embraced the freedom and licence her husband had afforded her, she refused to become Jasper's mistress.

"You've given me Lucy," Jasper said, touching the cheek of the sleeping three-year-old. With her head of titian curls, and her bright, engaging personality, she'd quickly wrapped Jasper, a constant visitor to the house, around his little finger.

Jasper had leased a cottage not far from Emsley House and was a regular visitor to Charlotte and Lucy, but he always returned to his own lodgings at the end of each day.

Charlotte knew how much he desired her. Nearly as much as she desired him. But the trauma of the past had taken its toll, and she was not prepared to throw away her reputation and condemn Lucy to public condemnation if her mother were to be branded immoral for her liaison with Jasper.

Now she tensed, waiting for Jasper to make some remark that indicated his dissatisfaction with the arrangement between them.

While he spent many days with Charlotte and Lucy, they were careful not to give the servants a reason for gossip.

Instead, he mused, "I wonder if Lucy will go dark, as you have, or if she'll keep her golden tresses. Her hair is surprisingly long for a child her age. Already she turns heads, my darling. Like you always have. I think Lady Leeson will be enchanted." He touched Charlotte's cheek, and she felt herself melt, wondering how long her resolve not to succumb to Jasper would last.

Surely Collingwood would sanction a divorce?

But the hope did not burn brightly. It would be a long, expensive and scandalous business that would compromise Lucy.

Collingwood would consider it losing face, and that was not something he would ever do.

Now, Charlotte's chief concern was their destination. "Jasper, I really don't know that you are right in believing Lord and Lady Leeson were not colluding with Collingwood to make me marry him. I don't know that I want to meet them."

"I believe you are mistaken," Jasper maintained. "They have always shown the greatest interest in your welfare and when Lady Leeson requested that I pay them a call to let them know how you fared, it seemed only natural that I offer to bring you and Lucy along so they could see for themselves. Lady Leeson is the kindest, most beautiful woman you could imagine. Even more beautiful than her portrait which you've admired for the humanity in her expression. Please, Charlotte, don't be upset. If you sense they are not your friends, we can leave. Will that satisfy you?"

Charlotte sighed. "I suppose so," she said. "I just wish I was going somewhere with you and Lucy where we could be alone."

"That is something you steadfastly refuse to do, my love." A flash of hope lit up Jasper's face and immediately Charlotte felt the need to retract her words, accompanied as they were with the familiar surge of fear that her actions would be construed scandalous.

"Jasper! Lady Collingwood!" Both Lord and Lady Leeson rose as the drawing room door was opened and the parlour-maid announced their arrival.

"So good of you to come," declared Lord Leeson. "We have been looking forward to meeting you since Jasper spoke so highly of you, and as we know you are in his care while your husband is away."

Charlotte dipped her head, embarrassed and unsure how to respond, Lucy clinging to her skirts.

"You did not bring her nursemaid?" Lord Leeson continued.

"I like to spend all the time I can with her," Charlotte murmured. Since Collingwood had departed, Charlotte felt she had so much time she needed to catch up on, given the years Collingwood had refused to allow her to be alone with her child.

"I think I would feel the same, Lady Collingwood."

Charlotte looked up to see that Lady Leeson had stepped forward for, while her husband had properly greeted them, she'd remained by her chair.

"Ah yes, you have three children, do you not, Lady Leeson?" Jasper asked.

Lady Leeson didn't reply. She moved forward to stand by her husband. "May I?" she asked. Charlotte was surprised to see that she'd put her arms out, as if she wanted to hold the wriggling child.

"Of course," she said, handing the little girl over.

"What a sweet child," Lady Leeson said, her smile fond as she stroked Lucy's curls.

"She has lovely hair," said Lord Leeson, and Jasper, seeming to enjoy the fact that Lord and Lady Leeson were so taken with the child remarked, "It is very similar to Lady Leeson's, is it not? The same colour, and the same curls."

To Charlotte's surprise, Lucy, who often objected in Charlotte's arms, seemed very content to be held by Lady Leeson.

"I think Lucy likes being made a fuss of," she said, warming to the couple of whom she'd initially been so wary.

"Perhaps the gentlemen would like to talk amongst themselves while we ladies entertain Lucy. I've had some toys brought to the window seat," said Lady Leeson.

Charlotte saw that near to where Jasper and Lord Leeson had seated themselves, a collection of dolls had been set out between a couple of comfortable chairs to which Lady Leeson directed them.

"Lucy might like to sit by the writing desk there and see which doll she likes. I'd be happy for her to take one home with her," said Lady Leeson.

"But what about your girls?" asked Charlotte, as her little daughter tottered over to the elegant French polished table and snatched at a letter Lady Leeson had obviously been writing. "Might your daughters not object?" she added, smoothing out the letter and replacing it with a glance at the elegant handwriting with its looped capitals. She blinked, then looked away, embarrassed that Lady Leeson might think her prying.

"The youngest is ten," said Lady Leeson, "and we both agreed during our talk yesterday, that it would be nice for one of her dolls to be given a new home if our little visitor took a particular shine to her."

"How sweet." Charlotte was revising her opinion of Lord and Lady Leeson all the time while her mind played over the unusual, familiar, looped capital letters Lady Leeson used in her correspondence.

"I daresay Lucy might like the company if she is missing her papa," Lady Leeson went on.

"Do you mean, does she miss Lord Collingwood? I don't think so," said Charlotte with a surge of bitterness which she ameliorated with a smile, though she knew it wavered a little. "He paid her little attention. Mr Creighton, however, is like a favourite uncle. She has enjoyed many outings with Mr Creighton since Lord Collingwood's departure. My husband is more interested in shooting large animals than entertaining little girls."

There. Let it be known to the whole world that Collingwood was as cold to his household as he appeared to society.

"It is fortunate Lord Collingwood survived the ghastly

business at the farewell ball," said Lord Leeson, pausing his private conversation with Jasper to interject. "I heard tell there were some who feared his injuries would be too great for him to travel."

"I think my husband felt that leaving England to persist with his hunting trip would be the tonic he needed," Charlotte said.

"His injuries were substantial, I heard," said Lady Leeson.

"Mostly face lacerations which I have no doubt that, as the years go on, he will say were incurred in Africa facing down the largest lion who ever roamed the African veldt." Charlotte knew she was being reckless to make her antipathy so clear but she didn't care.

She was with Jasper, and he made her feel safe. And in a surprisingly short time she had felt safe with Leesons.

Why had she been so suspicious? she wondered, as she watched the fondness on Lady Leeson's face as she knelt on the floor and played dolls with Lucy.

Lord Leeson was the consummate gentleman, still handsome, though going a little grey at the sides. He looked both distinguished and kind and as she glanced at Jasper she thought, too, what a good-humoured and handsome face Jasper possessed. Her heart gave a little skip.

He was the father of her child. He was the custodian of her heart. She loved him with all her being.

And yet they could not be together. The thought was powerful and painful.

Jasper looked suddenly sober. "My apologies, Lady Leeson, for our talk since of course, you lost your mother in particularly ghastly circumstances."

"As you no doubt know, my mother and I were estranged." Lady Leeson pressed her lips together. "She was not a kind woman." She appeared to struggle with her words and then said, "I thought of you often, Charlotte, after I heard that your father had made her your guardian following your—" She stopped, then reframed her sentence. Charlotte wondered if she'd been about to say 'elopement' in a reference to her rash escapade with Gilray.

Instead, Lady Leeson said, "When you left Miss Prism's academy, I was dismayed to learn that you were in Mrs Henley's care." She cleared her throat. "I did not think your father would have allowed it. But then, it would have been his wife, Beatrice, your step-mama, who encouraged him to agree. She had fallen under Mrs Henley's spell long before."

Charlotte blinked. She had not known the extent to which the Leesons were acquainted with the details of Charlotte's life.

She saw Lord Leeson look between them as he said, haltingly, "My first wife, Cassandra, was a good friend to your papa's first wife, Hortense, who also fell under Mrs Henley's spell and spent a great deal of time succouring the prisoners at the Marshalsea."

"You mean my mother?' Charlotte asked, moving forward, her heartrate quickening. "Do you remember my mother?" Mrs Henley had refused to speak of her mama, Hortense, saying only that she was a godly woman taken too soon, but that it was God's way of protecting her from the influence of her dissolute papa.

An uncomfortable look was exchanged between the Leesons before Jasper said, "Charlotte has always sought to learn more about her mother, whom she says her father refused to mention and whom, as she says, Mrs Henley never discussed."

Charlotte waited, surprised at how Jasper's words appeared to so discomfit Lord and Lady Leeson. As if they were unsure how to respond. "I heard you were all friends," she prompted. "That my wild poet father and my mother, his quiet, god-fearing wife whom I do not resemble at all, were friends with you and your first wife, Lord Leeson." She smiled at Lady Leeson, trying to put her at ease for surely there was something she was not being told. "When I saw your handwriting on the letter that Lucy snatched, it reminded me so much of my mother's. I daresay it was the fashion at the time to construct one's capital letters with such a flourish." Charlotte sighed. "Mama once wrote a letter to me which my father gave to me on my twelfth birthday. He said she'd written it when she knew she was dying and that it was my gift from the grave. It's all I have of her. Though everyone tells me she was so different to me her letter shows that she loved me dearly. I treasure it and carry it with me everywhere."

Jasper gave a short laugh. "Indeed, that's true." He was about to say more but Lady Leeson interrupted. She was pale and surprisingly tense.

"Do you have it with you now?" she asked.

"Of course," said Charlotte, reaching for her reticule and withdrawing the beloved and much-read correspondence. "Shall I read it? It's very short but it has given me such strength throughout many difficult times in my life."

"It has?" Lady Leeson smiled. "I am glad. And I would love you to read it."

Charlotte settled herself in her chair, smoothed the paper, and began.

My darling Charlotte,

I don't know if you will ever receive this letter,
    for it seems we are destined not to meet.
But I have faith that, some day, it will find its
    way to you so that you will know that your
    mother held you in her heart always. That

you were, and are, dearly loved, and that she
thought of you with every breath she had.

When you receive this, I do not know where I
will be, or where you will be, for that
matter.

I am trusting that your father will choose the
right time to give it to you. Perhaps that will
be when you are still a child; or perhaps
when you have children of your own.

If you are still a child, you can imagine me as an
angel looking down and smiling at your
antics.

If you are a mother, then you will know the
pain of being unable to hold your child if
circumstances have kept you apart.

Just know that you are, and always will be,
deeply loved.

Your mother.

Charlotte looked up to see tears in Lady Leeson's eyes.
Lord Leeson had moved over to his wife's side and his hand
was on her shoulder.

"When did your father give you this letter?" Lady Leeson
asked. Her voice trembled.

"I was twelve. I remember hearing that my stepmama was
unhappy and I didn't know why. I heard them in the
drawing room. I had my ear to the keyhole and then papa
opened the door and found me which made step-mama even
more disinclined that he give it to me."

"You were a naughty child?" Lady Leeson smiled. "So was
I. Mrs Henley was forever punishing me for it, telling me my
wild ways were unbecoming and I'd never find a husband."

She squeezed Lord Leeson's wrist. "Fortunately I found the best of men."

Mrs Henley was a strange bond between them. How could Charlotte have spent all those years in her care—or under her yoke—without knowing she was Lady Leeson's mother?

She felt a pang as she caught Jasper's eye. She wanted to tell the world that Jasper was the best of men, but of course the world would not sanction such sentiments. Jasper had merely been given the duty, by Collingwood, of looking after his wife while he was away.

But she would tell the company of his bravery.

"And Jasper Creighton is the bravest man I know," she said, "for he courted death to ensure my safety, and that of so many others." But then she caught Lady Leeson's eye and, remembering, clapped her hand to her mouth.

Lady Leeson pushed her shoulders back, looked at Charlotte and Jasper, and said, "Do not be afraid of talking of Mrs Henley in front of me for I do not mourn her any more than if she'd been some unknown, unfortunate woman who lost her life in unusual circumstances. She was cold and she was cruel." Before anyone could respond after the short silence that followed this, she went on, "Please, Charlotte, tell me what your father said when he gave you the letter."

It took Charlotte a moment to reconcile sweet, gentle Lady Leeson with her fierce words.

Jasper, too, seemed taken aback, though not Lord Leeson, Charlotte observed.

Charlotte glanced about the company. While she knew she ought to show respect towards Mrs Henley, she felt another tug of something inside her that released some of the tension she'd felt about this visit.

The more Lady Leeson voiced such similar feelings

towards Mrs Henley that Charlotte felt, the more she warmed towards her.

"Papa told my step mama it was my right to have it. I'd gathered it was a letter from my mama and was nearly expiring to have it so I told the biggest lie. I told my step mama I would love her all the more for knowing I had a mother who thought of me after death, as well as a step mama in life."

"You did not get along with your stepmother?"

"I always suspected she didn't love me." Charlotte watched Lady Leeson warily as she added, "When she made Mrs Henley my guardian, I *knew* she didn't."

Mrs Henley. Once again, they were talking about a woman who had recently died a horrible death. A woman who had been mother and guardian to both.

A woman whom, it was clear, they both detested.

Despite their respective ages, Charlotte was surprised at how quickly she was feeling such an affinity with this woman she'd never met before but who showed such interest in her. And in whose arms Lucy was sleeping peacefully. It was rare that Lucy took to strangers.

"She likes you, Lady Leeson." It was Jasper who spoke. Charlotte's darling Jasper, who made her heart sing and gave her hope for happiness. Not eternal happiness, for that was beyond her. Collingwood would return and Charlotte would no longer have Jasper's company on regular outings with Lucy.

Charlotte coloured as she found Jasper had now transferred his gaze to her. But she did not look away. No, as she gazed into his darling, handsome face, she realised that she had to take what happiness while and when she could. If Collingwood refused to countenance the scandal of a messy, expensive, almost unheard-of divorce, then Charlotte *would* enjoy Jasper's company while the opportunity afforded itself.

She swallowed, feeling herself tear up. She would tell him that. He'd kissed her passionately only once since Collingwood had gone away. The day after, in fact. But Charlotte had been so set on keeping up appearances for Lucy's sake that she'd told him she'd never allow such intimacies again. And he'd never pushed.

But now, seeing so clearly the love Lord and Lady Leeson had for one another, Charlotte realised in what short supply love and happiness really were.

Yes, it was something for which she'd take great risks. She had done so, after all, when she was foolish and naïve and didn't understand the consequences.

So why was she so afraid of throwing herself after happiness now?

Why? Because she knew how badly it could go wrong.

Yet as she gazed at Jasper, knowing now what she did not know then; knowing, too, how much he regretted not taking chances because he'd deceived himself with false dreams, Charlotte's resolve grew.

Yes, she could find happiness with Jasper. Even if it was for a short, sweet time only.

Her reverie was broken by Lord Leeson, who, in response to something his wife had said, laughed. "We were sure you and Jasper were going to make a match at one time."

"You did?" Charlotte blushed and looked from Lord Leeson to Jasper, who smiled and said, "Lady Leeson and I had no idea what kind of young lady you were until Jasper returned. He was quite affected by the encounter." He smiled. "But quite determined not to be."

Charlotte pressed her lips together. "I was a foolish, impetuous child when I was seventeen." Then she frowned, hesitant to voice her reservations. "May I ask you a question? Was I wrong in believing that you, Lord Leeson, went after me when I left Collingwood at the ball just before our marriage in order to—" She took a deep breath, before saying boldly, "In order to either take me back to Collingwood; or to deliver me to Mrs Henley?"

"Charlotte, how could you think either of those things?" Lady Leeson burst out. "My husband was trying to protect you from both so that you would be in a position to decide your own future."

Charlotte put her hand to her mouth and nearly wept. "I heard Lord Leeson was at the inn, enquiring, but I said I wasn't there because I believed you wanted to make me marry Collingwood."

Lady Leeson looked sorrowful. "I told Lord Leeson we should tell Charlotte the truth so that Charlotte would know who to trust. See what happened? She married Collingwood. First she endured all those years with Mrs Henley, and by God, I know what that's like. And now she's Collingwood's wife when she could have had Jasper Creighton." As she leaned into her husband's shoulder, she whispered, "I should not have spoken so freely, Charlotte. I apologise."

Charlotte was about to grant absolution, but hesitated. How did Lady Leeson know so much about her? Why was she so interested in Charlotte's welfare?

She glanced at her sleeping child, its little face cushioned peacefully upon Lady Leeson's shoulder. From the top of its reddish gold curls to the shape of her eyes, and the neatly shaped chin, Lucy could have been...

A close relative of Lady Leeson?

Charlotte rose to her feet. "Lady Leeson, may I look at that letter Lucy tried to take from you?" A sudden thought had occurred to her.

She took the letter Lady Leeson handed her, drawing out of her reticule at the same time, the letter Charlotte's own mother had written her.

And as she held the two up, side by side, she saw that she was reading correspondence, not similar, but identical.

Again her eyes ran over the words, the unusual formation of sentence construction, word creation, looped capitals.

And over the top of the letter, she saw Lady Leeson watching her intently, one hand to her throat, the other gently cradling the cheek of the sleeping child she held.

Lucy... Charlotte took a shaking breath as realisation dawned; as the similarity of features confronted her, and so many veiled allusions formed connections in her mind.

Lucy. Charlotte's daughter.

Lucy. Lady Leeson's grandchild.

This astonishing realisation must have been clear on her face for as Charlotte's mouth dropped open, and she half rose, Lady Leeson also stood, still holding the child as she took a step forward.

Jasper, aware suddenly of the changed, and charged atmosphere in the room, raised his head to look between Charlotte and his hostess.

"Charlotte?" He stood, instinct directing him to put his arm protectively about her.

And, instinct directing Charlotte to cleave to him, to rest her head against his shoulder while she cupped his cheek.

Smiling, as her mother's arm went about her shoulders and she said, softly, as she stroked Lucy's soft curls, "This, my darling girl, is what I have always dreamed of."

EPILOGUE

Charlotte gazed at the pink-tinged sky, revelling in the balmy summer evening as she curled against Jasper beneath their favourite tree halfway between the house he had leased and Emsley Manor.

"I'm almost in heaven," she murmured, stroking Jasper's cheek as she rested her head against his shoulder. Lucy had been put to bed an hour before Charlotte had slipped out for her usual evening stroll.

And, as happened nearly every evening, Jasper had been waiting for her here.

They'd been lovers for a month but careful to ensure they were rarely together beneath the same roof for Charlotte was adamant to protect herself and Lucy from the kind of whispers that would provide the vengeful and untrustworthy Collingwood with the ammunition he needed to destroy Charlotte's life.

And Lucy's.

Jasper didn't reply. It was as if he knew what was coming next, for Charlotte twisted suddenly in his arms, and burst out, "And in three weeks I'll be in hell."

For, in three weeks, Collingwood was due to return, and the brief hiatus from his cruelty would be at an end.

"My darling—"

Jasper's words were cut short by the sound of galloping hoofbeats as a rider cut through the woods near them in the direction of Emsley House.

They looked at one another, for there had been an urgency and intent in the manner in which the horseman had directed his mount that was clearly at odds with a casual visit, especially at so late an hour.

"Something has happened." Jasper rose and helped Charlotte to her feet. "Do you want me to come with you?"

It was late and would give rise to whispers if they returned together, but Charlotte nodded.

Together they hurried back, taking a shortcut through the woods that meant they were at the house just a few minutes after the rider who was now awaiting Lady Collingwood in the drawing room, Charlotte was informed by the wide-eyed parlourmaid.

"He says he has an urgent message for you, m'lady."

Charlotte gave Jasper's hand a quick squeeze at the door before she stepped forward, hope and fear coalescing with self-disgust that she should wish for another's death in order to ensure her happiness.

If only divorce were a simple matter.

The horseman, mud-stained from his race across the countryside, rose from his bow brandishing a sealed letter, which Charlotte took with shaking hands.

Jasper remained standing, watching her as she digested its contents. She felt the blood drain from her face as her beloved finally asked, "Is it Collingwood?" She heard the tense hopefulness in his tone, and tears sprang to her eyes as she shook her head.

"It's from Lady Leeson." She cleared her throat. "From my…mother."

Jasper was at her side in an instant. Lady Leeson wrote often, but clearly this missive differed from the usual.

"Papa is dead." Charlotte battled the rising sobs as she looked bleakly at Jasper, who asked, "And why is she passing on this news and not your step-mama?"

Charlotte frowned as she re-read the brief letter, trying to make sense of it, while Jasper paid the messenger, who muttered that he had no instructions other than to deliver the news in person.

"I can't imagine that my step-mama would be too happy that Papa left a villa in Milan to Lady Leeson," Charlotte whispered when the messenger had gone. She cleared her throat again. "To my real mother—" She tried to puzzle it out, adding, softly—"who was the real *Maid of Milan* in Papa's scandalous poem." She thrust the letter aside and put her hands to her eyes. "But Papa is dead. That is what Mama is telling me. That and—" She turned and put her hands on Jasper's shoulders. "Mama is gifting the villa to me because she says it's where I might have been born if she'd been allowed to marry Papa as she'd wanted to when she was an impetuous seventeen-year-old." Charlotte's laugh was tinged with hysteria. "She hopes it may give me the freedom to find the happiness *I* might have found as an equally impetuous seventeen-year-old."

Jasper clutched her shoulders and lowered his head.

"What are you saying, Charlotte?" He frowned. "You know I would live with you anywhere. In Milan, too, if it meant we could be together."

But the doubt in his tone echoed her own. Was the scandal worth it after everything they had done to keep Lucy safe from whispers and innuendo? What would it mean to their shared futures? No, it was not possible.

"Charlotte, I forget myself. Your father is dead. I am so sorry, my darling," he whispered as she began to cry and he held her close, kissing the top of her head.

"Lady Collingwood! Pardon me!" Another knock upon the drawing room heralded the arrival of yet another stranger, Charlotte realised as, shocked, she brought up her head and instinctively stepped away from Jasper.

At least, Charlotte had thought the newcomer a stranger until he removed his hat, and she saw through the sweat and dirt that caked his face that he was in fact Sir John.

"My dear Lady Collingwood," Sir John said again, advancing a few steps, his expression one of deep sorrow. "It appears you have heard the terrible news already, though I cannot imagine how, for I have ridden with the greatest haste from the docks."

Charlotte put her hands to her cheeks. "The terrible news, Sir John?" She looked at Jasper, adding as if it might excuse his presence so late, "Yes, I have just learned that my father is dead."

"My poor, good lady," the other man cried, gripping Charlotte's hands in a gesture that suggested that what he had to say might be more than she could bear. "Then I don't know how to break it to you that your husband is—"

The unsaid word hung in the air between them and Charlotte's closed her eyes as she anticipated what he was about to say, swooning so that Sir John had to catch her as he finished, "Dead."

Suddenly Jasper was there, and the two were assisting her to the sofa, Sir John instructing the parlourmaid who had scurried into the room at his cry to "fetch my lady's burnt feathers for she has had an unbearable shock."

But it was not unbearable.

It was a shock, yes, and it was profound like the shock of her father's death, which she was still digesting.

But as Sir John went on, "Sir Collingwood showed the utmost bravery right to the very end as he faced down the charging elephant, its tusks at least three hundred pounds apiece. So certain was he that his shot between the eyes would fell it, he did not move. And so he met his demise. My poor Lady Collingwood. Unflinching. Determined to the very end."

Oh yes, Collingwood had been determined until the very end. Determined that Charlotte would be his slave and his showpiece, his puppet and his plaything; the beautiful crown jewel in his prize collection, just like the elephant tusks that had ultimately cost him his life.

But now he was dead, and Charlotte had her freedom.

And a villa in Milan.

And a future swirling with possibilities.

"Sir John, you have ridden a great distance and are clearly in great distress yourself at what you had to tell me and what you witnessed. Millie!" Charlotte rose into a sitting position, suddenly clear-headed and as determined as her husband had ever been as she addressed the parlour maid. "Please show Sir John to the blue room where he must spend the night. If you'll excuse me, Sir John, this has been a very great shock. I have much to think about."

He seemed only too happy to be dismissed and as the door closed behind him, Charlotte rose to her feet, staring at Jasper who, not unexpectedly, failed to display the necessary sorrow at news of such a violent death as Charlotte whispered, "I am a widow," her heart dancing with joy, and relief, and expectation for a future she never believed would be hers.

"A widow who must serve out her twelvemonth of mourning before we can claim the happiness I hope you'll grant me." A smile tugged at Jasper's mouth, and then Charlotte threw herself into his arms.

Finally, the touch of his lips was no longer tinged with danger while the pressure of his arms around her truly did promise a lifetime of love and security. "Oh yes, my darling, Jasper. A twelvemonth of mourning that I intend to serve in my new villa in Milan," she declared as she twined her hands behind his neck, breaking her kiss to add, "But only if you'll come with me."

The fervour of his response was all she needed for his answer.

THE END

Passion Fever follows <u>An Unsuitable Alliance</u> and <u>The Reluctant Bride</u> from the *Dutiful Wives* series.

ALSO BY BEVERLEY OAKLEY

Daughters of Sin series

A steamy, funny, witty and dangerous Regency-set 'Dynasty'
featuring two nobly-born debutantes and their illegitimate sisters -
laced with political intrigue, scandal and, of course, dangerous
gentlemen.

1. Her Gilded Prison

2. Dangerous Gentlemen

3. The Mysterious Governess

4. Beyond Rubies

5. Lady Unveiled: The Cuckold's Conspiracy

Prequel (Scandal of the Season)

Scandalous Miss Brightwells series

A humorous, sometimes steamy, matchmaking series – with some
books sweeter and more sensual and poignant.

1. Rake's Honour

2. Rogue's Kiss

3. The Wedding Wager

4. The Accidental Elopement

5. The Honourable Fortune Hunter

6. The Courtship Caper (*Redone for The Soho Club*)

7. The Wilful Widow

8. The Gypsy and the Gentleman

Fair Cyprians of London series

A group of women who work in a high class House of Assignation find their unexpected happy-ever-after in a range of sweet to very steamy redemption stories.

1. Saving Grace

2. Forsaking Hope

3. Keeping Faith

4. Wedding Violet

5. Christmas Charity

6. Loving Lily

London Ladies in Peril (The offshoot series that follows Loving Lily)

1. Murder at Madame Chambon's

Hearts in Hiding

Historical romantic suspense, very steamy often showing the darker aspects of Regency society, including the dependence and subjugation of women – and how, against the odds, they find true love.

1. The Duchess and the Highwayman

2. The Bluestocking and the Rake

3. Duchess of Seduction

4. The Countess and the Cavalier

Scandalous: Three Daring Charades

Three sweet, yet intrigue-filled Regency historicals

1. Lady Sarah's Redemption

2. Lady Olivia's Butterfly

3. A Little Deception

Dutiful Wives

1. The Reluctant Hero

2. An Unsuitable Alliance

3. Passion Fever

The Soho Club

1. Hazard's Mistress

2. An Undesirable Alliance

3. The Governess's Secret Love

Writing as B. G. Nettelton

Wings over Africa (A murder mystery series featuring a pilot in Colonial Botswana and Lesotho)

1. Shadows over the Delta

2. Diamond Mountain

You can connect with Beverley on Facebook at https://www.facebook.com/AuthorBeverleyOakley

You can also buy her books direct from www.beverleysbooks.com

Remember, buying direct is good for you and helps the author.